HOUR OF THE TIGRESS

Also by Irene Lin-Chandler

The Healing of Holly-Jean
Grievous Angel

HOUR OF THE TIGRESS

Irene Lin-Chandler

HEADLINE

First published in 1999 by
HEADLINE BOOK PUBLISHING

10 9 8 7 6 5 4 3 2 1

British Library Cataloguing in Publication Data

Lin-Chandler, Irene
  Hour of the tigress
    1.Ho, Holly-Jean (Fictitious character) - Fiction
    2.Women detectives - Fiction
    3.Private investigators - Great Britain - Fiction
    4.Chinese - Great Britain - Fiction
    5.Detective and mystery stories
  I.Title
  823[F]

ISBN 0 7472 1923 0

Typeset by
Letterpart Limited, Reigate, Surrey

Printed and bound in Great Britain by
Mackays of Chatham PLC, Chatham, Kent

HEADLINE BOOK PUBLISHING
A division of Hodder Headline PLC
338 Euston Road
London NW1 3BH

With love to Jeanette Chandler in her 89th year. May you forever bloom!

With grateful thanks to Dr Su Tong-pin in Taipei and my miraculously patient editor, Andi Sisodia, in London.

Chapter 1

If you'd spotted the blood-red off-road Yamaha DT motor-bike streak away from the Old Bailey Wednesday afternoon, dicing the traffic like a demented sushi chef, you'd have thought: There goes Holly-Jean Ho. Miss Conviviality – *so* up herself – and why not?

After all, she's a *player* now.

Successful handling of traumas in the Far East have made her reputation: the *Sunday Times Woman's Section* has actually described her as 'gently lethal, the thinking person's private eye'. That was in April when the front pages were splashed with pictures of Sue Smith, the young nurse from Barnsley, emerging unharmed from the Muslim rebel stronghold in Mindanao in the Philippines – all thanks to our very own Holly-Jean Ho.

Surely that would be enough to turn anyone's head? Yes, it would. Plus there's a new swinging London, New Labour, new millennium, new Hong Kong, new office, new home . . . All of those are helping to put a smile on her face. Yet they are not the most important thing.

Does it have anything to do with *guanchi*?

Got it in one. Holly-Jean's *guanchi*'s just gone strat-ospheric.

Guanchi – the uniquely Chinese term for relationships, networks, connections, influence: the precious juice that powers the world's most powerful business conglomerate – the Overseas Chinese.

Not forgetting to mention the fact that she's also earned herself some sweet spare change. So she grins as she flashes by on her DT, and then pulls up at the lights . . .

★　★　★

1

Stalled at the High Holborn and Chancery Lane traffic-lights, Holly-Jean tore off the black silk tie and undid the buttons of her white Valentino blouse, formal attire befitting a court appearance.

Mid-October tomorrow and the Indian Summer was refusing to die. *Chyou lauhu*. Tiger-Breath autumn, the Chinese say.

A flash of reflected sunlight caught her eye to the right. She glanced at the black limo purring quietly beside her. Since the stretch black Cadillac was a car which Holly from long experience had come to associate with profound unpleasantness, it came as no surprise when the Caddie's rear tinted window slowly lowered and the lens of a video camera appeared. Spotting a slicked-back pompadour and Oriental smirk, Holly swore obscenely in Mandarin.

'*Chao nidr baba!*' (An invective involving one's father.)

The camera was instantly lowered and a clenched fist poked out of the window, thumb up and first finger extended. Slowly the thumb wagged a couple of times, miming the pulling of a trigger.

Holly duly returned the finger. Glimpsed black metal. Sudden loud crack. The Yammie jerked between her thighs like a snake-bit mustang.

'*Frock you!*' Holly yelled as the lights changed and she hurled the bike forward into the hot toxic sundae of London afternoon air. The trail-bike easily lost the cumbersome Caddie, but at the same time Holly also lost any lingering euphoria. Fear, rage, adrenalin and premonitions of doom permeated.

She powered left down Drury Lane, cut through Shorts Gardens, standing up as the bike bucked over the cobbles of Earlham Street, and braked hard across from Belgo, the huge basement mussels and Belgian beer restaurant, and skidded to a screaming stop amid a cloud of pungent blue exhaust.

She checked the Yamaha. A smooth furrow in the rear mudguard meant a replacement part. So they weren't using a spud-gun. Holly stood up, reached for the sky and stretched her tight neck and back muscles like a waking pussy-cat. It was just a nick, probably only some kind of compressed-air pistol. No lethal intent, then.

2

She hoped. No idea who they were or why. Holly-Jean was, however, only too familiar with the penchant among a certain type of Oriental male for random violence.

Her cellphone bleated. 'Yep?'

'Holly? Coulson here,' said the head of the Met's Chinese Community Liaison Committee. 'Need you at 43 Gerrard Street, Basement 2, ASAP. A very weird dialect, maybe Fujienese, or Chiu Chow? Anyway, he doesn't cop a word of my attempts.'

Holly sighed. *Frock*, just when she was looking forward to a hot peppermint bath and a nice cup of Oolong. 'Be right there.' She didn't need to ask any questions.

For as long as she could remember of her adult life, she'd been called upon to interpret between the two vastly different worlds her single tiny frame inhabited.

The only difference was that nowadays the exercise was cloaked in officialdom, she'd got a fancy title as Assistant Chair of the CCLC, and by now she'd discerned, by long peeking through the clouds of unknowing, that the two different worlds were actually two different *planets*.

She kicked the Yammie to screaming blue life.

Chinatown was brimming with locals shopping in the market and throngs of touristos – all of whom, oddly, were Oriental. Holly parked the Yamaha on the cobbled yard by the Lamb and Flag public house and elbowed her way through the dithering pedestrians to Number 43. A uniformed constable on the pavement outside checked her ID, spoke briefly into his lapel and a moment later admitted Holly through an iron gate and down ancient worn slate steps to the dank below.

'Basement 2?' asked Holly, pausing on the steps.

The constable looked down at her. As usual these days, he appeared to Holly's maturing eye as ridiculously young. Valiantly, his upper lip was adorned with ginger bum-fluff, but this and the acne only added to the impression of adolescence.

'Door to the left at the bottom there, Miss. Inside turn right and you'll see the lift. Just press the button, it only goes one stop, up and down.'

Holly entered the big industrial elevator and studied the

3

Chinese graffiti which was unshockingly violent and misogynistic as the steel box wheezed down the intestines of old London town. The doors cranked open to reveal a brightly lit subterranean cavern dominated by a giant machine, steaming and groaning Heath Robinson-like.

Holly looked around, keeping herself in the lee of the doorway. Uniformed officers stood about keeping an eye on things as the forensic technos set up their portable electronic work-stations. A photographer's assistant cussed loudly as a spotlight stand toppled over. Coolie toilers, seemingly oblivious to events, stacked huge poly-fibre sacks marked *Soybean* that were being slung down a flour-dusty chute from street level.

She spotted Cottingham the Medical Examiner fumbling with his briefcase. He looked marginally more hungover than usual, which wasn't surprising for a call-out late in the afternoon. The sun would be well over the yard-arm by now and by rights he should be imbibing. She and the M.E. were old familiars, their acquaintance forged in the untimely ends of others.

The noise was dumbing in intensity. Holly stepped forward. The air in the basement plant was sour and dusty and clung to the back of her throat as she clocked Coulson at the distant end of the cavern, gesticulating with a couple of plainclothes and an Oriental in a dark-blue suit of ill-tailored Mainland origin.

The tall, debonair senior policeman was looking harassed as he caught sight of Holly and waved her over.

'Hi, Mick.'

'Holly-Jean, thank God you're here. Can't seem to get a word of my Mandarin understood.'

'Infernal. But the hat will fit my wife,' replied Holly, shouting over the din.

'Oh, very droll,' said Coulson, reverting to English and mopping his brow with a green silk hanky taken from his Armani top pocket. Despite years of earnest endeavour Chief Superintendent Mick Coulson's Mandarin was execrable.

'They making *do-fu*?'

Coulson nodded. 'My ex's brand, actually.' He handed Holly a torn packet. *Flower of the East Nature Produce Organic*

Tofu. 'Company's owned by a big nob in the Chinoiserie. The guy's a billionaire and well-connected. Practically shagging the new politicos.' Mick looked sardonic. 'Why else would I've been bastard dragged down here. Had better things to do this afternoon.'

Holly's look of indifference clearly pained the Chief Superintendent.

'So would you mind telling me what we're actually doing here?' she said. 'I've had a rather heavy day down at the Bailey.'

'The Bailey?' said Coulson, eyebrows raised. 'Oh, right. The Shih case: Fat Chink with Billions. How'd it go?'

'Who knows? I just came and went,' Holly dissembled. 'So what's up with the *do-fu?*'

'We got a floater,' said Mick, jerking a thumb over his shoulder towards the far end of the factory where giant vats stood gurgling. 'Or rather a *suspender.*' He smiled mirthlessly. 'First off, love, can you please ask him to get this frigging monster shut down so I can hear myself think!' He pointed to the little Oriental. 'His name's Li, and he's the manager, apparently. Pretends he can't understand a word of English or any other known language for that matter!'

The plainclothesmen had backed off after giving Holly brief nods, and stood eyeing her warily as she began to interpret.

Holly tugged the manager over to one side and began trying out dialects. She knew he understood English perfectly well, but this was a game they all played when the law was around. To give him face she tried out Cantonese, Mandarin, Fujienese, Chiu Chow, Taiwanese and finally ancient Hakka, before he gave in and unleashed a torrent of verbal incontinence which mainly featured the shortcomings evolutionary-wise of the English police, and the inconvenience of their visit to his shipping schedule.

'I understand there's a dead body,' pointed out Holly in a reasonable manner when Mr Li paused for breath.

This elicited a sheepish grin from the agitated countenance of Mr Li.

'We need to shut down the plant!' she told him.

'No way,' said Mr Li. 'Got a big order going to Holland on tonight's ferryboat!'

Holly grabbed Li by the lapels of his ill-made suit and lifted him close to her lips. 'I'm not with the police, Li *shen-sen*. I represent the interests of the Chinese *community*.'

The magic slogan had its usual diazepam effect, but Li still seemed disinclined to cooperate. He whined on about orders.

Holly had had about enough for one day. First, the Old Bailey, then some monkey firing a pistol, ruining her beloved Yamaha's rear mudguard, and now this.

She reached for Li's ear-lobe, hauled it to her lips and enunciated in gutter Hakkanese: 'Old Man Li, you either turn that machine off this instant or you will be taken to the English dungeon where your delicate cherry bumhole will be rent asunder by the bulging warheads of the hog-spawned English criminals!'

Mr Li flinched, peered up at Holly white as a ghost. 'B-but . . .'

'Bristly hairs halfway down their shafts!'

Mr Li couldn't get the huge tofu-making plant shut down quick enough.

Mick thanked her, and while the technos swarmed and Coulson got busy on his cellphone, Holly made a quick study of the machines.

Dried soybeans went in one end, and by the simple addition of water, adjustments of temperature, pressure and a variety of processing methods, out the various other ends of the machine came the different product: sealed tubs of fresh soft beancurd, cartons of soybean milk, trays of even-dried tofu chunks and finally in a distant annexe, smelling like overripe Stilton, were glistening jars of fermented curd. Here were Holly's two favourites: plain *chou-du-fu* – literally 'stinky tofu', spongy cubes for deep frying or steaming, and *do-fu roo*, soft chunks of fermented tofu in spicy oil, somewhat like spicy goat's cheese.

Coulson called her name and waved her up to a gallery walkway overlooking one of the huge fermenting vats in the richly scented annexe. As she passed by, the M.E. Cottingham

6

managed a smile and a nod. Poor old sod looked about done in.

'Don't let 'em get to yer, Cotters,' she whispered, winking and chucking his chin. 'The Lamb 'n Flag's only two steps away.'

'Ah, dear Holly-Jean, join me?'

'You bet.'

She took the metal stairs three at a time. 'This it, Superintendent?'

'This is it, Holls – how's your gorge?' said Mick, warmly.

Coulson was a long-time unsuccessful suitor of Holly's. Theirs had grown into a steady friendship over the years. His yearnings and her rejections were worn comfortably like a favourite pair of Rupert Bear slippers.

They stood and watched as a small collapsible pulley specifically designed for this kind of task was erected and a man in a wet-suit and mask was lowered down into the thick creamy off-white goo.

'Looks awfully like—'

'Don't bother, Mick,' said Holly quickly.

Coulson cleared his throat. 'Yuk – what a way to go, poor bastard.'

'How long?' she asked, feeling squeamish. Holly loved her *tofu roo*. Least, she did until now.

'Got a call a couple of hours ago,' said Coulson. 'Seems one of the staff was doing a routine check on this tank, which is auxiliary and only used when they've got a big order on the books like now. Anyway, this guy was giving the old salty custard a stir when a baseball hat was churned up to the surface, followed by a woman's shoe and shortly thereafter, a foot.'

'Must have been a bit of a shock,' said Holly grimly.

'The man's still hysterical. It seems today's a bad one auspicious-wise in the Lunar Calendar, so reckons it's a ghost. We're waiting for Old Man Cottingham's injection to kick in, then when the lad's stopped jabbering, you and me'll ask a few questions.'

A hush fell, the coolies straightened their backs and everyone stood silent as the diver signalled to the pulley-operator and the body was brought up.

7

As the tofu drained off the swaying corpse, bodily features became visible. It was a woman with dark-amber skin.

'She doesn't look Chinese,' remarked Coulson.

'Filipina,' said Holly.

It was well past six o'clock when Holly got back out into the autumn air and straddled her Yammie once more. She fobbed off Cottingham with a genuine headache excuse and with a wave to Mick, powered off up Shaftesbury Avenue, cut across Charing Cross Road, turned right into Earlham, flew round Seven Dials' tiny roundabout and once more skidded to a pungent blue stop opposite Belgo.

Number 40. A two-hundred-year-old former spice shop. Intricate carved architrave to the twin arched windows. Across the glass the elegant scrawl in purple and silver: *Holly-Jean Ho and Associates, Software Intellectual Property Rights Protection Consultants and Private Investigations.*

Their new office.

As Holly removed her helmet she heard Gi-Gi the three-legged neutered Siamese tom calling from above.

'Who's my man? *Ai-yai-yai-yai-YAI!*' she called up at the tiny roof-garden of the fifth-floor penthouse.

Their new home.

They: Holly, Gi-Gi and Ho Ma-ma.

She glanced at her reflection in the Gianfranco Ferre showroom window just behind her, poked at her spiky black half-Chinese hair baked flat by the helmet, saw through to the disdain on an elegant face inside.

Chao tamen shrmau-dr pi-gu! Frock their Fashion Ass!

In her global village Holly-Jean Ho appeared just as she damn well pleased. She'd earned the right. And besides, when people tried to put the wind up one with pot-shots in the traffic after a hard day at the Bailey, followed by the unwelcome intimacy of a tofu-marinated corpse, the whole day bottomed off by the hysterical lamentations of a man who'd seen a ghost, it didn't exactly help one's mood.

Chapter 2

Minty the painter, up from the country for a few days, was manning the front desk of the office, sipping espresso from the new Gaggia and smoking his perennial joint, his mahogany Medusa head enveloped in a blue bonfire.

Holly footed the door closed behind her, arms batting away at the clouds of herb.

'Min-*tee!*' she said, with the exasperation of a toddler's harassed mother.

Minty puffed on his joint, and jerked a thumb at a name-card. 'Live-ish one. Said he'd call back in a half-hour.'

Holly glanced at the proffered name-card, slam-dunked her crash-helmet onto the hat-stand. 'We're honoured, are we?'

She planted her legs, breathed deeply, reached her clasped hands high above her head and very slowly arched backwards to touch the strip-waxed original oak floorboards behind her.

Minty said, 'Oh, and a Miss Frangipani Johns called. Said you'd know. Staying for a month in town at this number, 756 3345.'

'Frangipani Johns?' Holly breathed out. 'Doesn't ring a bell.'

As she held the pose, replenishing her *chi*, Minty smacked his lips lewdly. 'Nice sacro-iliac.'

She arched higher.

'Nice *nice*.'

'Ma upstairs?' asked Holly upside-down.

'Nope,' said Minty. 'Must be slaying the old biddies of Chinatown at mah-jong.'

The office manager, Polly Bruce, an expensive replacement for the much-missed, now retired, Mrs Pryce-Jones, was currently on a three-week holiday in Phuket. Holly's other full-time employee, Barrance T. Wong – Taiwanese, single, half man, half motherboard – was, as usual, out of sight, locked away in his pristine, air-conditioned space of electronic sorcery under the paving-stones of Earlham Street in what had once been the delivery chute for the barrels of spices. Following a complete nervous breakdown brought on by obsessional affection for a Cray supercomputer, the brilliant twenty-nine-year-old Cambridge PhD had been bequeathed to Holly-Jean by her old acquaintance, the Secret Society elder, Mr Plum Blossom. Time had shown that Barrance T. Wong had found a home under the cobbles.

Holly exhaled with a loud, 'Hoo!', stood up straight and began to rifle her post. It mainly consisted of bills and paper pollution. No cheques. Binnable. At the bottom of the pile a computer-addressed white envelope: *Deirdre H. Jones (197-), c/o Ms H-J Ho, 40 Earlham Street, WC2.* Inside was an embossed invitation from Camden School for Girls. The O.C. Society reunion for her A-level year, to be held at the Sugar Club in Notting Hill. *Le rip-off.* She'd go anyway.

Any chance to show her old world that Weirdre Deirdre had gone and done it on her own. Transformed herself from an awkward half-breed into a successful careerwoman who took no prisoners, brooked no crap. Least that was the idea, anyway. As usual life wasn't that simple.

Wheedling Welshly, Minty said, 'Taking the stand at the Old Bailey must have been harrowing enough. But getting up there and testifying *under oath* as to the good character of some Triad super-boss who makes Doctor No look about as evil as Bert Kwouk . . .'

'Not now, Minty,' sighed Holly. 'I've had rather a trying day. On top of the Bailey, I just got back from translating for a woman found in a vat of fermented tofu.'

'A dead one?' he exclaimed, eyes lit up through billows of smoke.

'What do you think?' said Holly, stuffing the unwanted mail into the litter bin.

'Tell me all!'

'Later, Minty. I'm too exhausted right now. How about this bloke who left the card?'

But Minty wasn't about to give up on his original digging. There was a bee in his Welsh bonnet and Holly knew only too well he'd hang on like a Jack Russell terrier.

'Anyway you don't fool me, Holly-Jean. Must have been bloody petrified. Scared shitless, you were, I reckon. It was the Old Bailey, after all.'

'Not really,' Holly lied as she squeezed by the giant fish-less tropical fish tank, positioned for auspicious providence by the geomancer and blocking access to the office bathroom.

Owing to Ma's *guanchi*, the *feng-shui* man had come amazingly cheap. When the fifth lot of fish bellied up, Holly had arranged plastic mermaids among the aquatic plants and kept the thing bubbling away anyway. If it didn't do much to soothe the slumbering Earth Dragon, then at least it saved Ma's face.

The problem with *guanchi* is, it works both ways. Last week, the same geomancer had come round to see *her*, on a matter of recalcitrant debt.

Feng-shui, literally Wind/Water, the ancient Chinese art of geomancy, was the current rage among the New Age Enlightenment mob, who are always on the lookout for the latest Wisdom of the East quick fix. And as always, practitioners aplenty had appeared as if by magic with oracular compass in hand to supply that demand.

Not that they were all a bunch of charlatans. But as a general rule, Holly recommended that you beware the pony-tailed type whose CV documents ten years researching the effects of gravity on the Balinese beach coconut.

Actually what you stumped up good cash for was the auspicious placement of objects of significance in your life. As Holly told the wine-bar chatterbox one night, what you're actually doing is trying to buy luck, sucker.

'Too true, darling,' came the reply, 'but we all know the Hong Kong Chinese literally live for *feng-shui* and, my dear, look at them – absolutely *frothing* with dosh.'

Then as usual, the same old tales would get trotted out, of the insane expense forced by reconstruction work before the HK Bank building was completed, in order to milk the best of the 'fragment harbour's' *feng-shui*. But did you know, Holly would tell the chatterbox, that these so-called 'ideal architectural coordinates' were actually arrived at by calculations based on the object's geometric relationship to the slumbering Earth Dragon?

'Earth Dragon, you say? Gosh, how quaint.'

Yes, Holly would go on, people are throwing perfectly good money at these geomancers, whose formulations claim to show the relationship between objects on the planet's surface and the Earth Dragon who dwells within.

Good-luck positioning means you end up doing nothing more disturbing than stroking the Dragon's soft underbelly. Bad *feng-shui*, on the other hand, means that every time you flush your loo, the Earth Dragon gets an earful of shit.

'Well, of course, darling, personally I don't believe in any of that Dragon stuff, but just look at the money the Chinese are making. There *has to* be something in it!'

Holly would end the conversation abruptly by pointing out that *feng-shui*, like witchcraft and other so-called black arts, has a dark and demonic side. In the wrong hands, indeed, it is lethal. You won't find many Chinese messing with it for the sake of the chance to flash the latest trend.

Besides all of which, the last thing Holly needed was bad debt collection. But she was Chinese – well, half-Chinese, and her caste was dyed.

Owing to this fashionable surge in popularity, Ma's *feng-shui* man had never had it so good. Unfortunately, a couple of months back he'd realigned a computer graphics company's office suite in Kensington and now they were refusing to pay, citing no visible improvement in their profit figures.

Could Holly-Jean intercede? the man had whined. Being a half-and-half, like, she understood the English better than any of the Chinese did, and since she was such a prominent member of our community . . .

The hint was enough: *Giri.* Duty.

Though loan-enforcement was not on her current list of life-goals, Holly had no choice but to agree to help. Word she'd turned away the *feng-shui* man would be all over Chinatown like a rash, tarnishing her hard-won *guanchi*. Besides, it wouldn't be smart to antagonise a geomancer. You never knew: he might go and invoke the curse of the thousand-year-old egg-fart.

12

★ ★ ★

Inside her office she straightened her desk, switched on the surveillance system and half opened a drawer by her right shin to check the monitor was working. The front door pinged and a man entered – presumably the client who had left his calling card.

Holly watched on the monitor as Minty led him into the annexe next door. The tall man sat down, reached for a magazine and methodically scratched his crotch.

She gave it a couple more minutes, doing some simple *chi-kung* breathing to bring her mind to order, then picked up the phone and said, 'Minty, would you show him in, please? And put out that joint!'

Holly rose as the door opened, reached across her desk and briefly took her visitor's outstretched hand as Minty announced: 'Brit-Hakka *Babe*. Year of the Tiger *Premier Cru*. Tiny in scale, but blazing in stature. Leddizangennulmun: Holly-Jean Ho, the Human Catherine Wheel!'

'*Gang-ying yang!*' was her riposte, too rude to translate.

'McIlvuddy,' said the gent with raised brows after Minty had closed the door behind him. 'Lord McIlvuddy.'

'Ho,' Holly said, sitting down. 'Plain old Ho.'

She studied her customer. Bespoke tailored country tweed stalking suit. Carved antler walking stick. Over six feet, aristocratically thin, full head of silver-hair, bright blue eyes. Long face, craggy and outdoors-toned. Large red weepy nose. Sixtyish, she guessed. A handsome dog who must once have made the gels swoon at the Hunt Ball. Still standing there, dithering with his stick.

'Do take a seat, Lord McIlvuddy.'

He finally folded himself into the client's chair.

'So,' Holly said brightly, 'how may I help?'

'A matter of ah tying up, y'know, um loose ends,' said her guest, producing a worn old gold snuffbox from his waist-coat pocket. In one fluid motion, His Lordship tapped, opened, pinched, inhaled two piles of lethal-looking black powder from the crook of his left thumb, then snapped the box shut and secreted it away.

Naturally appreciative of any devotional discipline, Holly smiled into the anticipatory silence.

13

Nothing happened. No sneezes. No curling of eyebrows. No perceptible reaction. Hardcore, thought Holly.

'You mentioned loose ends, Your Lordship?'

'Sad business. Family, y'know. Um.'

Two more quick snorts. Again no apparent reaction. Either the old geezer's nerves were really shot or he wanted her to think they were. Time to find out what's what. She selected naked-teen confessional mode. A little lost lisp.

'I can assure you discretion is our golden rule.' She fluttered her eyelashes. 'Absolute discretion.'

Lord McIlvuddy froze for a long three-count. Broken by a flurried spasm during which his legs jerked free, he harrumphed, ran a finger inside his collar, and began to fuss with a document from his jacket pocket whilst his other hand did the snuffbox thing. None of which prevented Holly from spotting the demon-flicker of salacity. OK, Lord Phallus-Brain.

'You have something to show me?' she asked with a frigid smile.

'Difficult business, y'know. A passing,' 'McIlvuddy muttered, handing over the document. 'A probate.'

Probate. Holly's smile dried and set.

Probate: the official verification of a will. In her opinion, nothing brings out the worst in human nature like the reading of a will. Nurturing families alchemised into mobs of frenzied hyenas. She didn't need the hassle. Nor the money. She dropped the paper back on the desk in front of McIlvuddy, and stood up.

'I'm awfully sorry—'

But McIlvuddy had already begun to read, ' "Proof shall be shown that every possible means have been undertaken to provide legal verification of the existence of all living descendants of the dearly departed. Such means should include the retaining of private investigation and missing person agencies . . ." ' He pointed at her. 'That's you, m'dear.'

He folded up the paper and put it back in his pocket. Out came the snuffbox. Two more piles effortlessly slid up the septum.

'Aah!' McIlvuddy bounced in his seat and shouted. 'Piece

14

of cake for a cloak-and-dagger gal of your calibre, what?'

Holly noted with interest that His Lordship's demeanour appeared to have undergone a sudden, radical change. The special snufftin?

Her curiosity piqued, she remarked, 'With respect, Your Lordship, in my experience these things hardly ever are "a piece of cake". Indeed, you're probably better off anticipating all sorts of problems.'

'Problems? Such as?' McIlvuddy barked.

'Oh, you know,' Holly replied blithely, 'the descendants of long-lost remittance men surfacing from the Antipodes just as the will is being read. The sudden revelation that a major beneficiary is a long-term resident of a high-security mental facility – the cretinous drooling progeny of in-breeding. That sort of thing.' She waved her hand insouciantly.

McIlvuddy snarled, 'Absolutely not. Nothing like that in our family.' He stared at her, pupils wildly dilating, then sneezed explosively.

'Bless you,' she said.

A crusty handkerchief appeared and was loudly trumpeted. The germ zoo so beloved of the English public-school man. A dangerous anachronism. Like the title.

'Sorry to disappoint, m'dear gal,' McIlvuddy ploughed on. ''Fraid nothing more hazardous than a jolly hike over to Somerset House or wherever they keep the big computer these days. Then a mere phone call to the Passport Office and a day or two's worth of "To whom it may concern" notices in the papers here and abroad.'

Holly inspected her nails. 'Might I know how you came to choose our agency? Domestic Probate is simply not our area of expertise. You may or may not know that we tend to operate in the international arena. Among our other services, besides the core business of software property rights protection, we are called upon to handle contractual negotiations, run security checks for the big ex-pat head-hunters, locate the occasional missing person, that sort of thing. You probably wouldn't know that,' she added vaguely.

McIlvuddy grinned. 'Oh, but I know all about you, Ms Ho.

Including today's heroics at the Old Bailey on behalf of an old chum of mine.'

Holly's face was set in porcelain, but her mind whirled. For a start, news sure travels fast in this town – she'd only left the courtroom a couple of hours ago! But more disturbing was her visitor's last comment. This seedy aristo and Shih Yang-fu *old chums*? Unlikely. But if true, what did that mean about the price of guppies? Things were getting murkier by the moment.

Holly waited in neutral, judging by the smug expression on McIlvuddy's face that there was more to come.

'Oh yes, I know an awful great deal about you, my pretty young maid.' Mid-leer, he licked his lips, revealing a black tongue.

At a speed precluding the naked eye, Holly recoiled fractionally, re-centred her *chi* and experienced two thoughts. One, so that was where all the goop ended up. Two, only demons have black tongues. (The latter originated in the Chinese part of her brain.)

McIlvuddy continued to speak, gloatingly offering up Holly's current CV as though privy to her underwear drawer. 'Holly-Jean Ho, formerly Deirdre H. Jones of Kentish Town. Your friends describe you as weird but lovely. Your teachers at Camden School for Girls said you were brilliant, but an uncut diamond. You eschewed a place at university even though you scored three grade A's in Economics, History and Art.'

Quick snort. Quick wipe.

'Instead you joined Whitelegge's Country Fair as assistant to Ramon Zarate, professionally known as Alcazar the Knife-Thrower. After which you hit the road as they said back then and travelled extensively all over the planet, spending much of the time in the pursuit of excellence in the martial arts. Your travels later included a spell running your own herbal remedy tea shop and kung fu *dojan* in the Lower East Side of Manhattan. You returned to London and took jobs in various computer-related companies rising to the glass ceiling in each case. Six years ago you quit at the age of twenty-nine, took your maternal ancestral name of Ho, and opened this agency. Your reputation for fixing things in far-flung places is excellent, culminating in last year's successful negotiation of the release of the Moro Liberation Front's hostages on the Philippine island of Mindanao.'

Substantial nasal blast. Substantial hanky swipe.

Holly felt intruded upon. 'So you read my press release. Which means you know we don't do probates.' Sure the tie-in to Shih Yang-fu was titillating, and sure the old geezer had definitely done his homework, but it was still a probate and thus far she wasn't biting. 'In fact, right now the agency's books are filled, Your Lordship, awfully sorry and all,' she said breezily, straightening some papers. 'However, I'd be more than happy to provide you with a list of suitable alternatives. I think I can say without exaggeration that I have personal contacts with the very best in the business.'

Squid-ink ejaculate in the twinkling blue seas of charm – high pressure frontal lobe system, rage predicted.

'By all means, delay,' he growled. 'Till you're freed-up, what? We'll discuss anon your fee.'

'I'm not taking your case, Lord McIlvuddy,' Holly said.

But it seemed His Lordship was already up, up and away in his beautiful balloon.

'Alas, duty calls, dear lady and I must hie to serve the ship of state! As my esteemed brethren in the Upper Chamber of the Great Mother of Parliaments like to say, "No showee. No doughee".'

McIlvuddy shouldered his deer-antler stick and held out his hand. Holly gave hers a touch askance. His Lordship wheeled smartly and flung open the door. Striding through the front office, he barked at a startled Minty: 'Of course we're all whores! What is life anyway, but one neverending refrain of "No monee, no honee, cheap Charlee!" what?' The front door slammed as the silver mane sailed past the windows up Earlham Street towards Seven Dials.

His Lordship was either one chopstick short of a pair. Or using.

'Blithering heck, what was that?' Minty said.

'Per diem,' said Holly, opening a tin of Oolong *cha*. 'Democracy's dozing allowance,' she added.

Minty stared at her, digesting.

'Clock-in money at the House of Lords.'

That did it. He jumped up. 'Bored with dry-shagging the yokels? Slaughtered one too many grouse? So hop on a train and spend a few days in Town. Skull out on *one's club's* subsidised wine cellar, taxi over to the House for an afternoon nap – and get *paid for it*! And while you're at it, should you so desire, you may participate in the ruling of the country!'

'So tell me,' Holly goaded. 'What great service to the nation merits this bountiful reward of a grateful citizenry?'

'*Just be in the right womb at the right time!* Their time's up, thank God.' The Wild Welsh Artist, part genuine, part agent's artifice – an effective marketing tool designed to sell paintings to the Philistine – collapsed back in his seat next to the Gaggia espresso machine and stared morosely out at the haute couture across the way. After a moment he sat up straight and said, 'What did you say the name was again?'

'McIlvuddy,' said Holly, making *cha*. 'What they call a "rum cove", I reckon.'

'McIlvuddy . . .' Minty scratched his Medusa curls. 'Got last week's papers hanging about?'

'Bottom drawer.' She pointed at the single filing cabinet.

Minty began to sort through the papers. A few moments later he flourished a page. 'Ah-ha! I knew it! Here it is: *DNA tests sought in titled paternity wrangle.*'

'Read on, Macduff,' said Holly.

It was a short piece on a page of international news round-ups. No by-line.

'You know,' said Holly, when he'd finished, calmly sipping her tiny cup of Oolong *cha*, 'England seems positively *Oriental* at times.'

She reached for the phone and while the Oolong's subtle charge – much less edgy than coffee's – kicked in, dialled up a number. After uttering a few terse words, she replaced the phone. Then redialled. This time she was asked by the patrician lady recording to enter her password.

She did so in Mandarin.

She then followed a complicated series of recorded instructions, punching in her coded responses. Replaced the headset, waited. The phone rang three times, she picked it up, pressed the zero key and heard a phone ring somewhere in Chinatown.

Having successfully navigated this miasma of electronic subterfuge, she finally reached Mr Plum Blossom, that handsome, suave, Oxford-educated assassin, her oldest acquaintance from the Societies and the other end of the conduit running from the Establishments to the UK's Chinese community.

The conduit which was her.

Mei Hua Shen-sen (Mandarin – Plum Blossom Mr), was a senior officer of the *Ju Lyan-bang* in London and north-east Europe. *Ju Lyan-bang*, better known to students of international crime as The Bamboo Union, is the oldest and by far the most powerful of the Triads operating in the global Chinese diaspora. Formed more than 200 years ago during the tyranny of the hated Manchu Ching Dynasty as a secret society of patriotic freedom-fighters dedicated to freeing the Middle Kingdom from the odious Manchurian Ching rule, the *Ju Lyan-bang* is probably the biggest criminal organisation operating on the planet today.

Most likely the richest.

Certainly the most heinous.

'And are you basking in the glory of massive face, Extremely Unmarried Miss Ho?' asked Plum Blossom in Mandarin. He liked to refer to Holly by this title. It was an old dig, light-heartedly meant to ride her into admitting the incipient approach of old maid-dom, and thus the concomitant – *he hoped* – surrender of her virtue to his manly charms.

In your dreams, China-boy, thought Holly, replying with due modesty, 'My inferior *guanchi* must take any and all the help that comes its way, Big Brother.'

'Well, you certainly scored big this afternoon. Shih Yang-fu is a mighty one. Just don't squander it,' said Plum Blossom.

'Squander?' snorted Holly. 'Not likely.'

Plum Blossom chuckled, 'OK, Extremely Unmarried Miss

19

Ho, since you never call me unless it is to beg a favour, tell me what I can do for you?'

'Hamish McIlvuddy, the Honourable. Ring a bell?'

'Should it?'

'Maybe,' said Holly, hesitating. 'He claims to be an old friend of Shih Yang-fu's. I'm wondering if there's any truth in it.'

'McIlvuddy? How do you spell that? OK, got it written down. I'll get back to you.'

'Thanks, Plum Blossom,' she said, then remembered. 'Oh, before you go, just one other thing. Any idea who Chinese-wise might be taking pot-shots at me and my Yammie from the back of a stretch black Cadillac?'

'You want that figure rounded off to the nearest ten?'

'Oh ha-bloody-hah,' said Holly. '*Ni shao-dr shang sah-mao!*' Which means you're about as funny as a dead cat.

She and Minty sat in silence, one in thoughtful repose, the other stoned, staring out the window at the *à la mode* catwalkers passing by.

'I've been thinking . . .'

'I know, I know, Minty,' said Holly, filling another tiny cup with Oolong and placing it in front of him. 'You've finished the show. Life's all shit.'

They raised their cups with both hands. Chinese etiquette came naturally to this pair of old mates.

Holly smiled at her old pal and went on, 'You never want to paint again. You've got to get back to the real world and do some real work.'

Minty's eyebrows disappeared under his corkscrew curls. 'Sheesh!'

But it was always like this after he'd finished getting a show together. Ever since Holly had first met him – too long ago to contemplate – when he was at what used to be called Hornsey Art College before it got tarted up by a desperate Ministry of Education trying to cook the nation's academic books and rechristened the University of Muswell Hill or whatever, the pattern of Minty's artistic life had been the same.

First came a period of fretful inactivity, leading eventually to deep drink and drug-addled depression, broken at last by the combined urgings of wife, Jemima, agent, Sadie and close friends like Holly.

There followed six months holed up in a Devon cottage, painting till all the craziness had been squeezed out of the tubes of acrylic and become the magic on the canvas.

'Lord Snuffy's probate. All yours,' said Holly. 'You sleep under the stairs.'

'You know I love you, Holls,' said Minty.

Chapter 3

In the office bathroom she cleansed her face of London grime. Wetted her hair under the cold tap and scruffed it up the way she liked it. Fixed her minimal make-up and stood back from the gold-tint mirror that had formerly graced the ladies' powder room of the Embassy Club.

She looked at her body. The soft steel anatomy of an adept of martial arts. Tiny, but never small. A beauty, men said, but one tough titty.

She looked at her face. The lustrous long eyelashes – from her Dad – neon to her shallow Oriental lids. Pupils dark as wells of blood. Porcelain skin like fresh *tofu*. Her best feature.

She stared into her eyes, dove deep and felt the electric stroke of goose-pimples. *Chi-pi.* Chicken-skin, the Chinese call it.

Delayed reaction.

Minty was right, of course. She *had* been scared shitless.

Taking the stand in the hallowed courtroom of the Old Bailey, she'd felt a sudden childlike, abject terror.

Mounting the dock steps, something – the brain lobe marked 'Chinese' playing tricks probably – had made her stop and look up. For one chill ticking of the clock, the ceiling of Number One Court slipped out of focus and in the pulsating ether there hung an animate tapestry of that sad, ancient room.

Spectres of the countless mangled hearts and shattered lives that had passed through the great gate of justice began to leer out from the carpet-weave of murder and lies, and as she looked up, paused on the steps to the dock, they began their dance.

Spastic necks tethered to a Black Cap sky.

With no outward sign but total composure, Holly had wiped her mind blank with a *chi-kung* manoeuvre, and blazing a confident smile, she had raised her hand to take the oath.

'I swear by . . .'

She'd been called to the London Central Criminal Court as a character witness for the defence in a case brought by the Serious Fraud Office against a Chinese trader, Shih Yang-fu.

Shih's alleged crime – a paper-money scam, moving non-existent product from one EU country to another and picking up demurrage refunds from Brussels each step of the way – had allegedly been operating for more than twenty years and had netted sums that were so mind-boggling that at one point the Old Bailey crowd let out a spontaneous cheer – a rare moment of levity in otherwise bad-tempered proceedings.

The intricate prosecution case was so numbingly complicated and the heat in Number One Court so oppressive that even the élite prosecution team – following their recent failures the SFO had been forced to hire the very best – were looking punchy by the lunch recess.

Returning for this afternoon's session, Holly noted that each of the prosecution team wore an identical rictus of real ale, a half-stewed show of teeth that was meant to exude confidence but came off manic. To sobersides like Holly, who'd enjoyed a quiet meditation in nearby St Paul's Cathedral, it was sadly obvious.

The fancy skills had finally apprehended what everyone else in Number One Court had known since last Monday morning, about three minutes into the prosecution's opening statement. That there was more chance of a sphere of impacted snow surviving the incendiary motif of eternal chastisement common to many cultures than the jury understanding a single word of their case.

The prosecution's confidence wouldn't have been helped by the gin-wattled judge's apoplectic interjection back on that first day: '*De*-what!'

'Demurrage, Your Honour.'

'I would remind Counsel for the Prosecution that until the

dictatorship of Brussels finally vanquishes this Island Race, the Queen's English will be used in my court.'

'Quite so, Your Honour,' said the QC, meekly. ' "Demurrage" is a technical term, meaning the amount of rate payable to a ship-owner by charterer for failure to load or discharge shipment within time allowed. In this case, the accused, by means of shell companies, was owner, charterer and customer. He thus owned the entire chain of transportation – the ships, the trucks, the container *and* the product.'

'Yes, yes, yes. But the *crime*, Counsel,' spluttered the judge. 'Would you please be so good as to tell me the *crime* we are judging here?'

'Certainly, Your Honour.' The sweat streaming from under the QC's wig was clearly visible to all. 'Since the earliest days of the EU, the defendant has conspired with a vast global network of corrupt customs and port officials to cause apparent "unavoidable" delays in shipment in order to claim the demurrage refunds under existing EU regulations. Following which he has then gone on to ship the product to its destination and reap those normal, legal profits as well. It is purely and simply a case of nefarious and most wicked greed.'

'Indeed, Counsel. Your task will be to prove that statement in clear and simple terms to the full satisfaction of the Bench.'

'It is my intention so to do, Your Honour.'

There followed days of technical testimony by the prosecution, with the public gallery of Number One Court peopled by snoozing derelicts and hungover journalists.

Today, by contrast, was the first time the defence were to call character witnesses, and Holly found herself facing a packed, buzzing courtroom.

After swearing the oath, she had been asked to formally identify herself. Her reply, 'Holly-Jean Ho, formerly Deirdre H. Jones, also known as Ho Shao-lan,' apparently tickled Lord Justice Reamer, presiding.

'Thrice-named! Thrice-blest!' he declared with an unlikely rogueish twinkle, as if this were the first enjoyable moment of the trial. 'The third name, unless I'm mistaken, would be Mandarin?'

24

'It would, Your Honour,' called the defence counsel.

'Then I would like to assure the young lady, in the light of my recent remarks regarding the Queen's English, that the court will bear no malice towards the use of the ancient language of the esteemed Han race. Might a translation be forthcoming?'

'Little Orchid Ho, Your Honour,' Holly bobbed a smile.

Within its horsehair wig frame the judge's knobby visage deepened to a vermilion hue. To the prosecution's audible groan and a titter from the gallery, he commented, in wavering emotion-loaded tones, 'My lifelong work outside the court has been to raise that jewel of nature. Among my sins I count orchid-fancier, my dear, and I can say without hesitation, that the face, in this case, splendidly fits the name.'

Cheers erupted all round.

The barrister for the defence began. 'This witness is of outstanding character and achievement, Your Honour, actively contributing to a highly positive degree, both within the Chinese ethnic community and in society at large, and as such is uniquely qualified to testify as to the defendant's good character.'

The judge beamed as the defence continued.

'Ms Ho, amongst her diverse talents, is Deputy Vice-Chairperson of the long-established, recently revamped under a new name, Metropolitan Police Chinese Community Liaison Committee, the CCLC. She is also a lifetime UK delegate to the International Athletics Association, a selector for the English tae kwon do team, and a master exponent of the martial arts.'

The barrister paused, looked around the court, adjusted his wig and smiled. 'Ms Ho is also a successful entrepreneur in the software arena and a personal affairs management consultant whose reputation for getting things done in far-flung corners of the globe is well-established.'

Humbled by such excess, Holly had lowered her eyes.

Then, straightening her spine in response to the defence questioning, she had quietly but clearly listed the defendant Shih Yang-fu's worthy acts. His generous contributions to Chinatown schools, hospitals, social clubs, and Taoist temples. The free consultations at herbal and acupuncture clinics for the needy, the travel bursaries to obscure martial arts schools in provincial China and so on.

During the expert and at times, vicious cross-examination, she answered at some length detailed questions about Shih's business empire.

'Just one more question remains, Your Honour,' said the prosecuting QC, winding up. 'Understandably, the witness makes no mention of the vast international crime organisation, the Swatownese Triad called *Tien Tao Meng*, The Gate to the Paradise Way, for which the defendant, Shih Yang-fu, as Paramount Leader, has the Mandate of the Gods of the Tao-ist Underworld.'

There was immediate uproar, with the entire defence team on their feet yelling, 'Objection! Mistrial!'

The public gallery erupted into riotous shouting and stamping of feet.

The judge, banging his gavel, thundered, 'Silence in Court! *Silence!* I will have this chamber cleared unless this disgraceful exhibition ends immediately!'

Eventually the noise died down, and the judge upheld the defence objection, ordering the prosecution's remarks to be struck from the record. The focus shifted back to the witness.

Holly adopted a perplexed look. 'Swatownese Triad? Mandate of the Underworld?' She shrugged contemptuously. 'The tired old myths are still doing the rounds, are they?'

The QC smirked at the jury. 'Oh come now, Ms Ho. Triads, Chinese Secret Societies . . . I think we all know they exist. I would say most intelligent, informed opinion understands that the criminal element within the Chinese diaspora is probably one of the biggest if not *the* biggest criminal business organisation on the globe. And I emphasise business, because with these people it's always a cloak of legitimate commerce under which they hide their evil doings!'

He paused for effect, turned slowly with outstretched forefinger to point at the defendant. *These people*, thought Holly. He gets one for that.

The QC declaimed as from the pulpit, raising his voice to a righteous vibrato, finger jabbing, 'And that man, the defendant in this case of outrageous dishonesty, Shih Yang-fu, is a vastly powerful leader of that corrupt and evil business organisation where murder and mayhem are commonplace and all morals enter the maelstrom!' Again he paused for effect. The courtroom was riveted.

'A *Tswei Da-gr* is the exact term, if I have it correctly.' He looked at Holly with gloating eyes. 'The Biggest Brother! Yes, the man we see before us today, that innocuous-looking gentleman sitting over there in the perfectly cut suit and polished British shoes, is, as you Chinese so euphemistically say, the Biggest Brother. Or in plain simple English if you prefer it, and I know *I* do – Shih Yang-fu is their Boss of Bosses!'

He swung round to Holly. 'Possibly even *your* boss too, Ms Ho?' With a derisive, 'Nothing further,' he sat down.

Again there was immediate vociferous objection from the defence bench. Once more, after the judge had brought the court to order, he had the prosecution's comments struck from the record, adding for Holly's benefit, 'The witness might feel entitled to consult with Counsel concerning the possibly slanderous comments recently made by the prosecution, whom I fear have nothing less than insults left to their case.'

The defence barrister stood up. 'No further questions, Your Honour.'

The judge thanked Holly for giving evidence, and told her she could step down.

But Holly was not yet ready to take her seat. She felt oddly serene following the prosecution's savagery and the public outbursts. Her esoteric disciplines had filtered the pandemonium and throughout the cross-examination she had *maintained*. Now she raised her head and addressed the court.

'I'd like to say something in response to the learned counsel's comments, if I may, Your Honour?'

The judge nodded. 'Proceed.'

'Objection!' called the prosecution.

'Overruled.'

Holly said, 'Hollywood's favourite bogeyman is the evil Oriental. I expect the learned counsel watches too many late-night videos when he gets home after a hard day arguing the drier points of financial law. And judging by the aridity of

27

this week, who can blame him?'

This elicited an ironic cheer from the public and a bow of acknowledgement from the prosecution.

Holly went on, 'Actually I'd hoped Charlie Chan had finally joined his ancestors. But apparently not. Which makes it rather tough for people like me whose entire life has been spent on the bridge over the abyss between two opposing worlds. Derided by both sides.'

She looked at the jury one by one. ' "Not-quite-white! Touch of the Yellow Peril!" – the jeer from one lot. And it's just as bad from the other side: "She's a banana – yellow skin maybe, but white inside!" '

Holly continued, 'I only know that if you're ever around young Jimmy Lee, you'd better not call Shih Yang-fu a gangster or even intimate that he's remotely connected to evil organisations such as criminal Triads and secret societies – should they in fact exist. Because young Jimmy might just demonstrate some of his new-found skills on you!'

'And who, pray, is young Jimmy Lee?' enquired Lord Justice Reamer.

The prosecution barrister was instantly on his feet. 'With respect, Your Honour, I can hardly imagine what relevance—'

But Holly had the judge's rapt attention.

'Your Honour, Jimmy Lee is a sixteen-year-old with cerebral palsy and a dream. Five years ago, Jimmy began studying martial discipline at our *dojo* – our training centre – and confounded the doctors who'd written him off as a hopeless drooler, a spaz.'

'I must protest!' shouted the prosecution, over the jeers of derision from the gallery.

Holly ignored him. 'Jimmy Lee's dream is to represent Britain at the Olympic Games for the Physically Challenged, but he could go no further with our teachers.' She paused, looked around at the silent court, the faces still, expectant. 'Shih Yang-fu was guest speaker at our Open Day this July. He watched the students, among them, Jimmy, put on their display. Last month, Jimmy Lee and his single-parent mum were flown in a private plane to the world-renowned Shao-lin Temple in Mainland China. There, thanks to the generosity of Shih Yang-fu, young Jimmy, with his beloved mum for company, is to spend the next two years under the guidance of the Shao-lin monks preparing for the Games.'

The almost imperceptible nod from the accused as she'd stepped slowly down from the dock while the gallery cheered and clapped was what had sent her *guanchi* index soaring.

Shih Yang-fu, a multi-billionaire from pearls to petroleum, a legend in the legend-lagged Chinese, diaspora, owed her. Holly-Jean had just saved his face in front of the international financial press and the public gallery of the Old Bailey, the world's most famous courtroom.

Guanchi didn't come any better than that.

Holly stepped back from the gold mirror on her bathroom wall and grimaced. She should have remembered the problem with *guanchi* – it works both ways.

'Come on, Minty,' she said, grabbing her bag. 'Shut the shop. We're going out to get smashed.'

'That Miss Frangipani Johns called again. I said you were busy.'

'I wonder who the heck she is?' mused Holly by the door. 'But let's get our priorities right. My throat's desperate for a swim.'

Chapter 4

Midway through Thursday morning's hangover, her fore-finger, on its third and final attempt, shakily keyed in the number of Holly's best journo *guanchi*.

In its cradle next to a police speed-trap radar detector disguised as an air freshener mounted on the dash of a silver Mercedes SLK two-seater heading west on the M4 just past the Newbury exit at 118 mph, the phone began to trill.

'Hi, Shirl, it's me, Holly-Jean. What's the skinny on Lord McIlvuddy?'

'In exchange for an exclusive interview with the girl who saved the Yellow Peril billionaire's arse?'

'Done. Can you get into the clippings library this afternoon?'

'No, but my Friday-boy can. I'm on the way to the Quantocks.'

'Work or play?'

'Gimme a break. Two jobs: *The Legendary White Hart Returns* and *Legacy of the Hunt – Mad Fox Disease*.'

'Sounds perfectly rabid.'

Shirley Jacquet, writer of the *Lady Muck* gossip column for the *Now* tabloid, had her office assistant or Man Friday meet Holly early afternoon in the marble, steel and glass lobby of the hulking new Thames-side headquarters of International News Incorporated, the world-dominating empire of media mogul Boris Ocker which counted *Now* among its many other publications.

The glaring white sunlit river and skyscape smelled of ripe ocean. Holly shuddered in the chilly river air as she parked the Yamaha and locked her helmet away. She walked past the

Rachel Whiteread sculpture of a lifesize upside-down Rolls-Royce moulded in plain concrete and up the thirty-six marble steps to INI.

Jed Van Hoorhuis, Shirley's harassed assistant, was summoned by Reception and arrived at a run.

'Completely frazzled. I'll have to leave you to it, that alright?' he gulped confidentially in his sing-song Dutch as they doubled down corridors and out of elevators to the clippings morgue.

'No problem,' said Holly, breathing hard. 'Just point me.'

Jed saw her to the morgue and left with a smile and a wave.

The clippings morgue of INI was a quiet air-conditioned room on the sixth floor. Holly's memory tape instantly rewound to the hot summer library at Camden swatting for A levels and dreaming of Bowie.

Two long rows of computer terminals and ranks of metal shelving holding cardboard file boxes were manned at the front desk by a cheerful-countenanced lady of middle age, wearing pince-nez on a gold chain and a floral dress with generous cleavage more suited to the point-to-point than Grub Street-on-the-Thames.

'Lord McIlvuddy? Young rogue but bags of charm,' she smiled mischievously. 'Knew the father. Same mould. Lovely dancer. Marvellous polo player. An utter dog.' She laughed gaily and waltzed away, returning a few minutes later with a large box and a carton of disks. 'There's rather a lot, I'm afraid. Some on disk, most on hard copy. The case caused such a stir at the time.'

Looking away, she added, 'What a waste to society the sixties turned out to be. Such a *destructive* age, I always think. So many lives *ruined* . . .' With a shrug and over-bright-eyed smile, she turned back to Holly. 'I'll put you over there at Terminal 9. It has a lovely view of the river.'

Somebody's history, somebody's sorrow, thought Holly, thanking the sweet lady.

She quickly got down to work. The McIlvuddy story, she discovered immediately, was fascinating enough to evaporate any remaining traces of her hangover. For a start, Hamish McIlvuddy was no Lord, just a mere Right Honourable. The

31

actual title – 'McIlvuddy of That Ilk, Lord of the Isle, High Chieftain of the Clan McIlvuddy' – was currently in dispute as Minty had remembered from last week's newspaper.

The previous Lord, eldest of two brothers and two sisters – Hamish being the second male and next in line for the title – had died some six months ago, allegedly succumbing to sudden cardiac occlusion in the palms of a fifteen-year-old trainee masseuse on her solo audition at His Lordship's Fountain of Eternal Youth massage parlour in Pasay City, Manila. The story had made the newspapers because Jonny McIlvuddy, sixty years old at the time of his death, was still the subject of a warrant for arrest on charges of breaking the conditions set for bail and absconding while bound over by the Shropshire Magistrate's Court.

The original charge, first filed in 1974, was conspiracy to manufacture and distribute for reasons of profit a Class B narcotic, the chemical compound lysergic acid diethylamide-25, *aka* LSD. In the celebrated case which came to be known as Operation Rachel, Lord McIlvuddy and some old pals from Christ Church College, Oxford, had set up an acid still in the depths of mid-Wales and begun churning out quantities of LSD which swamped UK and Europe throughout the early 1970s.

Among the group was the brilliant young chemist, Pietro Bonetto, who, after completing his custodial sentence, went on to a distinguished career in bio-medics and indeed was mentioned last year as a possible Nobel candidate.

Owing to the dogged efforts of Detective Inspector Paul Suttoh, the lab was busted and the conspirators taken into custody. Most of the gang were denied bail and eventually received fairly lengthy prison sentences, much reduced later on appeal when all the public furore had died down.

On the mistaken grounds – brilliantly argued by one of London's most successful and expensive QCs, Sam Sangster-Choate – that he was but a minor player in the game, the judge had granted Lord McIlvuddy bail. Setting the sum at a quarter of a million pounds – an astronomical figure for those days and symptomatic of the hyperbole surrounding the trial – the judge had felt confident in letting the young aristocrat walk free.

After surrendering his passport and making bail with the help of the family-connected merchant bank, Shadwell's, Lord McIlvuddy had jumped in his yellow Morgan Plus Eight and spun gravel from the court car park directly to St Mawes in Cornwall, where he moored his yacht. Accompanied by his then girlfriend, Moonbeam, and two others not known, he set sail on the evening tide and passed into tabloid legend, never again to set foot on English soil. Thereby sacrificing his branch of the family's dividends from Shadwell's Bank for the next few years and causing the Home Farm near Chipping Sodbury to be sold at a discounted price.

The famous acid-bust case was, however, just a taster of the McIlvuddy shenanigans. Holly's juices were flowing. Reading the McIlvuddy file was like broaching some ancient septic tank full of family murk. There were reams of faded clippings from the society pages and gossip columns of yesteryear, featuring different members of the aristocratic family. Much-decorated heroes in far-off skirmishes, empire-builders caught with their pants down in Simla, Ooty and Happy Valley. Legends of sporting prowess, military brilliance and valiant rogering. Aside from the Rachel Case, the most mentioned family member was the father who won a VC at El Alamein, rode with the Exmoor Forest Staghounds and a winner at the Grand National, drove a Bentley at Le Mans during the marque's glory days, and was killed by a landmine in Malay on the family rubber plantation.

Jonny, seven at the time of his father's death, spent his childhood either away at boarding school, Christ Church Cathedral Choir School at Oxford, followed by Eton, or with a nanny at one of the family houses, while his mother, American soap heiress, Barbara-Ann Curtis, migrated from one luxury watering-hole to another in order to mate.

When the librarian called by with a cup of Earl Grey, it was past three and Holly was late for her next appointment. She made copies of what she needed and was just closing up the last clippings files when a slip of sepia newsprint fell out from behind the flap. It was from the William Hickey gossip column of the *Daily Express*, dated 29 September, 1974;

green felt-tip ringed a tiny piece entitled, *Bun in the oven for Bounder?*

Holly read:

Rumours from drop-outdom in the Far Orient have reached our ears recently, the juiciest of which hints that the erstwhile lady companion of disgraced peer of the realm, Lord Jonny McIlvuddy of That Ilk, the young bohemian gal charmingly known only by the sobriquet, Moonbeam, may be expecting His Lordship's bairn. This would of course make the sprog next in line for the vast McIlvuddy fortune. More on this as we hear it . . . Pip Pip!

She made a photocopy of the clipping and left the morgue with reams of hard copy. It was three-thirty and behind schedule she raced the Yammie across Blackfriars Bridge through Elephant and Castle and cut across to Brixton Gaol.

She hurried through the entry procedures and was hastily escorted to an interview room where a Legal Aid solicitor and his client were waiting for her to interpret. The case involved a Chinese merchant seaman who'd jumped ship at Tilbury and had been accused of shoplifting and assault with a deadly weapon, namely a six-bladed throwing star called an *i-shang sao*.

Discovering that the Shantungese sailor had family in Rotterdam, she suggested to the solicitor that the man plead guilty to a lesser charge and accept deportation to Holland and asylum on grounds of political persecution back home.

The solicitor had no idea what would be made of this suggestion by the courts, but Holly at least had done her bit. She got out of Brixton as the rush hour was well under way but weaved through to the office before six.

Ma and Minty, with the help of Barrance T. Wong's deft fingerwork on the keyboard, had already garnered quite a file on Hamish Peregrine Vere Andrew McIlvuddy.

When the consensus declared stomachs empty around seven, Holly told the others to leave it for the night and go and eat dinner. She locked up the office and took the whole pile of paperwork upstairs to the fifth floor. Gi-Gi had gone out, probably on the sniff, and she had the place to herself.

Lying in a Balinese hammock suspended between two hooks on either side of the little conservatory extension, sipping a glass of icy Alsace Gewürztraminer, she rapid-scanned every scrap of information they had garnered on the McIlvuddy clan.

With a fresh glass of the raisiny nectar to hand, a new bottle on ice within reach on the floor and nibbling from a whole, perfectly ripe but slightly chilled, 200-gram Camembert, which she held like a bun in her left hand and occasionally dipped into a bowl of virgin olive oil, minced garlic and a chiffonade of fresh basil and oregano, she methodically re-read each piece of flimsy.

By the time she'd finished, around nine o'clock, she knew three things: a lot about the Clan McIlvuddy; that getting down a 200-gram Camembert required the better part of two bottles of Gewürztraminer, and that such indulgence while lying in a hammock resulted in the equivalent queasy shame as had the three ice cream Mars bars she'd eaten while watching *Cinema Paradiso* on the box in the early hours of last Sunday morning.

Luckily for an advanced disciple of the esoteric arts, Holly-Jean needed only to turn left out of her front door, walk the block to St Martin's Lane, left down to Trafalgar Square, traverse by the fountains – pausing for a nod at Horatio on his column – through Admiralty Arch to find herself, ten minutes along the Mall from her front door, in St James's Park.

She ran for one hour, practised her skills for another and ended with thirty minutes of *chi-kung* in a secluded pondside pathway. The last being sadly curtailed when a man roller-bladed out of the twilight and by the beam of a pen-lite showed her his genitalia.

Perhaps owing to the remaining excess of blood sugar in her system caused by her earlier indulgences, Holly failed to restrain herself and delivered the whirling spin-kick to the groin known as 'Ironing Flat the Precious Trinity'.

It took her ten minutes of *shiatzu* – applying deep pressure to the secret meridian points – to quieten the unfortunate man's whimpering and to assure herself he would not be needing immediate medical assistance. Despite which irritations, as she made her way home to Covent Garden, Holly's mind was crystalline and revving.

Crossing St Martin's Lane her mobile buzzed. It was Mr Plum Blossom.

'Hamish McIlvuddy lived in Hong Kong for many years. He was an agent for Shih's mainland China trade during the Cold War years and through the Cultural Revolution upheaval.'

Holly's pulse raced. 'How'd it work?'

'Shih had good *guanchi* with the Communists, McIlvuddy had good *guanchi* with the roundeyes in Hong Kong.'

'Cosy.'

'Very. And not to mention profitable. Shih owes his fortune in the early days to McIlvuddy's connections.'

'So what's the agenda for his choosing me to work the probate?'

'No idea, but there's more. They had a big falling-out, over some girl . . .'

Holly listened for a while longer, standing in the lee of Stringfellows nightclub.

'Thanks, PB I owe you one.' Her stride quickened to a jog as she dodged through the Thursday-night crowds back to Earlham Street.

The McIlvuddy Probate had her hooked.

Despite the lateness of the hour, Minty had returned to the office and sat, feet on a desk, the files open beside him, the air sweet with herb. Behind him perched Ma, kneading his neck.

'Forget all that *cherchez la femme* bollocks,' said Minty. 'It's the money, stoopid.'

'Pots and pots of it,' added Ma.

'An awful lot of loot,' Holly agreed. She'd been stunned to discover the extent of the McIlvuddy fortune.

'Did you see the land?' Minty put in. 'Vast tracts in Scotland, England, Australia and Argentina. Then there's the blue chips traded on Wall Street, London and European Bourses.'

'Not to mention the single-malt distillery,' said Ma. 'Nor the hotels and golf courses.'

'I rather like the ferryboat service between Shetland and the Scottish mainland. But seriously,' Holly said, 'if our preliminary research proves correct, Minty, this fat an inheritance precludes a peaceful probate.'

'I agree,' he said. 'The sheer magnitude of the estate gives me the wobblies.'

'You foresee inevitable skulduggery, daughter?' said Ma.

Holly looked at them both. 'Maybe a skull's already been duggered.'

'Obscene wealth like that,' Minty scratched his chin, nodding. 'Worth killing for.'

'Fratricide!' hissed Ma with grim relish.

'Going rate for a post-mortem certification in Manila?' said Holly, winking.

'Probably less than a hundred US,' cackled Ma.

'Right. Down to business,' Holly said, handing round steaming cups of fresh Oolong *cha*. 'What was the exact extent of Lord McIlvuddy's involvement in the family businesses over the years of exile?'

Ma said, 'As far as we can tell, the entire estate was and still is run as a private trust by a group of City finance eminence, some of whom are related to the family, some not. No details here, but presumably the Pooh-Bahs managed to get some kind of regular remittance to him.'

'How about Hamish, our client, Lord Snuffy himself?'

'On his uppers,' shrugged Minty. 'Filed for bankruptcy a few years back after failing to pay his tab at the bookies and is currently being sued by the Goodwood Racecourse Management for failure to sub up. Apparently Hamish Peregrine Vere Andrew likes the odd flutter.'

'Not to mention the special snuff,' said Holly. 'And that Peruvian tube-cleaner doesn't come cheap. So how about the sisters? We'll need to talk to them.'

'One's on Exmoor,' said Minty, checking the file. 'Hawkridge Manor, near Dulverton. That's Henrietta, the elder sister. Mad as a hatter by all accounts. The other, Titania, lives in a ramshackle castle turned sporadically open pub in Shetland.'

'How'd she end up there?'

'Married a local laird made bad.'

'So we schedule next week for visiting. We'll need to go and see the City eminences, the sisters and maybe Manila. How're you fixed, Minty? The painting show going to keep you busy long?'

'Not if I can help it. After I get pissed at Monday night's opening I'm gonzo. Think I want to stick around to read the reviews?'

'Good,' Holly said. 'We'll split the travel between the three of us. We can work out the exact schedule later.'

'I have a question,' said Minty.

'Fire away,' said Holly.

'Why wasn't the LSD case closed down long ago? Surely the statute of limitations has been long, exceeded.'

'Normally, yes. But,' Holly-Jean said, 'every five years or so, till his eventual retirement from police service in 1993, the courts had been petitioned by the policeman who'd led the original bust team – D.I. Paul Suttoh – to renew the charges and reissue the arrest warrant.'

'It sounds like an obsession,' said Ma.

'A highly enjoyable not to mention lucrative one.'

'What do you mean?' said Ma.

'Well, every other intervening year or so, acting on "information received" and with enough accompanying tabloid fanfare to wake an opium tribe on the morning after the harvest festival, Suttoh would set off for foreign parts with extradition papers and fat cheque from the gutter press in hand . . . only to return empty-handed.'

'Is Suttoh still alive?' Minty asked.

'Died last year,' Holly said, picking up a brand-new hardback book off the desk. 'I stopped by Dillon's on my way back from Brixton.' She quoted the title: *Scent of a Blighter* by D.I. Paul Suttoh. 'Haven't had a chance to read it fully but it seems like quaint stuff.' She turned to the last page of the book. 'Listen to this. The book ends with a quote from an entry in the detective's diary, dated 17 June, 1985.'

Holly read with mock solemnity: ' "Like a pair of doomed lovebirds, we constantly circle the globe. Me the ardent one, his nibs the shy. Too ruddy shy by half." The End.'

'So he never made the collar of a lifetime,' mused Minty.

''Fraid not. His nibs outlived him, but only for a while. Tell me what you dug up about the paternity suit,' Holly said, pouring more Oolong.

Minty picked up another file. ' "Neither marrying nor procreating, Lord McIlvuddy devoted his life of exile to the wholehearted pursuit of hedon in the form of constant momentary gratification. Following his death without an heir, the title should have passed automatically to his brother, Hamish," – your man there – "but for the sudden and unlikely emergence of a son, allegedly borne Lord McIlvuddy by his most recent Filipina live-in, a young woman by the name of Marybel Lacsina. Hence the paternity suit and the request for DNA testing. According to reports, the suit would fail." '

'How so?' asked Holly.

'A Filipino doctor, a Manny Devesfrunto, has stated for the record that, despite eschewing all forms of birth control, and rigidly following a schedule of a minimum once-daily ejaculation into an average of five new partners a week, Lord McIlvuddy's seed had never taken root.'

'So far, so good for Hamish,' said Ma. 'If the DNA test fails to prove the connection with his elder brother, he's mostway home.'

Holly pulled out the press clipping from the William Hickey column. 'What d'you make of that, guys?'

Ma and Minty perused the short piece.

'I think: velly intollesting,' said Minty.

'The trail leads to the East,' chuckled Ma.

'I think I'd best have a word with Doc Devesfrunto,' said Holly. They sipped their Oolong thoughtfully.

Minty said, 'There only remains the obligation to fulfil the stipulation of the will: that the services of a PI agency be employed to show every effort has been made to turn up any other missing heirs.'

'Which is where we come in,' said Ma.

'Hasn't something struck you as odd?' Holly said. 'Why are we talking about a will in the first place?'

'What do you mean?' asked Minty.

'I thought in matters – and here I quote today's instant

research – "of progeniture pertaining to hereditary title", the inheritance is decided by pre-set rules. Salic Law.'

'Salic what?'

'The law that excludes females from dynastic succession.'

'You're right,' said Ma. 'Surely all these Ilks and Head Chieftain-whatnots are decided by historical laws. Nothing to do with an individual's dying wishes at all.'

'It's all changing, getting freed up by Parliament. Girls can inherit. But anyway make a note of that,' said Holly. 'Visit the heraldry people.'

'Burke's Peerage?' added Minty.

'Both, if necessary,' Holly said. 'And another thing. Assuming the will is genuine and effective, it begs the further question: why us? Have we suddenly become known as the cowboys of the trade?'

'No way,' snorted Ma. 'We have a damn bloody good reputation!'

'Since the last thing oddbod Hamish wants is for us to actually turn someone up . . .' Holly reflected.

'You're absolutely right,' Minty said, puzzled. 'This agency's red-hot right now. Especially if someone had his brother murdered in Manila and made it look like a handjob from hell,' he joked. 'After all, you're known as a Far East specialist, Holly-Jean.'

'Frock, I was forgetting something!' Holly told them about Plum Blossom's phone call, Hamish's Hong Kong connection to Shih and the subsequent falling-out, 'over some girl'.

'What does that signify?' asked Minty.

'Haven't the foggiest,' admitted Holly. 'But don't worry. I'll get to the bottom of this murky little pond.'

Ho Ma-ma slapped her tiny, wrinkled hand on to the desk. 'If you ask me, this whole thing pongs like three-month-old *chou do-fu*.'

'What's *chou do-fu*?' Minty asked.

'Fermented stinky beancurd. Toff-oo to you.'

'Yikes.'

'Tastes like ripe Stilton,' said Holly, absently. 'Y'know, I suppose it could have been a genuine heart attack. Dissolute lifestyle in the Tropics. Wet rot in the House of Exile. The old roué and the young masseuse.'

'The hands that heal. Permanently,' Minty murmured, his eyes a thousand palmfronds away. 'Gawd, some of those young Filipinas are angels.'

Ma joked, 'We Chinese say: "Old cow eats young grass".'

'A fatal attack of indigestion?' said Holly-Jean. 'Doubtful. I like the idea of murder.'

'As my friend Paul Carless the trucker used to say,' said Minty, still musing on distant delights, ' "she was only fifteen, but she had the body of a twelve-year-old".'

'Thank you for sharing that,' said Holly. 'How is Paul, by the way?'

'Propping up the bar of the Cider Tap in Dulverton, by last reports.'

'You'll be going down to Exmoor to see the mad sister so get in touch with Paul. I've got a feeling we'll be needing him,' Holly said.

Minty made a note.

'Now listen, you guys,' said Holly, 'I agree with Ma. This thing stinks to high heaven, there's huge money involved and maybe Triad *guanchi*. Therefore, I think it'd be a sensible idea that we should, where our rear fundaments are concerned, from now onwards, maintain extreme vigilance. Understood?'

'Perfectly.'

'They're welcome to try for a piece of mine,' snarled Ho Ma-ma.

'Yeah, right,' laughed Minty. 'Old Chinese witch. You'd scare the living daylights out of the average Chinkie gangster.'

'You'd better believe it! Now then, fellow pilchards,' added Ma, 'what about me? Don't even think for one minute that I'm going to be left out of all the fun.'

'Don't worry, Ma,' Holly dissembled. 'You're going to be absolutely vital to Operation Snuffy.'

'I'd better be.'

When the others had finally left – Ma to an all-night mah-jong session in Gerrard Street, Minty off somewhere into London's Thursday-Night-Slight-Temperature – Holly sat alone in the upstairs flat with the files containing the financial structure of the McIlvuddy legacy.

41

The autumn wind had finally arrived from Norway and the ancient window-frames of the old spice merchant's shop rattled and groaned. Holly-Jean found she couldn't concentrate on the lists of numbers and got up to put on Carlos Jobim. Middle-aged attention deficit disorder, she reckoned.

As Jobim's soothing rhythms filled the room, she let go of the day. Inside her head she looked out onto a tropical night: a silvery stretch of sand, and beyond, the ocean – empty, calm, starlit . . . and suddenly full of foreboding.

Chapter 5

Next day, Friday, Lord Justice Reamer announced after the lunchtime recess that, in the interests of saving the taxpayers' money (and his pre-booked tee-off time the following morning) and due to lack of conclusive evidence, he had ordered the jury in the Shih Yang-fu Fraud Trial to acquit before the close of session. This news reached Ho Ma-ma before it did her only daughter.

Sitting with her *lau pengyous* – her old mates – in a basement social club off Gerrard Street in the rabbit-warren heart of Chinatown, surrounded by tables of players and the clack-clack of shuffling mah-jong tiles, she acknowledged with apparent seemly restraint the loud congratulations. Ignoring the biddies, she busied herself with her mobile phone.

'*Ai-yo!* Ho Shao-lan has really done it this time!' said one old granny.

'Fancy saving Shih Yang-fu's face!' said another.

'Might as well have won the lottery!'

'*Bitswei!* Close your lips!'

'*Dwei-la!* Bad luck to talk about it so close to Saturday's drawing!'

'What is it – three weeks' run-over? Forty mill!'

'Didn't we say don't talk about the lottery!'

'Anyway, your unmarried daughter is certainly someone to be very proud of in your old age!' This was addressed to Ho Ma-ma.

'*Tamada ni!* Whose old age, you self-abusing she-monkey!' shouted the widow to her left.

'Ho Tai-tai's just middle-aged like all of us,' said another.

'Yes, but as for her daughter's marriage – it's a terrible

shame but true even so – who'd have Shao-lan now that she's her own *lao-ban*, her own boss, making more money than most men?'

'Anyway, she's probably past childbearing already.'

'You're just jealous, spider-egg.'

'Yes, but even so, it would be an unbearable sadness not to experience the joys of grandchildren.'

'And inauspicious! Who will pay for the underworld upkeep of the lineage when you've both gone?'

'No one to burn paper-money or offer up choice goodies at the twice-a-month ritual. You'll have to beg from us in the afterlife!'

The lady to Ho Ma-ma's right, sensing that the moment of triumph had been well and truly vanquished, and concerned to avert genuine hurt, slammed her palm down on the table, upsetting the four-square lines of tiles. 'Will you turtle-turds shut up and play mah-jong!'

Lee Tai-tai, a recent addition to the group, could be forgiven for her misplaced concern. She didn't know the tiny Chinese widow on her left very well. Knew nothing of the switchblade intellect, the spitting temper, the wit as quick as a cobra's strike – and just as venomous. Had no way of knowing that in Taipei, the Ho clan called her: *Lung shang huli i-yang jao-hua.* The dragon that's as tricky as a fox.

Ho Ma-ma: Holly's awkward bundle. Who, having finally made a very bad connection, was now yelling into the mobile phone, '*Gung-shi Ni!* Congratulations, Shao-lan!' She paused. 'What! You haven't heard?'

The line went down. 'Hello? . . . Hello?' Ho Ma-ma shook the cellphone angrily. '*Yang-wei houtze!* Self-abusing simians!'

She tried again. The line was shrouded in static. 'Shao-lan? Little Orchid? Are you there? Well, whether you can hear me or not, for tonight's celebration I'm inviting this gang of dried-up parrot pudendae.' To which announcement the ladies cheered.

Holly put down the phone with a puzzled look. 'Ma's finally gone bonkers,' she said to Minty who'd just returned from a hanging. 'Something about masturbating monkeys and parrot's private parts. Least I think that's what she said, it was a terrible connection.' She noted Minty's sour expression. 'How're they hanging, kiddo?'

Minty grunted. 'Hah.'

With his show opening Monday at the Kaiserman-Soho Gallery, Minty had spent the day with Sadie Kaiserman and his agent overseeing the hanging of the paintings in the exhibition.

'On-on, lad,' she urged cheerfully. 'Nothing like a well-hung show.'

But Minty had other stuff on his mind. That was obvious to his oldest and best friend, and she had a pretty good inkling as to what.

Sure enough he started in. 'Holls, wasn't it great in the old days at the Lock?'

He meant Camden Lock, where he and Holly had been neighbours and where in the agency's infancy he'd been her occasional part-timer. Professionally speaking, that is. As friends they were closer than lovers, but never physically so. Minty was married with daughters, and Holly was, well, off all *that* at the moment.

She smiled at Minty. 'You mean when hippies ran Bokhara stalls at the weekend and the nights were raucous at Dingwalls.'

'Right!' said Minty excitedly. 'Fan-fucking-tastic pub-rock – Ian Dury, Brinsley Schwartz, Graham Parker and the Rumour. Neglected soul maestros like Arthur Conley and Wilson Pickett.'

'Which was before the Lock became London's third biggest tourist attraction after the British Museum and the Crown Jewels,' said Holly drily. 'Before the cobblestones bordering the old canal became inundated night and day by a neverending flash-flood of the planet's fashion-victims, frenziedly craving their fix of *Camden* street-cred.'

'Exactly.' Looking around, Minty said, 'Some place, this.' He gestured at the state-of-the-art Gaggia, the surveillance system. 'Top-of-the-line. Like the Hardom-Kardon hi-fi, the electronics. Granted the fifth-floor penthouse is just two tiny bedrooms above a single studio space, but two properties in this expensive and prestigious backwater of Covent Garden? Must have cost an astronaut's arm and leg. How about the other tenants, Holls?' he asked.

'London pieds-à-terre mostly,' she replied. 'Heard of Betrina Isley?'

'The African-American contralto diva.'

'First floor,' said Holly. 'Away most of the time singing at the world's best opera-houses. On the second there's a Lebanese arms middleman whom we never see.'

'Convenient.'

'Yup,' Holly said. 'Third floor; young yahoos. Leave their kids in the country for a couple of nights on the Town every week. Old Prof. Harrison lives on the fourth. Retired plastic surgeon who pioneered liposuction. Single gent and quiet as a mouse except for the odd spot of bother some mornings when his rent-boys refuse to leave gracefully.'

'All loaded to the gills, then,' noted Minty with an exaggerated Cymru lilt.

Holly knew exactly his thoughts: Where was all the dosh coming from? Of course, he'd reason, there was Ma: what with the Taipei stock-market going extraterrestrial, the old Hakka peasant was probably worth a bob or two.

Even so . . .

'Don't get me wrong, Holly, old girl, but didn't we get the exact same buyout deal? Jolly generous, but y'know . . .' He meant the compensation paid to residents before the steel-ball flattened the old warehouse at the Lock.

'Enough with the snide, Minty,' said Holly. 'Out with it.'

He whistled the intro to Otis Redding, then changed the words as he sang, 'Sitting on the Dock of the Old Bail-ey, getting pa-ay-aid to lie.'

'Not funny,' said Holly.

'Your business,' shrugged Minty.

'Right.'

But the thing once released hung in the air like a poison toadfart. While Minty busied himself rolling a joint, Holly bit her thumbnail and asked herself for the umpteenth time *why* she had agreed to give evidence for Shih Yang-fu.

Which was when a gleaming black extended Cadillac pulled up with a swish of air on the cobbles of Earlham Street outside the twin-arched windows and, though Holly froze in anticipation of the stocatto spray of automatic weaponry, it

46

was nothing more than Chinese bearing gifts. Two young Oriental boys in white shirts, black pants, white socks and black shoes, began carting in hampers of Chinese epicure, the cases of Kao-liang wine, the huge floral disc supported on an easel which spelled out in chrysanthemums the character *syingfu*, Eternal Happiness.

While Minty nodded sardonically, Holly-Jean tried to refuse the gifts in traditional Mandarin etiquette. Her efforts were naturally ignored. There was a moment's embarrassment when one of the boys adopted a formal pose, bowed and enquired in correct Mandarin as to Holly's requirements: 'Regarding the height, girth and length of the young male selection for your evening's pleasure.'

'Not necessary, thank you master, most humbly and effusively,' replied Holly, blushing.

'Perhaps your friend . . .?' He indicated Minty.

Holly looked at Minty for a moment. Biting her lip to stop the giggles, she bowed her head and said in formal Mandarin, 'That would be most generous. The choice shall be left in your hands.'

The boy backed out of the door, and the limo surfed away.

'What? Whaaat?' demanded Minty.

But Holly couldn't stop giggling.

Even as Earlham Street suddenly became jammed solid with TV news outside-broadcast vans and a scrum of cameramen and microphone-wagging reporters burst through the office door with shouts of, 'Who is the mystery girl involved in the collapse of yet another case by the Serious Fraud Office and the predicted cost to the taxpayer of more than five million pounds!'

Around midnight the chic denizens of that part of Covent Garden, the after-theatre crowd, the pre-nave E mob and a blasted bevy of provincial lager-louts were startled to see a group of elderly Chinese ladies in their best party-cheongsams spill out of Number 40 clutching open bottles of strong-smelling clear spirit and whole wind-dried ducks as they cackled their way back the three blocks to Chinatown.

Up on the roof, Ma, Holly and Gi-Gi – the last so stuffed with salted pollock roe that his single front paw kept buckling

47

under his stuffed belly and he had to be carried to bed – retired discreetly.

The three of them leaving Minty to continue his futile attempts at getting the gorgeous painted courtesan fresh off the illegal immigrant boat from Fujien Province to comprehend that he wished her to share his other joint as well.

The paper one.

Chapter 6

Holly spent a quiet Sunday futzing around the top-floor apartment with the place to herself. The way she liked it. Following Saturday's all-night mah-jong, Ma was on her regular visit to the home of Holly's Dad's only sister, Auntie Glad, in Welwyn Garden City. So Holly was alone.

Phone on answer-machine with the volume turned down. Chet Baker in the hi-fi. The serious Sundays spread all over the floor. Chilled Alsace varietals to hand and a defrosted sack of *ma-lah ho-guo* – numbingly spicy hotpot – simmering away on the stove.

The lethal chili-oil-swimming concoction – a Taiwanese speciality that made the heat of a mutton vindaloo seem like kid's stuff – was offered by only one establishment in Chinatown. All the London Taiwanese knew the place but few indigenous inhabitants were aware of the mad delights of *ma-lah ho-guo*'s tongue-blistering tastes.

Any adventurous local souls who venture in off the street by chance may sample at their peril the red-brown sludge of separated oil and liquid. With chary chopsticks they may pick from the accompanying dishes of raw ingredients to dunk briefly into the stew bubbling over a table-flame and singe before tasting.

The waiting staff kindly serve a pot of mild-brewed jasmine tea to soften up the hot-pot when it gets to napalm strength. Should unwitting virgin epicures, spice-buds intact, attempt this dish, they will relearn the old adage that pleasure in life comes at a price. As Holly would tell friends, 'Beware the Morrow.' Or at the least make sure your toilet door has strong hinges.

Fiery by nature, Holly-Jean was addicted to the stuff. She

49

had to have it at least once a month, lest she go into decline.

She reckoned it a sex substitute.

Gi-Gi arrived mid-morning, obviously exhausted from a night on the tiles, lapped up some of the tea-diluted *ma-lah* and after a howled shudder of fur-standing pleasure, hopped up on his three legs and draped himself over Holly's lap.

While Holly scanned the papers, left her hand absently fondling his soft furry stump, Gi-Gi purred like a buzz-saw. Stories about the Old Bailey fraud case and the acquittal of Shih Yang-fu were mostly featured in the financial sections. Though Atticus mentioned her appearance in the dock, describing her as 'the black-belted exotic Anglo-Chinese beauty who last year negotiated the safe release of the Mindano hostages'. Thus the day drifted by.

At eight in the evening Holly went for a walk around Covent Garden Piazza, watching the tourists and the buskers. A man stepped out from behind one of the big columns fronting the church in the Piazza and said, 'Hi, darling, long time no see!'

He put his arm round Holly's shoulder as though greeting an old friend, and in the act of kissing her cheek, whispered with a menacing but perfect enunciation, 'You will fail conspicuously, spectacularly and of course, utterly, in your earnest endeavours to locate any living heirs to the McIlvuddy estate. Is this clearly understood?'

His fingers had clasped a knot of hair at the nape of her neck and tugged hard, causing Holly to wince as her right hand snaked between the man's legs and grabbed his gonads.

Her captor gasped, 'OKOKOK!' as his grip instantly released her neck.

'Hakkanese stand-off, sucker,' said Holly, squeezing hard. The man sank to his knees moaning, tears streaking down his cheek.

Holly gave her wrist a last flick and pinch before setting him free. She looked down at him writhing on all fours, no one giving him much attention in that parade of street freaks and performance nutters. He was some kind of Chinese, not obvious which – but a sophisticated type, judging by the fashionable clothes and the clever English.

'Who sent you?' The man didn't answer so Holly remarked quietly, 'You would prefer another lychee handshake?'

'No, no,' the man began babbling. 'Honest, Little Miss. They never said. Just another client.'

'Client? What is your business?'

The man climbed to his feet and scrabbling in his pocket brought out a card-holder. In the instant Holly noted the metal strip lining the small wallet, she ducked, felt her hair parted by the blade, delivered a rapid combination of left-right-left to the man's meridian points and as he crumpled, reached out to hold him from falling and pinched the nerve to the carotid artery in his neck, inducing immediate ebbing of consciousness as blood to the brain was halted.

'Who sent you?'

A scream of high-revs accompanied the blow from behind as the motorbike's tyre sent Holly sprawling. As she looked up from the ground, the bike and its driver were racing away with her new acquaintance on the back. She jumped to her feet. Frockit!

For a moment or two she berated herself angrily. She'd been sorely lacking in diligence. Worse, she'd momentarily lost her concentration, assuming the man was alone. Her years of advanced training should have prepared her for the bike's sudden arrival, even here in the middle of the Piazza and some distance from the road. But she'd misused her hard-won discipline and had indulged the glee of victory. Bad, bad work.

Time she paid the *dojo* a visit. Time to rehone. Less than perfection was unacceptable. In her chosen line of work it could be fatal.

Her eye noticed the bladed wallet lying on the Piazza's cobblestones where it had landed. In their scramble to get away, her attackers had overlooked it.

Holly walked over and picked it up. It was empty. They'd hardly leave a calling-card, now would they? Besides, it was obvious the men had been sent from one of the Societies. The talk of clients was mere flim-flam. There *were* no

51

Chinese freelancers. It was as simple as that.

Fingering the razor-sharp edge, Holly-Jean walked home in deep thought to a last dish of *ma-lah* before a narcoleptic chili-tranced sleep of searing nightmares.

Chapter 7

The true extent of the tycoon Shih Yang-fu's gratitude was revealed well before lunch on Monday when Mr Denzil Nuttall, a solicitor, arrived at the Earlham Street office with a cardboard box wrapped in auspicious red silk and a bundle of documents for Holly to sign.

The documents proved to be share certificates of stock in a bewildering array of trading companies, mostly based in provincial China. The well-augured red box proved to be crammed full of crisp new fifty-pound notes.

'Oh,' said Holly. 'Maybe I should return that one.'

'Nonsense. I'll stash that,' said Ma briskly.

Over coffee, Holly and Ma spent the next hour carefully checking all the papers, while the solicitor did *The Times* crossword.

At one point Holly said incredulously, 'He's really just giving away these shares?'

'*Ai-yo*, but are they worth the paper they're printed on?' remarked Ma, waving a sheaf. 'This stuff looks like it's been recycled from left-hand usage.'

Putting aside his newspaper, Nuttall intervened with an oleaginous smirk. 'Might I suggest that perhaps your mother would prefer to relax with a cup of tea upstairs and leave the two of us to handle the paperwork?' he said smoothly, addressing Holly-Jean. 'I am instructed to deal with the sole individual, known legally as—' here he consulted a notebook '—Deirdre H. Jones, Holly-Jean Ho, Ho Shao-lan. That is to say, yourself, madam. In my long experience, these matters are often better conducted in a more, shall we say, *private* environment.'

'Forget it, buster. The Witch of the East stays.' Ho Ma-ma

stood up and cackled horribly, elbowing the solicitor out of her way.

'Shao-lan, I'm a regular visitor to Taiwan and the Main-land, right?' she appealed to her daughter. 'Believe me – it's like magic over there nowadays. All these bankrupt state-owned businesses have been privatised and cash raised out of thin air. Pouf!' She flung her hands out wide. 'Their trick is to use prestigious international financial consultants to launch the public offerings. These economic high-fliers are wined and dined, shown around the same gleaming, high-productivity factory, the same huge tract of prime "special economic zone" acreage, shown the same provincial planning-approved multi-billion-dollar infrastructure plans for subways, canals, high-speed railways, airports . . . Over and over. The same project, different name. They just change the presentation print job!'

Ho Ma-ma paused for breath after delivering her punch-line, then added sagely: 'The beauty is, even if the trickery is discovered, nobody wants the bottom to fall out of the market, so nobody's telling. Meanwhile the state officials have sold high, pocketed some nice change and moved to Vancouver.'

'So we get some worthless B shares on the Shenzhen stock market. Who knows, one day . . .' said Holly brightly.

At that point they came across a document that purported to be the deeds to the complete ownership of a certain Nan-Yang Pescatorial Corporation.

'Now this *does* seem fishy,' joked Holly, handing the documents to Ma.

'*Ai-yo!*' exclaimed Ma, after scrutinising the paper care-fully. 'What in the name of the gods is the turtle-brained idea of giving away a whole deep-sea fishing company, lock, stock and barrel?'

Nuttall, the solicitor, explained that Holly-Jean would be doing Mr Shih an enormous favour in terms of UK tax management by accepting the nominal and very temporary ownership of this and certain other companies.

Holly called her accountant to confer.

'Touch those with a two-hundred-foot barge-pole,' said the woman on the other end of the phone, 'and it'll be me doing the character witness bit and you the Serious Fraud Office's playmate of the month.'

Holly then called her connection with the Bamboo Union to gauge the probable effect on her *guanchi*, not to mention her general health and welfare, of such a refusal.

After the usual delay piercing the miasma of electronic subterfuge, she reached her old acquaintance, Mr Plum Blossom, gentleman and according to Ma's sudden hissing in her ear, just recently inducted *bi da-gr*.

Holly assumed that her old pal had been promoted to the office of Older Elder Brother on the strength of many removals. Human and otherwise. As usual he addressed her as 'Exceedingly Unmarried Miss Ho'.

'Ho *Shao-jye*, in the light of your recent efforts on Shih Yang-fu's behalf, a refusal will not offend. On this *one* occasion.'

'Are you sure?' Holly said.

'I am sure. However,' he added, 'I strongly urge you not to make it a habit.'

Thanks a lot, thought Holly, questioning for the umpteenth time why Fate had decreed she be split between two worlds.

'By the way, Mr Plum Blossom, who do you know who fits this description?' She described the two men from the Piazza.

'Nothing immediately comes to mind but I'll look into it, Extremely Unmarried Miss Ho.'

'Would you? That will definitely set my *chi* at ease. Meanwhile if you should come across a lad in Chinatown seeking treatment for blue testicles . . .'

Mr Denzil Nuttall seemed anxious to leave following the latter telephone conversation. Loosening his collar, he watched closely as Holly signed receipts for the various stock certificates. He made no comment when she declined to accept the transfer of ownership documents. Those he stowed away in his case, leaving one small bundle.

'There just remains one more thing, madam. If you wouldn't mind signing here.' He indicated a dotted line on a single sheet of paper.

While Holly hesitated, Nuttall held out a tattered document.

'This one is yours,' he urged. 'It comes with absolutely no

55

strings attached. A gift, as they say, and I'm assuredly no Greek. I think you'll find it more of a cosmetic afterthought, perhaps designed to appeal to the feminine in you from someone who is genuinely grateful.'

'You read it, Shao-lan,' demanded Ma.

With difficulty Holly deciphered the smudged-ink print job of Chinese characters on the off-colour, lowest-quality paper.

' "*The Harmonious Friction Entire Wedding Service*",' she read.

' "*Nuptial Dress-Hire, Beauty Salon and Photographic Studio. Customed Portraiture of Historical Romance. Uniformed Chauffeur with Foreign Limousine. Additionally: Supreme Herbal Tea of Fragrance with Vitamin Supplier. P.O. Box 378. Urumchi, Sinkiang Province, People's Republic of China*".'

She put down the deeds with a huge grin and looked at her mother. 'A wedding salon and tea dealership in Sinkiang, Ma!' she exclaimed. 'It sounds absolutely brilliant!'

'*Oo-loo moo-chi*, Sinkiang?' Ma erupted. '*Tamada!*'

Holly was shocked. Ma's language was usually colourful but rarely quite so iridiscent.

'*Shema wen-ti?*' she asked. 'What's the problem, Ma?'

'Urumchi's full of Muslim splittists and liquorice allsorts: Uigurs, Kazakhs, Huis, Kirgizes, Xibes, Tajiks, Tartars, Uizbeks and Daurs. The only thing in common that lot have is they hate the Han Chinese.'

Barrance T. Wong was passing by at that moment on his way out to lunch, and quite exceptionally he stopped and spoke.

'Urumchi. The exact geographical centre of Asia.' Behind the bottle-thick lenses, his eyes twinkled with a far-off gleam. 'It is the location furthest away from the oceans to be found anywhere on the planet,' he announced. 'A strange and wonderful place. There you may find the most sublime alpine landscapes and swan lakes juxtaposed with the harshest desert on earth – the Taclamacan. Which in translation means, "The desert you go into, but do not come out of." A place I have often dreamed of visiting.'

A speech of such length and emotional content from the lips of the entirely pleasant but normally silent cyber-sorcerer left Holly and Ma stunned.

After an embarrassed pause, Holly unscrewed the cap of her Parker pen and waved the two halves about. 'Well, who knows, Barrance?' she said. 'Perhaps you shall visit Urumchi one day. Sooner than you might expect.'

Barrance T. Wong paused with his hand on the door. His habitual look of pained bafflement had returned.

'The saltmarsh of Lop Nur is also nearby. That is where the Chinese conduct the underground nuclear testing. Moreover, many of the *lao-gai* are located in the vicinity.' He shut the door carefully behind him.

'*Lao-gai* – forced labour camps! The Chinese gulag!' crowed Ma. 'Little Orchid, you don't want to know. It's the Wild West!'

'Ma, it's a *Shop on the Silk Road* and it's ours!' said Holly, signing her name to the deed.

'*Ai-yai-yai-yai-YAI!*' muttered Ma.

When Mr Denzil Nuttall had finally left, Holly and Ma shut the shop and walked over to Gerrard Street. At a fifth-floor establishment overlooking the bustling street they ate steamed vegetarian dumplings and drank Oolong. After lunch Ma had business to attend to in Chinatown, so Holly strolled back to the office at a slow pace, reflecting on the morning's happenings. The heatwave was over, and the October sun was silvery in the Nordic wind. As she meandered through the crowds, the phrase *Harmonious Friction Wedding Salon* echoed on the breeze.

Holly-Jean was a true Londoner and she loved Covent Garden with its European street-café atmosphere. Considered herself extremely lucky to be living in what some would say was the best place in town. But recently she'd begun to wonder if she'd someday break out for a period.

Move to Asia, try living in Chinese society for a while.

Dig into the buried half of her schizoid soul.

Had Fate in the form of a Wedding Salon in distant Sinkiang decreed it thus?

As she reached the office a Chinese gentleman was waiting by the door. Not again, thought Holly, bracing herself for sudden violence. But no, this man removed his black Shanghai fedora, and said politely, 'Ho *Shao-jye*, humble felicitations and greetings from Shih Yang-fu. Might I have a quick word?'

Holly unlocked the door and let the man in ahead of her.

'I will be brief,' he said, when Holly had closed the door behind her and offered the man Oolong *cha*. 'It has come to my patron's attention that you have become involved in a certain legal matter, pertaining to what or whom it is not necessary to elaborate, except to say that it concerns a probate and the identification of any extant beneficiaries.' The man looked at her.

Holly looked back and said nothing.

He continued, 'My patron has requested that I pass on his personal message of support. Indeed, he wishes you every success in your venture to locate any living descendants of the deceased.'

Holly raised an eyebrow.

The man cleared his throat. 'That is to say, my patron believes that you will undoubtedly be successful in this endeavour, and that you will indeed discover the existence and whereabouts of an heir or heirs to the estate in probate. He furthermore offers any kind of assistance that may be needed at any time and in any place. Is this clearly understood?'

Holly had had enough of these personally delivered questions of comprehensive clarity.

'Tell your patron ta, thanks, and not necessary.' She saw the man out and sat at her desk trying to concentrate on routine office crud.

About three in the afternoon, Shirley Jacquet arrived and Holly-Jean spent an hour or so giving neutral answers to the tabloid journalist's muck-raking questions about Shih Yang-fu. Acutely wary of divulging any information that might offend the tycoon, or disaster of disasters, cause him to lose face. Holly explained to Shirley that all myths, rumours and allegations to the contrary aside, as far as she knew, the man was practically a saint.

'Don't give me that guff,' was Shirley's predictable response.

'Look,' snapped Holly, somewhat weary of the world, 'just because I'm half-Chinese doesn't mean I'm privy to every arcane secret of the Orient.'

'Maybe not,' Shirley said, 'but as Holly-Jean Ho, private

clit, conduit to the Chinese, the best person in town to turn to if you've got a problem of a – shall we say – yellowish hue, you know a damn sight more than you've given me so far. C'mon, Holly, spill the beans!'

'Might get me into serious trouble with the hierarchy.'

'Hierarchy?' Shirley enthused. 'Now you're talking!'

'I mean Chinese UK society, nothing more.'

'Give, girl.'

'Well, all right then, Shirl, since I owe you,' Holly said with feigned reluctance. 'But this comes with a price-tag, agreed?'

'Agreed.'

'Any rumours of heirs or heiresses to the McIlvuddy estate surface in your world, let me know.'

'Natch. As long as it's quid pro quo. Any turn of events connected to that vat of dosh, you let me know firstest.'

'Done.'

Though Shih Yang-fu's bio was a matter of public record in Asia, Holly knew that in London, until the trial had thrown the unwelcome glare of the public spotlight upon him, few outside the sphere of Asian financial expertise had even heard of the man. Atypically of the Chinese super-rich, who traditionally flaunt their wealth, Shih Yang-fu lived a highly secretive life. The turning world outside the walls of his exclusive spaces dotted around the globe, remained for the most part completely unaware of the man's existence.

Adding exotic embellishments from her own imagination, Holly recounted for the benefit of Shirley Jacquet's copy, the legend of Shih Yang-fu. His rise from the first breath of life between the thighs of a dying thirteen-year-old waif on the rat-shit banks of the fetid Wangpoo River in war-time Shang-hai to the pinnacles of global wealth. His starved pot-bellied days as an orphan refugee of the civil war between the Nationalist forces of Chiang Kai-shek and the victorious Communist army of Mao Tse-tung.

Serving glasses of chilled Muscat d'Alsace, Holly told the journalist how Shih Yang-fu had smuggled himself into Hong Kong as a toddler under a consignment of frozen skipjack tuna and how his tiny, blue, stiff body had been dumped on the harbourside of the feet of a Bible-hollering nun from the

Methodist Mission who had thawed him back to life over a charcoal brazier.

The boy had begun his entrepreneurial life by collecting for the Mission from the offices of round-eyed businessmen and Chinese traders. Wooden box in hand, he had walked the streets of Hong Kong from dawn to dusk with unfailing diligence and with the zeal of the rescued, calling each day just before the noon cessation of stock trading, at the offices of a broker where he invested half the proceeds.

The young lad was such a successful elicitor of funds that the Mission never suspected his perfidy. By the time he was seventeen, Shih Yang-fu had already made his first million.

'The rest, as they say,' Holly declaimed as she poured Shirley a third glass of wine, 'is money, money, money.'

'Bunkum, bollocks and bullshit,' replied Shirley, shaking her head in exasperated admiration. 'You're such a great little liar, Holly-Jean.'

'But it is adequate copy?'

'Adequate,' conceded Shirley ruefully. 'But what about the Triads, Holls? Can't you throw in a secret ritual or two? Maybe a little Chinese torture? Y'know the sort of thing: "*The Death of a Thousand and One Tumescent Cockroaches*" No? Then how about the drugs . . . illegal immigrant smuggling? Worldwide prostitution?'

'Choice racial stereotyping there, Shirl – very nice,' said Holly-Jean sarcastically. 'But even if I did know about any of that stuff – and I'm not admitting to it – I'd be a wee bit stupid to have my name quoting it all down in your rag, now wouldn't I?'

After Shirley had gone Holly-Jean reached for the phone and called Professor Janet Rae-Smith. A reformed alcoholic, Jan, Holly's best friend, was now a member of the Prime Minister's shadowy but influential clique of advisers known as the Merlin Group. Holly left a message on the beeper and Janet called back a few minutes later.

'Hi, Jan!'

'What's up?'

'I need a financial whizz-kid's brain for an hour or so.'

'Pertaining to what, might I enquire?'

'The McIlvuddy estate.'

Jan whistled appreciatively. 'You handling that? Good one, girl.' She paused, muttering to herself over the line. 'Let's think . . . floods of filth floating thereabouts. I know! Charlie V. He'd just love to stick his dirty great proboscis into that trough of fat. Holly?'

'Yup?'

'I'll set up a meet.'

'Ta, thanks, Jan.' She jotted down some details on a notepad.

Janet said she had to rush. 'We'll do Parliament Hill some time soon.'

'I'll bring the kite,' said Holly.

Chapter 8

Monday night's private view for Minty's show at the Soho-Kaiserman Gallery in Greek Street was packed with the artsy-fartsy crowd.

After a word of welcome and requisite posturing with Minty's agent, Sadie Kaiserman, a lacquer-taloned Manhattan hardnut, Holly-Jean and Ho Ma-ma left Minty at the hands of the mob and did the rounds with glass in hand, Holly rejecting the acidic Riesling after a sip for a Pernod and water on ice, Ma opting for a schooner of Beck's and a comfy seat on a black leather sofa from which to peruse the art. Holly wandered, unlike most of the liggers, actually looking at her friend's work.

'Uh-oh, look who's here,' said a voice. It was Chief Superintendent Mick Coulson of Scotland Yard, senior Diplomatic Squad officer and Met CCLC boss liaison.

'Hi, Mick,' said Holly. 'Still avoiding tofu?'

'Me and health food's like Captain Haddock and water – makes me poorly.' He swigged his bottle of Beck's, gestured at the wall. 'Nice big colourful paintings. Got things in them I actually recognise.'

'Natch. It's our mate Minty wot done it.'

They drifted slowly by the huge gaudily hued canvases.

'ID that body yet?' asked Holly.

'Nope,' replied Coulson. 'But your guess was spot-on. The victim *was* a Filipina. We found the labels on her clothes originated in Manila. Apart from which, a big zero. Nothing on Missing Person here. And as yet we've received zip from Manila.'

'Don't hold your breath. Even the Philippine government admits there are no reliable birth records for about half the country. You want an identity in the Philippines, you make one up. There are little printing shops in every major *barrio* running up new papers. Still, someone must be grieving for a missing relative.'

'Well, to be honest,' sighed Mick, 'we haven't the resources to spend time on this one.'

'Right,' snorted Holly. 'What's another Flip here or there? After all, the planet's swamped with them – domestics, dancers or prostitutes. Servile positions of absolutely no political value or influence.'

'All right, all right, don't get your panty-liner in a twist. I promise to keep an eye on it.'

'I'll check on that.' Holly poked him in the chest.

They stopped by a giant canvas and gazed. The policeman changed the subject.

'Listen up, Holly-Jean,' he said in grim tones. 'Following your act of sabotage at the Old Bailey last week, I've got some muckers in the Serious Fraud Squad who are just a wee bit miffed with you, to put it mildly. You must know the SFO works hand in glove with the Inland Revenue . . .'

'Oh really?' Holly feigned boredom, but knew the hateful taxmen could make her life misery should they choose to do so.

'Yes, really,' said Coulson. 'You'd better watch that sweet pert behind. I heard nasty rumours of an "imminent penetrating scrutiny of your current tax status". And that's one area where I can't help at all. If they want revenge, those dickheads can dig it up somehow, somewhere.'

'So maybe it's time for a bag-job on the nightboat to Rotterdam. Stash the cash in Luxembourg pronto.'

'Hush your mouth, sweet girl of my dreams.' Trouble with Coulson was that he perpetually saw himself as Holly's knight protector, she his fair damsel in distress. Reality was Holly picking up *his* pieces. By her reckoning, he owed her at least a third of his career.

Hang on – something funny about the picture in front of them. It depicted an image of a tiny intense female figure with grotesque spiky black hair, pushing apart or holding back the seas of two globes. Under the layers of colour there were charcoal-smeared Chinese characters on one global shoreline, and English print on the other. International currency denominators could be seen emerging from the layers of acrylic. Below the woman's struggling dangling body was a blacker than black abyss.

Wordlessly Mick pointed at the title on a card stuck to the wall. Holly leaned forward and read: *My Best Friend.*

'The blood snake in the grass,' muttered Holly, as angry shouting broke out somewhere near the front door of the gallery.

Mick and Holly turned towards the source of the commotion. The milling crowd suddenly parted. A woman shrieked as a group of half a dozen or so black-leather garbed, pony tailed Chinese boys broke through the guests in a swagger, swigging from green bottles of Ching Tao beer, flicking their cigarette butts about them, and spitting gobs of blood-red betel-nut juice on the polished wood floor to splatter onto the designer threads of the terrified glitterati.

Shouting a mix of English and Mandarin obscenities they were gone in a few seconds.

By the time Holly had shoved her way through the suddenly babbling crowd, only the screaming of high-revved two-strokes and a cloud of acrid blue exhaust were left hanging in the air of Greek Street.

'Wow, heavy art critics or what?' joked Minty above the hubbub.

'*Sunday Times*, mate,' called a wag.

Coulson stood by Holly in the doorway. 'What do you make of that?'

'*Shao lyoumang* – little gangsters. The youngest rung of the Triad ladder.'

'What did they want?'

'No idea,' replied Holly, looking down the street as the last wisp of exhaust evaporated, 'but they had Shanghainese accents.'

Chapter 9

Through her old chum, Professor Janet Rae-Smith, Holly had arranged an appointment with Charlie Villiers, Investment Manager at Ardossan-Burge.

She parked the Yamaha DT in a bike space overlooking the river and was shown to her seat by the female maitre d' in the vast glass and chrome eating-pit known as The Lido just over Blackfriars Bridge. The place was packed with City suits and power-dressed women.

'I'm Charlie – you must be Holly-Jean. Well, Janet said you were gorgeous. She was understating. Hope that doesn't offend. Can't be bothered with the PC rules.'

'It doesn't offend,' said Holly, smiling. Villiers was a handsome jelly-roll himself.

The waiter came and took the order for drinks.

Charlie smiled expansively. 'Champagne, I think, don't you?'

Holly thought.

'Now as for the food, it's edible here. My advice is think "Millennium!" and go boffo,' said Charlie. 'It's OPM.'

'OPM?'

'Other people's money.'

'Isn't that immoral?'

'Not in the slightest,' said Charlie, ordering Beluga caviar and roast venison. 'I tend others' money; make it grow. They do nothing. Now and then I hand them a vase of freshly picked cash. They're happy; I'm happy. For lunch today you be happy too.'

'Righto,' said Holly. 'I'll have Loch Fyne oysters followed by barbecued red snapper in banana leaf.'

'So,' said Charlie when the waiter had gone, 'Jan Rae-Smith

says I'm to be yours for an hour. Anything you want to know. Barring the speak-your-weight machine, of course.'

'The McIlvuddy wealth.'

Villiers whistled appreciatively. 'Think Croesus. Apart from the blue-ribbon portfolios, and the multitude of businesses, the monster in that estate is the land holdings. Untapped minerals, uranium, platinum Down Under, vast stretches of the undeveloped coastline of Western Australia. Think, in fact, unseemly drool.'

'It's that big?'

'Think Godzilla.'

Holly's snapper was smothered in coconut juice, lemon grass, galangal and fresh coriander, and melted like butter in her mouth. Charlie stuffed his face with venison with all the trimmings, and spoke of the wealth generations of McIlvuddys had acquired during the days of Empire.

After lemon and carambola sorbets, Holly wiped her lips with the linen and said, 'So the matter of inheritance is likely to be fraught?'

'Think Mike Tyson in a jacuzzi full of piranhas.'

'Worth killing for?'

'Think utterly.'

Holly sighed, threw back her head and tipped down the crystal flute of Krug.

Think: It ain't so rough. Occasionally.

For the well-hung length of Charlie Villier's post-prandial Havana, Holly and the charming City gent took a stroll by the River Thames. The sun had thrown a handful of diamonds onto the surface of that old stretch of water. Tugboats and gin-palaces rocked on the gentle tide. Paddle-steamers converted into tourist traps collected barnacles and slimy green algae.

Fortunately, no pop star had decided to launch his latest release by some vulgar publicity spectacle. Instead, moving with stately majesty upstream from the North Sea was a five-masted tall-ship, sails reefed, gleaming woodwork, Cyrillic lettering on its prow and crew standing at stations.

Holly said, 'All ship-shape and Bristol-fashion.'

'Aye, aye, Master Mate.' Charlie saluted. 'Break open the cabin-boy!'

Inspired by the October sunshine, Holly decided as they strolled along to filch as much information as she could from Charlie Villiers about her recently acquired Shenzhen B shares, the Sinkiang trading company, and China prospects in general. But first she needed something else.

'Charlie, is the McIlvuddy Probate the key to the treasure-chest? Because if it is, you've got motive for murder right there.'

'Whose murder?' Charlie rubbed his chins.

'Uh-huh.' Holly shook her head.

'Well, actually, the probate is not really the key. In fact, the McIlvuddy Trust does its level best to keep the wealth way away from the family stiffs. The probate really only amounts to a decision about title and the residences, plus the odd annual dividends and stipends. But for the details you'd better have a talk to their in-house lawyer. I know the chap, name of Willy Sangster-Choate.'

'Heard of his dad,' said Holly, recalling her day at the clippings morgue.

Charlie was riffing through his Dunhill leather name-card pouch. 'I'll call and let him know who you are. Here's his number.'

'Thanks, Charlie,' said Holly, stowing the name-card. 'One more thing, since I've got you in a relaxed frame of mind: what's your take on the Shenzhen B market?'

Charlie threw back his head and roared with laughter. 'You're some girl, you are, Ms Ho! Rae-Smith warned me you'd wring me dry before the brandies. Shenzhen, eh? Tell me more, Holly-Jean.'

The City financier's reaction was guardedly enthusiastic when he'd heard the details of Holly's recent acquisitions. She was careful not to divulge names and figures, just that a benefactor had seen fit to be generous. If Charlie was on-line he'd know who.

'Hold on to those shares,' he said. 'When you get the chance to pay a visit, go take a look for yourself.'

'I heard there's a lot of flim-flam, stage-prop manufacturing plants.'

'Absence of reality is a problem in China, undoubtedly,' said Charlie, blowing huge blue ski-jumps of Havana. 'As a general rule, from the moment the wheels of the plane touch ground, think everyone in China's lying.'

Holly smiled. 'Charlie, you're talking to a girl who can trace her Hakka heritage back to Chiang Cheng-chi-sr's rape of our homeland.'

'Chiang Cheng-chi-sr?' repeated Charlie.

'Genghis Khan.'

'The Apocalyptic Horseman,' said Charlie. 'Nasty chap.'

'So began the Hakka diaspora. Despised and forced to move on after our homeland was burned. Survival of the fittest. Became the Jews of China. With one difference: we're all Chinese in the end. And my mum drilled me with the Confucian ethic: family comes first.'

Charlie looked somewhat bemused, like – So what's your point?

Holly explained. 'The Chinese are programmed from birth to devote themselves to promoting the future well-being of the family above all other considerations, including what we call honesty. It's ingrained and it's different to the rest of the planet. With the Chinese all rules are suspended. 'Think anarchy, based on a categorical imperative: me and mine first.'

Charlie chuckled mirthlessly. 'It'd be cute if it wasn't so terrifying.'

Holly shrugged. 'Chairman Mao tried to force the substitution of Party for Family, himself as the Great Helmsman, in other words, Big Daddy, but it didn't last.'

' "Smash Rotten Thinking of Long-Dead Thoughts",' Charlie remarked sombrely. 'Twelve-year-old Red Guards denouncing their own parents. The Cultural Revolution is the unsung genocide of the twentieth century.' He carefully sculpted the ash from his cigar along the crumbling stone wall above the Thames.

Holly looked at him, the glittering river reflected in her eyes. 'But that's neither here nor there. The crucial bit is: the dragon is only just awakening. One in four on the planet are Han, Mandarin is the most spoken language in our world, and when you get that diligence and acumen combined with this ethic . . .'

'You mean non-ethic.'

'No, I mean different ethic. That's the mistake the rest of the world makes. As a Chinese pal of mine put it to me when I was studying for my A Levels in the course of an offer to set up a tiny two-way radio in my fountain pen: cheating and lying aren't wrong if it's for your own good. Since this is a universal given in Chinese society, anyone who gets cheated is judged a failure. The other guy was just smarter.'

'And did you cheat in your A levels?' asked Charlie, watching a couple of seagulls squabble viciously over a Big Mac wrapper above the rippling Thames.

'No way,' laughed Holly. 'The guy wanted a hundred quid. A fortune back then.'

'But would you have?'

She pondered that one for a short second. 'No, I don't think so. I was already deep into studying martial arts by then. And that stuff teaches you spine, discipline, will. Or else.'

Charlie opened his palms to the sky. 'This thing about the world turning Chinese. Don't get me wrong. There's never been a straight world – business, I mean. But we tend to get along just about, what with rules and overseers and recourse to impartial, unbribable law. I mean, look at Hong Kong. The only reason it stays successful, that people have confidence in doing business there at all, is because of the rules we British set in motion. For as long as they're upheld.'

'So, maybe the Hong Kong disciplinary approach will be seen to be the key to market success and spread throughout China. A subversive renaissance.'

Charlie shook his head. 'Just plugging holes in the dyke of global corruption. Whole new crap-game. New rules. No-rules. Greatest good for me and mine, and the rest of you, Jack, go fuck.'

He puffed a blue cloud of his thigh-rolled leaf and looked out across the river. 'So we learn Mandarin,' he added with a cheerful shrug, 'and keep reminding ourselves. "The myth that life was always going to get better was just a con dreamed up to keep the masses striving".'

Holly turned to see if Charlie was joking. 'Paranoia in Threadneedle Street? Cripes.'

'Cynicism each day keeps disillusion at bay.'

69

'But the lolly keeps rolling in, right?' Holly quipped.

Charlie laughed. 'By the way, that boy of yours, Shih wotsit. You'd better keep that connection well-oiled, y'know – *gwanji.*'

'*Guanchi*,' said Holly. 'Why – what have you heard?'

'He's the one behind the consortium financing the big dam. Shih delivers East China's power for the next decade. He's tofu of the month.'

Lest the Krug had made Holly loose-lipped, she changed the subject. They walked on, chatting about Jan Rae-Smith, discovering mutual acquaintances, exchanging gossip. They'd reached the end of the riverside walkway when Charlie suddenly stopped and clasped her arm.

'It occurs to me I'm getting bloody addled in my old age, Holly-Jean.' He stubbed his cigar violently on the old stone and flicked the mangled butt high out onto the sparkling water. 'Were you aware, dear girl, Shih Yang-fu made a heavily disguised but unsuccessful takeover bid for the McIl-vuddy Group last year?'

'No, I wasn't,' Holly replied, biting her lip. *Frock me.* 'So what does that mean about the price of guppies?'

'Haven't the foggiest,' said Charlie as he hailed a black cab. 'Have I been of any use at all, Holly-Jean, dear girl?' he called out of the window.

'You've been unfeasibly brilliant, Charlie. Bye-bye!'

Perched astride her DT tilted on its stand overlooking the river, Holly called the office by mobile phone to check on Minty's progress.

It had been decided at yesterday morning's pow-wow that after the dust had settled on his private view, he would go down to Exmoor to see the Hon. Mrs Henrietta Pitcher, née McIlvuddy, the eccentric sister. His brief was to rattle a few bones and see if any skeletons were lurking in the mahogany wardrobes. And of course, to discover if indeed there were any other existing heirs to the estate.

Though Ma had protested vehemently, it was finally accepted that her job would be stay in Town to guard the fort. Not without a battle to save face, though.

'I'm no office *shiao-jye*, some green-eared virgin who makes *cha* and *kr-tou*'s every time she sees the boss,' she'd shouted, steaming mad at the idea of being left out of the action. 'A silly dolly-bird – all right for a few drinks after work and a lesson conjugating horticultural verbs!' (It doesn't translate well, but the essence is 'deflower'.)

Ignoring Minty's catechistical 'Why green *eared*?' Holly-Jean had pointed out that with her office assistant Polly Bruce still absent and showing no signs of returning from her holiday in Phuket, Ma's position as 'Office Chairperson and General Manager' was absolutely vital, since Barrance T. Wong refused to have anything to do with the public.

'So you see, Ma, we really do need you here,' she said. 'Besides, you're the only person I can possibly think of entrusting with the hard-earned Ho family jewels, *ker-boo ker-yi*?'

'*Ker-yi*. OK-la, I suppose so, Shao-lan,' Ma had finally conceded. The requisite face-saving had been accorded, but the banter masked a sad dawning. They all knew Ma was getting beyond high jinks.

'But Little Orchid, my one and still unmarried daughter,' Ma poked the air with her sharp, rock-steady forefinger, the skin tight, pale and unspotted by liver deterioration, 'I only agree on the condition that my *lao-pengyous* come over during office hours to play mah-jong. *Ting-r dong ma*?'

'Got you, Ma, *ting-r dong*.'

Then all there was left to do was just toast Minty good luck with snifters of Remy and see him away to prepare for the opening of his show.

He'd been in a chipper mood. But that was yesterday. Before the show. Before the critical reaction. And before last night's unsavoury visitation by Shanghainese fine-art connoisseurs of unknown provenance. Which meant today would be a whole different story.

It was now two-thirty in the afternoon. Holly calculated that her friend would be in terrible shape.

Sure enough, Minty only answered after twenty-four rings. There was a desperate groan. A clatter as the phone was dropped, fumbled for. Swearingly retrieved. A nasty fit of coughing culminated in a croaked, 'Ministry of Infinite Remorse?'

71

'Hungover are we, sweetie?' shouted Holly as loudly as she could. 'Time to sling yer behind down to Exmoor, pronto. *Dong-bu-dong?*'

'*Dooong . . .*'

He'd better understand all right, thought Holly, calling her travel agent to check her ticket was issued ready to collect for the early evening plane to Sumburgh Head, the world's most dangerous airfield according to some. (Most drunken oil riggers returning to the North Sea, by the look of the departure-gate mob at Heathrow waiting to board along with Holly.)

Being the only female on the plane, Holly-Jean was not short of attentive society.

'Aye, ye've never heard tell the one aboot the chains-man, Pissful Pete from Peterhead, coming off two-weeks' home leave?' said one straggle-bearded hulk wearing Red Wing oilman's boots.

Holly confirmed, as the plane strained up to altitude, that somehow that particular vignette of Celtic petro-chemical lore had passed her by.

'Och, absolute plonky!' said the man to her left. 'Pussed to the fucken gills, he staggered across the Tarmac and lurched full-face into the propellor of an old Dan Air DC3.'

'What yin call the paraffin budgie.'

'To-tally obliter-ated! Munce-meat!'

'How awful,' said Holly, sipping her Pernod and water.

'Raight enough,' said the straggle-bearded man. 'They say three of his mates walking behind him at the time were covered fray head tae toe with the man's remains.'

'Aye, they all ended up in the loony bin.'

'Trauma-fucken-tised.'

Holly finished her P and W, and shuddered. 'What a dreadful story.'

'Nay worries, lassie. Pissful Pete never felt a thing.'

'Aye, he wuz comin' off a fortnight of perpetual boozing on accoont of arrivin' home a wee bit early and catchin' his missus in bed with the vicar.'

'That must have broken his heart.'

'Raight enough, the vicar wuz one of they new-fangled wummin-priests.'

Nose pressed to the smeared airplane window Holly could see a fringe of beach, more ocean and a huge pyramid of black cliff. So, if the brakes failed or the reverse thrust faltered, it would be fire or ice.

The Shetland shuttle plane came skimming over the white-capped navy ocean to bounce and jerk in the cross-winds as it swooped down on the tiny landing-strip, a wrinkled layer of tar on top of a blanket of heather and peat.

On the last approach, feeling pinpricks of panic, Holly-Jean shut down her mind by *chi-kung* technique and only resurfaced when the little plane had come to a complete standstill. Far healthier than taking beta-blockers, Valium or Prozac.

The taxi from the airstrip at the southern tip of the main island of the Shetland Isles took two hours to reach Lerwick, the capital. The single Tarmac road meandered across the treeless, peat and heather strewn landscape of this northern latitude while the autumn evening sun kept slowly gripping and ungripping the sky in gold-purple claws. Heaven's Siamese cat, thought Holly-Jean.

They drove slowly into the low-rise town of Lerwick, passing a fiord, vernacularly, a *voe*, where the oil-rig supply ships, the giant tugs and the hardy little Norwegian sailboats, rocked on the gentle sheltered swell. A solitary Viking long-boat faced to the west in all its sunsetting splendour.

Bonny-looking children with rosy cheeks and carrot hair were tearing about in little groups, buttoned up against the wind. The few shops were shuttered. It was eight in the evening.

The air was chill, honey-ocean sweet and intoxicating as Holly slammed the door of the taxi and stood for a few moments, dizzy with pure oxygen breath, stretching long and low her back and legs.

'Here we are then, Holls,' she said aloud, hitching her shoulder-bag, and making the crowd of kids gathered to watch her, giggle.

Chapter 10

The Queen's Hotel, Lerwick, was a forbidding dark stone building with its rear wall rising deep from the ocean tide. From the window of her cosy little single room, Holly-Jean could see across the narrow voe to a smooth, khaki-coloured, treeless, wind-honed island. In the Northern Latitude evening sunlight, an old bent man cut peat, while his wife stacked the rich, sticky sods of ancient timber to dry out for the winter fires.

Trees become peat becomes coal becomes diamond. Simple alchemy through the unrelenting pressure of the earth's crust. Holly wondered if the pressures of a lonely life would reduce *her* in the end to a hard little unpolished gemstone.

She thumped her thighs with her fists. From which sulphurous peephole did that doomy idea slither? On such a lovely night, in such a lovely place. She shook her head to flick away the demons and recalled her Dad's oft-repeated slogan: 'Just remember, my girl, self-pity's the one luxury you can't afford.'

She opened the mini-bar and found miniatures of gin and tonic. Sipping her drink she looked out again on the island opposite, at the couple of peasants about their work at the edge of the world, on the turn of the millennium.

Nothing much changed since Breughel.

Or Bosch.

Showered, hair still damp, Holly-Jean wandered downstairs to the lobby of the Queen's Hotel looking for a meal, and was directed with a casual wave by the girl running the front desk to a door on the left. Little did she know as she turned the wooden handle and entered the Bar of the Queen's Hotel, Lerwick, Shetland that she was stepping into legend.

★ ★ ★

Ear-bleeding noise, rainforest hair canopy, steaming body
odours. A stained banner hung from beams above the throng:
The Blamelsss McCacophony.

Holly-Jean was tiny, but she rarely ever felt so. Inside this
bar, however, she was instantly dwarfed by the unruly mob.
For a moment, effaced by the close-knit communal ribaldry,
she was hesitant.

A female bumped into her. Holly-Jean pulled back, space
invaded. But instead of moving away, the girl gently insinu-
ated and entwined her body parts, smiling and stroking
Holly's face in such an animal gesture of friendship that her
rigid stance melted away.

'There, you see?' said the girl.

'Uh, thanks,' said Holly, not really knowing why.

The girl looked twenty-plus. A beauty. But a feral presence.
Dread-knotted, green-dyed locks festooned with pink ribbons
and bead-bedecked hairpieces. Piercing blue eyes, pale-silk
skin and luscious raspberry-stained lips. Unsettling. Hugging
Holly's arm and talking non-stop something, gibberish
maybe. Now laughing merrily, the girl proffered an embroidered Rajasthani cotton shoulder-bag.

'This is what you're looking for.'

Holly glanced down and in an instant her memory was
fast re-wound to the autumns of her youth. The bag was
full of freshly picked liberty cap mushrooms, some still
creamy-white, others, crushed, sodden and crawling with
maggots.

'Magic?'

'From the fairies.'

Holly just shook her head, smiling now, infected with the
girl's virulent happiness. 'Which way's the ethanol?'

The girl pouted unhappily, then pointed over the mob and
Holly shoved off through the sweaty press of dancing, singing
and shouting. Fingers in her ears, she elbowed her way to the
bar, and when she finally received the attention of a barman,
enquired about food.

'Meat pie wuth neeps and tatties,' shouted the huge
bartender, a ruddy-faced Viking with twin plaits of golden
hair reaching down to his waist.

'Tastes like shite,' said a body beside her. 'There's the McDonald's doon the road.'

'In that case, would you give me a Pernod and water, please.'

When the drink arrived, the body next to her moved off a barstool and Holly sat herself up and surveyed the frenzied bacchanal.

In the far-left corner of the long L-shaped room there was a traditional fiddle and accordion band pounding out the flailing jigs and reels of this Celt-Viking island.

An old man, wind-etched, ruddy-faced with snowy stubble from tonsure to chin, led the band, pumping his fiddle like a bellows. Holly watched, entranced, as his work-callused fingers flew up and down the cat-gut, fiercely tender and strangely erotic. Hawk nose dusted with rosin from the bow, temple-veins pulsing with music-driven life, his sea-blue eyes seemed locked on some far-off shore. A magnificent man.

Meanwhile, elsewhere in the bar, a jukebox counterposed on full volume with incessant deafening jungle.

Holly was just starting on her second Pernod and contemplating with no great enthusiasm the meat pie with boiled mashed parsnips and potatoes, when a great shout went up. All heads turned towards the tall picture window at the left end of the bar, still streaked with flames from the saga-length northern sunset.

'What's happening?' Holly shouted at the bartender.

'It's only the old crack – jump oot the windy intae the water and survive . . . and ye's drinks're on the hoose.'

'Survive? You mean . . .'

'Aye. It's friggin' Arctic Ocean oot there, baby. Ye's dead withun three minutes.'

'Oh.'

A likely story, but who cared? Someone grabbed her round the waist and she found herself in a Highland Fling, her glass of Pernod and water describing a milky arc over the heads of the crowd. The place was awash with spilled drinks, and a never-ending supply of brimming glasses were thrust at her all night long. The jigs reeled on and within moments Holly's black cotton shirt was soaked with sweat.

It seemed the old fiddler was supplied with endless energy. Every time the other band members stopped to wipe the juice from their brows and sup their pints of heavy, he'd be off bowing away again, the dancers cheering and leaping about.

At one point in the long evening, exhausted from the dance, Holly found herself in a back room at the other end of the bar with a microphone in her hand and hush fallen as she sang 'Sukiyaki' with a bunch of Mainland Chinese fishermen off a Shanghai factory ship – the only song in the karaoke book she could find that would satisfy the crowd's request for 'a Chunky-Chonky numburr'.

Later, when the sky outside the picture window was slowly darkening to violet and mauve, the girl with green hair came by and sat with her for a time, and once again proffered her embroidered cotton bag of patchouli-perfumed liberty caps.

'Free from the fairies,' she explained with a serious smile.

Was she fanatic zealot or merry prankster? Holly-Jean noted undertones of aristocratic English as the girl kept urging, 'The Viking priests used magic mushrooms in religious rituals.'

'Yeah,' said Holly, 'and they fed it to the lads just before landfall. Juice them up for an away win of rape and pillage.'

The girl shook her head violently. 'No, no. We came out of the dark into the light. Everyone here tonight has eaten them.'

New tack. Holly glanced around. The Shanghainese looked dilated. 'What, even the old man on the fiddle?'

'How do you think he plays that stuff all night?'

To which Holly-Jean shrugged. If you can't beat them . . .

Around seven o'clock in the morning, wincing in the harsh sunlight clanging off the water like a fire siren, Holly-Jean slowly paced back along the voe to the Queen's Hotel.

Yawning cavernously, she stripped off her clothes and entered the tiny en-suite bathroom. There she rigorously showered, then using a Vedantic silver chain from Shri Ma's ashram in Kerala, she cleansed her nasal passages. This involved dropping her head back, inserting the chain into a nostril, letting it pass down into the throat behind the epiglottis, reaching in her finger to hook the chain and then pulling the two ends in a sawing motion. She bent to the sink and ingested fresh icy water, then expelled them in two fine jets.

She turned her attention to her molars. She flossed violently and scrub-brushed her teeth. Using a Yunnan tongue-scraper she roughly harvested the greenish tundra of poisons from the back of her tongue to the tip, leaving it bright red and vibrant. Finally she Q-tipped her ears and got dressed.

Her way of evacuating all the toxic shit of the night before.

She hadn't slept a wink, she'd eaten nothing since she couldn't remember when and her calf-muscles ached from the jigs and reels as though multiple-stabbed.

And she felt great.

In the vague twilight hours, on a velvety peat hill overlooking the North Atlantic, she'd seen a dozen shooting stars. This, she decided, had to be a good omen.

Auspicious morning.

Checked out of the hotel, Holly was waiting on the cobbled street for her taxi to arrive when she spotted two Chinese in a Mitsubishi Pajero with rental decals parked a little way down the road. One of them was talking into a cellphone, the other aiming his impenetrable sun-shades at her. Auspicious *frock*!

The taxi took her onto the roll-on roll-off ferryboat at Mossbank for the short crossing of Yell Sound, a deepwater voe, to the island of Yell. No sign of the Pajero. No other road. This the only one north. OK. The taxi, a battered Volvo, sailed on the winding empty roads traversing the island of Yell northwards to the crofter's hamlet of Gutcher and the last onward ferry of the United Kingdom: to the isle of Unst.

Unst, the Roman Empire's furthest northern outpost.

Ultima Thule: the End of the World. The Recalcitrant Centurion's nightmare.

They made a stop at the Post Office in the scattered handful of crofts called Uyeasound to buy lunch of cheese and biscuits washed down with Irn Bru, fizzy glucose pop – the taxi driver's insistent treat. He left Holly sitting on the grass, eating ravenously, for 'a wee while, to do my messages' – which turned out to be half an hour. Her empty stomach

78

partially filled, Holly-Jean dozed in the crisp lightly chilled sun.

After lunch the road wound on to the north. Some twenty minutes later, the taxi driver set Holly down on the wild grass verge of the roadside.

'Yon's the laird's.' A scattering of semi-habitable stone buildings lapped around a central tall castellated edifice in the nearish distance.

The taxi three-point turned and drove away, leaving utter silence, broken only by the distant baa of sheep. Holly stood rooted. All around her, a seascape of wind-softened hills, towering cliffs, ocean coves and inlets was unfurled as though she bestrode a giant living map wearing ten-league boots.

She sniffed and sucked in deeply. The air was iced cherry-wine.

A flock of seagulls suddenly wheeled overhead, screaming their demands for food, and finding none tumbled on across the big sky. Holly-Jean hopped from tussock to tussock across the spongy peat, joined a path through the scattered stone outbuildings and stepped across an uneven ancient flagstone courtyard.

A huge carved wooden door was set in the stone wall of the tower building. She pulled down on a rusting iron bell-rope. A peal could be heard echoing inside. Then silence. Somewhere in the distance, the same sheep, baa-ing his freedom.

Holly yanked on the bell-rope again and the door opened. It was the green-haired girl from the night before.

'Come on in, we've been expecting you. Did you take Andy's taxi? And did he make you stop for cheese and biccies at Uyeasound Post Office? I bet you he did, because he's having it away with the post-mistress, Caroline Haroldson, and bully for them too because it's nice to know that love can bloom at any age, don't you think? And how was last night? Did you enjoy yourself? Did we make you welcome here in Shetland? My name's Morag-Rose, which comes from both sides of the family, and you're called Holly-Jean which is American, Deirdre which is Celtic, and Ho Shao-lan which is Mandarin for Little Orchid, aren't I right?'

Holly mumbled appropriate sounds and trailed after the girl as they passed through a boot-room full of discarded wellies, peaty Doc Martens and mouldy raingear. Stepping into a vast hall as high as a cathedral, hung far up with regimental flags, dark and dusty with cobwebs. Lower, at the height of the hanging cast-iron candelabra, the heads of proud stags sprouting impossibly huge and intricately pointed antlers looked down with glass-eyed insouciance.

Crossed claymores and moth-eaten tartan circular shields were nailed on each of the four walls. Giant bookcases with mobile step-ladders attached to a rung on the top shelf were placed variously around the chamber. A peat-fire smoked in a walk-in fireplace. Blackened pots and what looked like a whole sheep being smoked hung from hooks inside the thick soot chimney.

'Come, Holly-Jean, look. It's the speciality of Baltasound Castle!' beckoned Morag-Rose, standing inside the fireplace and pointing up the chimney.

Holly ducked her head inside the blackened orifice and looked up to where, far above, a perfect blue rectangle of sky gleamed. Odd, her knowing my name, thought Holly fleetingly, but Morag-Rose was only drawing breath.

'Terribly smoky when the wind blows the wrong way, which it does nearly all of the time, and in the winter the rain just falls down in buckets and soaks the whole hearth, but Dad won't fix a cowl or a proper flue system. He says if it was good enough for his ancestors, it's good enough for us, notwithstanding poor Mum's bronchitis, though she does smoke a tremendous number of Balkan Sobranie cigarettes every day which we get delivered from Edinburgh by the box-load monthly. Of course I don't live up here on Unst all the year round, only in the summers. I help in the pub – that's when it's open. We only open when we're wanted by folk. The bar's outside in one of the barns, did you see it? I love the summer light – you know, the midnight sun. All that extra energy. And the fairy food. And the fresh air and the sheep. I just adore this place on the edge of the world, so clean, so bright. So far from the city.'

She stopped mid-whirl and looked suddenly heartbroken. 'I'm afraid it'll be time to be going back down south soon, now that the nights are drawing down. Autumn's such a wee sad time I always think, but it's so very beautiful up here in

Shetland, on Unst. And it's the mushroom season, too . . .
Well, well, anyway, I'll see if Cook wants to make us some
tea.'

She tripped off the carpet, opened a door and calling out,
'Mary!' disappeared.

Holly sank down onto a worn cord sofa, and let her head
fall back. The dark vaulted ceiling high above was full of
sprites.

Morag-Rose came back with a tea-tray and sat down on the
sofa opposite.

'Actually it's your mother I'm hoping to speak to,' said
Holly. 'That is, if her maiden name is Titania McIlvuddy?'

'Yes, that's Mum, all right. But you can't see her, she's not
here. In fact, she won't be back today. Depends.'

'Depends on what?' asked Holly, sipping her cup. 'Lovely
tea.'

'Earl Grey, Lapsang Souchong and Typhoo. She's on the
sheep.'

'The sheep?'

'Yes, it's the annual herding. They've all gone – all the men
of Unst and some of the madder women like Mum and, of
course, all the dogs, and some whisky in flasks and blankets
for the sleepy, and mutton and mustard sandwiches. Everyone's out on foot around the whole island to drive all the
sheep up to the big pens in the north-west for winter.'

'Ah, so the dogs have gone,' mused Holly. 'That's why it's
so quiet outside.'

'You're observant, Holly-Jean. I always say it's like a silent
movie around here when they've gone for the sheep,' said
Morag-Rose. 'And they could be days more. One or two of
those sheep are genuinely feral. Although they've been bred
for centuries by humans, up here they're left to their own
devices from year to year. We just borrow their wool every
summer, to make the beautiful Shetland sweaters from the
beautiful Shetland sheep. You should see them, they're wild
loons, they climb down to the most impossible ledges off the
steepest cliffs. You can't bear to look down at them. Makes
you giddy and sick with fear.'

'But they do survive?' asked Holly, suddenly worried about
sheep, talking to this green-haired elf in a stone castle on the

northern-most island of the nation.

'Oh, of course. Somehow they got down – and get back up they will,' said Morag-Rose, adding, 'Though not until the dogs and everybody have long gone home. Ha-ha!'

'So let's forget the sheep for a second, shall we,' broke in Holly. Reality was on the end of a soaring kite and she was reeling in the line with desperation. 'For a start, when I arrived here today you said you were expecting me. You even knew my name. What's going on, Morag-Rose?'

'Oh, that's simple. My Aunt Henrietta e-mailed me at tea-time yesterday. Your colleague – Mr Minty, is it? – had been to visit her about Uncle Hamish's will and she said that we were to expect a visit from you. Sure enough, here you are.'

Holly held out her cup while Morag-Rose poured in fresh tea.

'Thank you,' she said. 'OK, your Aunt Henrietta e-mailed you. And you don't need sleep. Seems perfectly reasonable. So what can you tell me about your uncle's affairs, since your mother's out herding the sheep?'

'I can't tell you much,' Morag-Rose said, 'other than to say Uncle Hamish is as mad as a hatter, which I'm sure you know already since you've met him, though from all accounts he's not quite as utterly crazed as his elder brother was.'

Holly nodded. Now the big question. 'Has anyone ever mentioned – y'know, family gossip, rumours of such – that Lord Jonny had any illegitimate children?'

Morag shook her head. 'No, sorry. I know this is crucial – why you're here – Auntie Ett told me that. But nobody talks much of Uncle Jonny.' She stopped and clapped her hands. 'I know. Let's look through the family photo albums!'

There were at least fifty green leather-bound albums on three of the bookcase shelves. The years recorded within were gold-embossed on the spines. Holly pointed out to Morag-Rose the years she guessed were relevant, and they spent the rest of the afternoon sitting on a stone terrace overlooking the courtyard going through the family pictures while Morag-Rose provided breakneck commentary.

It was in the 1979 album that Holly found what she was

looking for. There were a series of the same group in different poses. Morag-Rose agreed to let Holly have one of the photos on the condition that she guarded it with her life and returned it unsullied at a later date. 'And whatever you do, please don't mention it to Mother.'

Then Morag-Rose stood up close, looking down at Holly. 'It occurs to me there's something I should be asking you, Holly-Jean,' she said diffidently. 'Like, would I myself, little Morag-Rose, be coming into any of the McIlvuddy money from all this detection you're doing?' She waved her hands airily at the scattered, tumbledown stone buildings amid the intense beauty of that stark Desolation Row.

Holly said she really had no idea. Just working the probate, searching for the last of the eldest brother's line, was all.

Morag-Rose continued, 'We're all pretty broke, up this end of the family. And it's a damn long way from those City folk who manage it all. Oh sure, they're doing their best for the future generations of the McIlvuddy clan, but I could surely handle some cash right here and now.' She took on a faraway gaze. 'Would dearly love to ride a BMW Paris-Dakar trail-bike.'

'Now you're talking,' enthused Holly-Jean. 'My kind of horse. Go anywhere in the world with one of those. Where would you go if you came into the dosh?'

The answer came immediately. 'Overland from London to Sulawesi.'

'Why the heck Indonesia?' said Holly, amused. 'Your bum would be that sore you might as well go the whole hog and reach Australia.'

But she never got to hear Morag-Rose's reasons for dreaming of Sulawesi, because the noise of cars, people and howling dogs suddenly filled the courtyard below. The herding of the sheep was over.

'Quick, we've got to put these albums away,' said Morag-Rose, jumping up. 'Then we'll open up the pub. You must help me behind the bar, Holly-Jean. They'll all be as thirsty as smoked fish!'

Van Morrison was singing 'Wild Night'. Holly-Jean was nodding her head and singing along, her hand on a beer-pump, glass tilted to catch the frothy liquid. At dawn someone asked her if she was having a good time.

She replied, 'A night not to forget, a night of newfound old friends, newheard old stories, newborn old lives.'

Whatever that meant.

A few hours later, Andy the taxi driver came to collect her for the long drive back to the airfield at Sumburgh head and the afternoon flight. Only Morag-Rose was up to say goodbye, the rest of the household were sleeping it off.

'I hope you'll sort everything out, about the will and all. Can I come and see you when I'm down south?'

'Of course. Here, I've got a card somewhere.' Holly dug out a creased name-card from her totebag. 'Come and see me – I'd love it.'

Morag took it. 'Thanks, Holly-Jean. And here's something for you. From the sheep with love.' She presented Holly with a gorgeous Shetland knitted sweater; among the ancient intricate pattern were purples, scarlets, yellows and blacks. Holly loved it and reached up to kiss Morag-Rose's ruddy cheek.

Morag stood back and said, 'You know the family legacy? Well, they've got literally millions of sheep on the McIlvuddy land in Australia. I went to visit when I was ten years old and one day we flew in a little two-seat airplane over one of the farms. Took a whole morning to cross the farmland. I reckon after I get bored in Sulawesi it'll be time to say hello to the family sheep.'

'Morag-Rose, I hate to disenchant you,' said Holly, stifling a yawn as the taxi was about to pull away, 'but this isn't about sheep.'

Morag looked at Holly. 'You don't think I'm obsessed too, do you? Everyone round here thinks I'm batty about sheep.'

'Obsessed?' Holly made a wry face. 'Overenthusiastic, perhaps. Still,' she added as the taxi began to roll away, 'I can think of worse things than sheep to spend your time worrying about.'

Morag trotted along beside the open window, 'Like what?'

Holly shrugged. 'Oh, old Chinese men and the corrupt

murderous power games they play to replace their withered libidos.' Holly turned to look out of the back window.

Morag stood, hand raised, her silhouette stark in the empty seascape. Lonely as a lighthouse.

Chapter 11

In the narrow seat on the plane south she opened her passport-wallet and pulled out the faded photograph. Examined it closely, editing, projecting, fantasising. Her stomach ached. She put the photo away, and as she did so, the dog-eared corner of an old black-and-white photo peeked out from her wallet.

It was her talisman, without which she never travelled.

Carefully she slid this photo out. Blurred and spotted with the damp of age like liver-spots, the photo showed a tall man in an English Army uniform, while beside him, half his size, stood his Chinese bride, dressed in white and carrying a bouquet of dark blooms. Both looked into the camera with a gravity, as though they could already see the troubles they were expecting ahead of them down the rocky road of inter-racial marriage.

It was London, in the postwar era of ration books and austerity. No place for a pair of miscegenetic lovers.

Holly kissed the photo and carefully replaced it in her wallet.

Holly-Jean Ho would be the first to agree that hers, though rich, varied and tightly knotted as any decent tapestry of life should be, had almost always lacked a solid, long-term, emotional and physical partnership. Any old other: significant, sigillary of Sikh. She had none.

Not that it normally bothered her. As an entrepreneurial woman she was exceedingly proud of having made it in the shit-wide world. Holly-Jean Ho, Private Clit, Millennial Woman. That hard-won title had been achieved alone, without the help of either gender.

As for the rest of human contact – love, babies, sex, all that sticky stuff – she'd long ago declared it generally offside, and somehow, till now, she'd mostly got along just fine, trotting down the middle of the field, minding her own business and avoiding the ball.

Occasionally there came a clash of hearts and minds. Even the odd rapturous release of her most secret self. But it was only ships that pass. She figured orgasms were easy diddled and life was not.

Holly-Jean Ho was just too complicated to share. And it didn't take Wittgenstein to extrapolate that one.

Her dad, Mr Jones, a gentle Christian with an unwavering faith in the triumph of Love despite three years in Changi (he was awarded the DSC for his courage in helping other POWs survive), was a terrier of a rugby wing-forward for the Harlequins who, while Holly squirmed in her seat beside him, would shed tears at the cinema and didn't care who saw. Handsome, dashing, soft-spoken, reticent at times, with his only daughter he was helplessly in paternal love.

Her childhood was his hugs and Ma's nags. Not a single day of her adult life went by when Holly did not recall the burnt-toast smell of his armpits. Dad Jones was her English oak.

Her mum, Ho Ma-ma, was, is, a Hakka hardheart with a wily, wiry intellect and no time for sentiment. Whose idea of affection was a nasty pinch on the arm that left a blue bruise. But who was irrationally committed to her only daughter's future.

Holly-Jean was weaned and fed on opposing logics, her destiny a zig-zag of opposing genetic predispositions. Even the sentence structures of Mandarin and English were completely opposite, and Chomsky posits that acquiring sentence structure forms the mind.

Thus, her parents, united only in their unconditional love for her, had bequeathed Holly-Jean a split set of values, a split epistemology, a split soul.

And sometimes (trapped like this in a narrow seat in a narrow tin tube 20,000 feet above the earth while the black clouds played volleyball with her gullet), Holly-Jean faced the fact that she was lonely.

That her success in bridging the abyss had come at a huge price.

That in the end she was just another schizoid half-breed.

That it was only her obsessions; her work and her people, which barely kept the midnight wolf at bay.

'Her people.' She thought about that one.

Ho Ma-ma, her awkward bundle. Her best male Minty, happily married elsewhere. And though Ma and Minty had a special affinity which sometimes left Holly as an onlooker, and though they had all-in spats which turned ferocious, the threesome were best pals.

And then there was Barrance T. Wong. A wounded child, content to merge with his electronics and flee the world.

The point was, the whole caboodle worked. Her people. Holly-Jean, the Mother Goose and they her unruly brood. Upon whom she depended for it all.

But as Peggy Lee asked in despair, 'Is that all there is?'

On this odd gloomy body-function day, in an airplane in a storm, Holly-Jean felt a deprivation. Was this the first afternoon of the rest of her life? And as she pondered this one, the old insidious dream of having her own family beckoned and called with such power it tore through her chest and left her aching for the things other people take for granted.

Walking a daughter to the school gate, attending the panto, helping with homework.

Families kneeling together for Midnight Mass on Christmas Eve before going home to open the presents under the Christmas tree.

Families lighting each other's joss-sticks to kowtow before the gods at the Tao-ist temple before eating Mooncakes and building a barbecue under the night sky on Moon Festival. (Even Holly's fantasies had split personalities.)

Oh, to be Mama Bear. Deep in the shelter of the cave, the air dense with the breath of her cubs, the scents of kindred sweat, the tender heat of enfolded fur, the secure snores of hibernation. *Safe*. While outside, the cruel winter snow comes howling in.

There were Holly-Jean's teeth-grinding, no-sleep thoughts as the Lerwick plane banged down into the grey soufflé of chill autumn tea-time in West London.

Chapter 12

Holly-Jean picked up her Yamaha DT from the short-term car park at Heathrow and dialled through to the office. Ma answered with a booming croak.

'*Wei?*'

'For the umpteenth time, Ma,' complained Holly, still crabby from her meditations, 'it's "Holly-Jean Ho and Associates. Good Afternoon, may I help you?" Not, "*Wei?*".'

'Whatever you say, Only Daughter,' Ma said frostily, obviously offended. 'You have some kind of lousy trip?'

For some reason, Holly couldn't stop herself dumping on Ma. 'So where the frock's Minty?' she asked curtly.

'Haven't heard from him yet.'

'Dickhead should've been back last night. Did he leave a message on the answer-machine?'

'I didn't check.'

'Well, go and check.'

'Chill, child,' said Ma, then quoted Mandarin: 'The scissors of anger will snip off life's toes.'

'Yeah, yeah,' muttered Holly uncharitably. 'Heard it all before.' She waited while Ma played the answer-machine tape back into the mouthpiece. Minty's voice came through crackly.

'I've discovered nothing of importance or sanity on Exmoor. The Honourable Henrietta's as mad as a bat on benzedrine. On my way back to Town. See you guys later.'

'Did you get that?' asked Ma.

'Yes, thanks.' Minty's voice made Holly feel contrite. 'Look, sorry about that just now, Ma. Lack of sleep. So where is he?'

'You worried, Shao-Lan? You think maybe something's

89

happened?' asked Ma, sounding worried too. 'Something connected to those cuss-mouthed Shanghainese monkeys turning up and ruining his show?'

We've got Shanghainese coming out the bloody woodwork these days, thought Holly.

'I'll call Sadie Kaiserman,' she said aloud. 'She should know where the boy's at. Maybe he's on a bender. It's happened before after a show, depending on the reviews.'

But the New York art agent hadn't heard from Minty. She sounded antsy. 'Find him. Tell him I need him here. There's a bunch of Japanese corporate buyers who are talking bulk orders for office decorations.'

'Good news,' said Holly. 'I suppose.'

'Why the hell not?' demanded Sadie.

'Nipponese office walls are hardly the right showcase for Minty's creations.'

'So it ain't the Louvre, honey, but this is bono sponduliks.'

'Of course you're right, Sadie. Tell him to get in touch, you see him. I'm beginning to get a wee bit nervy.'

'The Welsh whacko does seem to inspire worry.'

Holly asked, 'How were the reviews?'

'You haven't read them?' said Sadie incredulously.

'Been away, sorry.'

'Well, homegirl, it's true: there really ain't no such thing as bad publicity. Those Chinese gangbangers who ran riot hit the *Evening Standard* front page, brought in a huge payload of curious public,' enthused Sadie. 'Done Minty a priceless PR job.'

'And the serious critics?'

'Not too shabby. Sewell calls him the Last Hope for Figurative Art.'

'Excellente!' said Holly. 'Listen, Sadie, I've got to go. I hear anything I'll have him call you. You do the same for me. Copacetic?'

'You trying to say *capisce*?'

'No, copacetic.'

'Whatever.'

As Holly cut the connection, the cellphone chirped in her hand.

'Holly? It's me, Paul.' It was Paul Carless, the trucker from Dulverton, calling as requested.

'Hi, Paul. Got time to earn some back-to-the-Tropics money?'

'Thure sing,' said Paul. 'When do you need me?'

'How soon can you get up here?'

'Minty was down here yesterday and called by The Tap. Told me I might be needed, so I'm packed and ready to go. I'll be in Town tonight and at your shop tomorrow at ten, OK?'

'Good chap. Listen, before you go, Paul, did you happen to see Minty today? He should be back here by now but no one's seen him this end.'

'Nope, not today,' said Paul. 'As I said, yesterday we had a few lunch-time bevies. Then he was off to Dulverton Manor to see Her Madness, Lady He'tta.'

'He's probably wasted somewhere,' said Holly, nerves beginning to grate. 'Look, Paul, if you have time to spare tonight when you arrive in Town, do me a favour and take a scout around for the hopeless git. You know all his old wetting patches.'

'Do I ever.'

'I'll see you tomorrow morning at the office. Got the new address?'

'Minty gave it to me.'

'Bye then.'

'Addis Ababa.'

Holly drank a can of iced coffee from the Heathrow car park vending machine. Minty missing? What with the threats implied by various occurrences since she'd got involved in the McIlvuddy probate, her imagination was fertile. With edgy perceptions, bone-weary frame and cramps in the nether regions, she rode the long haul via the A4, Hammersmith, the Embankment and up Whitehall back home.

There she made her peace with Ma with a few contrite words and then, with the onset of exhaustion and worse cramping, she made one last connection before calling it a day.

This one was to Mr Plum Blossom, her wisest longtime

Chinese friend and ally; her *guanchi* with the Bamboo Union and bulletin board to the Secret Societies.

After a polite exchange of ritual greetings, Ho Shao-lan *shao-jye* enquired as to any information that might have come to light about the pot-shot taken at her Yamaha on the way back from the Old Bailey last Wednesday.

'Extremely Unmarried Miss Ho, Little Orchid, my humblest apologies.' Mr Plum Blossom indicated that he was superficially distraught. 'I have no solid information, and thus am only able to speculate that this was an arbitrary, spontaneous action by young undisciplined elements of an inferior organisation.'

Arbitrary? Spontaneous? Only nearly blew her frocking leg off. Something odd here. Plum Blossom always knew everything.

'And how about these other visitations?' She told him all about her two opposing threatenings. One to lay off the McIlvuddy Probate and fail publicly to locate any living heirs. The other to succeed and find one.

PB was silent for a while. 'You are muddying the clear waters, Ho *shao-jye*. Be sure not to disturb the fishing grounds.'

'Meaning?'

'You are my dear friend, Shao-lan. You must be fiercely vigilant.'

'Oh, thanks, that's a great comfort,' said Holly. She mentioned the Shanghainese boys causing trouble at Minty's show. The other vague sightings in Shetland.

'Shanghainese?' Mr Plum Blossom's voice betrayed no undue concern.

'Most definitely,' replied Holly. 'Ma heard their accents too. Fresh off the snakehead shuttle.'

'Excuse me.' Mr Plum Blossom was suddenly busy elsewhere and took his leave, assuring her first, 'I'm certain this is neither significant nor connected to your other affairs, but naturally, I would be most happy to look further into it, Extremely Unmarried Miss Ho.'

Holly said that would be hunky dory, and for once didn't believe a word her acquaintance had said. Less than reassured, she took comfort from the fact that at least now she had called it all in. The Society had been informed.

Now she could close down for the day.

But preparing for bed she found her mind was racing, overwired and flashing with glittering images from the wind-swept north and the confusion the probate had percolated. She tried to relax using her esoteric techniques, but to no avail.

When she got like this, Holly-Jean knew there was only one way to fix things.

The *dojo* on Highgate Hill was Holly's place of refuge. Her space where the world stilled and became a deadly ballet.

It was eight in the evening when she walked in the door. The place was busy with students and adepts. She changed quickly, and after working out in front of the mirror until loose and sweaty, she spent an hour practising the basic moves of the discipline she'd chosen for the evening, *wing chung kung fu*.

Finished, she towelled herself dry and sat down with legs folded under her alongside the spectators lining the edge of the tatami mats of the main darshan space.

A strapping young East End Bangladeshi was bowing to his *lao-shr* ready for a bout. The two squared off. The boy moved. There was a flurry of rotor-blade limits and the fight was over: the boy spreadeagled on the rice straw tatami mats, the teacher bowing to the crowd.

Holly felt good, relaxed, at home. That is, until some bright spark called out, 'Teacher Ho is here tonight. Let someone raise the challenge.'

Quickly the call was taken up. 'A challenger for Teacher Ho!'

After much persuasion a white male of about twenty-five with a buzz-cut and tattoos climbed to his feet. Squat, bulldoggish, with a low centre of gravity, the man took up position staring balefully at Holly. This was the very last thing she needed. But with the crowd unanimous and baying, and she the founder and owner of the gym, Holly realised she had no choice.

Problem was, the guy looked to be about three times her body weight and dimension. On the other hand, there was nothing the Tiger girl liked better than a physical challenge.

She rose to her feet and stepped onto the tatami. She flexed her aching muscles, bowed once, twice before moving swiftly backwards and letting her feet begin their dance.

The two combatants circled each other warily, then the man feinted, swerved, lashed out and caught Holly's knee in a vicious lock, the palms of his hand pummelling her down. Holly flattened, spun on her belly, flicked away her legs, and sprang up.

They circled again. Again the man lunged, this time spinning into a rotary kite which caught Holly full-square on the jaw. She saw stars and buckled. The man moved in for the kill. Holly reached out her right hand in a vague waving gesture. There was a loud snick, and the man's head snapped backwards. He stumbled sideways, dazed and losing motor control.

Now Holly moved. All the disquietude, the frustrations, the despair bordering her life these last months, boiled up and over in a flurry of strikes and blows. The man wilted under the onslaught, sank to the mats and collapsed with a loud groan before subsiding into stillness.

The *dojo* was silent. Holly bowed and dropped to her knees to examine the prostrate form.

Immediate hubbub broke out and the mat was suddenly swarming. One of the senior *lao-shrs* on a year's contract from Shao-lin Temple examined the lad, then straightened, pushed his way through the crowd and took Holly to one side, his eyes full of confusion.

'The young man is unconscious, Teacher Ho. Your last strike, unless I'm mistaken, was Cockerel Crows at the Crescent Moon – one of the Forbidden Secret Techniques. What could you have been thinking? It is by good fortune only that he is not dead.'

Holly exhaled her breath, dropped her head and said, 'I am abject, *Lao-shr*. I admit I was wrong to use the technique, but I believed I was in total control of the delivery. I had no intention to seriously hurt. My timing was fractionally off – hence the injury. He will recover shortly.'

'That is as maybe. What is more important is that you have

broken the sacred rules entrusted to you when the secret techniques were revealed.'

Holly nodded. 'Through my lack of control I have committed a grave error in front of the students. This is unforgivable. I will atone.'

When the man was revived and taken back to a cold shower, the *Lao-shr* clapped his hands and called for quiet. The students took their places and the teacher gave them a little lecture on the overriding importance of controlled use of the learned techniques. He called upon Holly to say something.

'I apologise sincerely to you all. What you witnessed tonight was ill-disciplined. Never seek to emulate such a loss of control. Our knowledge is in the cause of peace. Not war.'

Despite which she was given a standing ovation and many admiring comments as she pushed her way through to the dressing room. 'Showed the facker!'

Sighing under the shower she wondered whether the *dojo* was fulfilling its spiritual role in teaching a higher way. Or just churning out another batch of brutal nightclub bouncers.

Back home she took an aspirin and a mug of hot milk to bed. Before she dropped off, she had a last look at her prize from Baltasound Castle's family album.

The tableau of badly cut long hair, flares, platform boots, Indian-print Granny dresses and John Lennon mirrored specs drew her into the faded photo. She examined the blurred faces closely, trying to read the emotions, the mouths open in reaction to something, the laughing lips of one who must have just spoken.

Holly imagined what words were said as the camera shutter clicked.

At last she yawned and let the photo drop from her fingers as through the open bedroom window, tripping across the rooftops of Covent Garden from somebody's hi-fi, came Procol Harum: 'We skipped the light fandango, and turned cartwheels cross the hall . . .'

Perfectly apt, thought Holly-Jean, falling headlong into the henna-stained arms of an androgynous Morpheus.

Chapter 13

She slept like a creosoted log and woke at seven feeling groggy. Three double espressos form the Gaggia and concentrated effort on her office computer catching up with routine crud did nothing to alleviate the Nagasaki Rats.

At nine Holly-Jean called Shirley Jacquet.

'I need your databases. I'm messengering over an old photo. Guard it with your life.'

'And A Bright and Breezy Good Morning to you too, Holly-Jean,' said Shirley drily. 'How old a photo?'

'About 1979.'

'*That* old,' said Shirley. 'You might be lucky. Data'll be a bit thin on the ground but I'll do what I can. I suppose this has nothing to do with the Triads' sudden interest in your employee's creative output?'

'You know about that?' asked Holly, dullard-brained.

'What am I, chopped liver?' Shirley said. 'I'm a journalist, Holly, news is how I make my living. So what's the photo's connection to the little Chinese gangsters who raided Minty's show? From what I heard they were cute as dolls.'

'Cute as anthrax, you mean. No connection to the photo whatsoever,' said Holly. 'This is purely identification of all parties present, known documented facts – historical, hearsay, related gossip-column entries.'

'Got you: the complete carpaccio.'

'That's raw meat.'

'It is? This photo: anything usable?'

'No, nothing. Private affair.'

'I'll be the first if and when, right, *shao-jye*?'

'Right, Shirley.' She didn't bother letting Shirley know that there was a connection to the McIlvuddy Probate. Her friend was bound to know all about that already, Holly was sure. She left her office and greeted Ma, who was sitting behind the front desk drinking Oolong *cha* and reading the *Financial Times*.

'Still no sign of Minty,' Ma commented as she underlined a stock listing. Holly went to pick up the phone.

'Don't bother,' Ma said. 'I already called that over-painted Brooklyn Barbie doll agent of his. Nobody's heard a thing.'

Holly put down the phone.

Without looking up from her stock pages, Ma said, 'Me, I'd bet on Hastings. There's a bunch of those ex-Hornsey/St Martin's Art School riff-raff living down there by the sea, smoking dope and bringing up babies.'

'Now how would you know that?' Holly gaped at the little old woman.

'Minty and I go *wa-a-a-ay* back, dincha know?'

When the messenger arrived Holly despatched the photo, then checked her post, electronic, voice and paper. There was a Shadwell's Bank cheque for the standard retainer of £1500 endorsed by the account holder, the Rt. Hon. Hamish McIlvuddy.

She checked the rest of the mail. Only one of interest – a hand-delivered envelope with blue ink writing. She tore it open. *Emburey Hotel, WC1* stated the letterhead. '*Looking forward to hearing from you soon. Love, Frangipani Johns.*'

Holly frowned as she folded the letter and stowed it in her shoulder-bag. Who was this Frangipani Johns? Never heard of the girl.

Just then Paul Carless sauntered in. Quite a sight. Antique denims, battered leather jacket, blue-mirrored Ray-Bans. Long blond hair turning dusty with middle-age. Tall and lanky, skeletal thin. Huge, thick blond Zapata moustache and blue eyes just beginning to lose their sheen after a lifetime of alcoholic abuse. His denim shirt was open to reveal a typical un-PC T-shirt: a Big Mac truck, a half-naked slut with enormous mammaries and the legend, *No road too tough. No muff too rough.* Holly flashed Carless was the living embodiment of Freewheelin' Franklin from the Furry Freak Brothers.

'Hi, Paul. Know Croydon?'

'Shithole off the M25.'

'Got a job for you there.'

Ma found some paper-money from the office safe for his running cash, and Holly handed Paul one of the company credit cards.

'Try not to melt it, Paul.'

'Keep the baby, Faith.'

Holly smiled and shook her head, grabbing her bag and bike keys. This buy was a living relic, a blast from the past. Shooing Paul out of the door ahead of her she said, 'Off you go. Remember to stay in touch at regular intervals via Ma who's holding the fort here. Agreed?'

'Ougadougou.'

Closing the street door to the office, Holly-Jean was about to insert the keys into the Yammie when she noticed a neat pile of white grains formed into a perfect pyramid about a foot high, carefully assembled on the old wooden ledge of the twin-arched windows to *Holly-Jean Ho and Associates*.

She reached down for a piece of grain. With effort it powdered between her fingers. She dabbed it on her tongue. Sea-salt.

Feng-shui.

But good or bad? Frock knew. One thing for sure, someone was messing with hers. She turned back to the office and was about to call Ma outside to take a look, when something made her hesitate – a sudden strong feeling that it would be a bad idea to draw Ma's attention to the sea-salt. Holly-Jean scratched the Brillo at her nape. No need to frighten the old dear.

She wheeled the Yamaha on to the cobbled street. Turned the key, kicked over the start and revved the engine to a satisfying scream. Second thoughts: better get rid of it. Abruptly she turned off the engine, put the bike back on its stand.

But why not tell Ma? She knew why. It had just hit her that Ma had a weird thing about *feng-shui*. Although like most Chinese the old woman allowed one or two of the geomantic symbols around her dwelling – the fish tank was supposed to

98

bring in business – she never discussed the subject.

Since Holly hadn't been bothered one way or the other, neither a believer nor an unbeliever, she'd not given it a thought before. But this dopey morning, Holly-Jean suddenly apprehended the fact that over the years Ho Ma-ma had never talked about *feng-shui*.

Standing on the pavement looking at the sparkling white pyramid, Holly had the certain revelation that something connected to *feng-shui*, something unpleasant, had happened to Ma in her past. Holly knew full well from stories around Chinatown that *feng-shui* had a dark side.

With a quick glance around to make sure no obviously be-goatee-ed Oriental shaman type was observing her from a purple cloud hovering over Karl Lagerfeld's boutique, she swept the pyramid of sea-salt off the windowsill and blew the remaining crystals into the wind.

Stuffing away incipient terrors, she viciously kicked the Yamaha's goolies to produce a high-C keen of pain that rattled the fancy windows of dandy Earlham Street, and tugging back on the handlebars Holly wheelied all the way up to Seven Dials.

Willy Sangster-Choate, the in-house lawyer for the McIlvuddy Trust, had agreed to give her five minutes between 9.50 and 9.55 meetings in his own law firm's office on the 37th floor of the NatWest Tower.

A pretty red-haired secretary in a Monsoon print ankle-length cotton dress that had to be twenty years out of date, showed Holly-Jean into the glass-windowed corner office. Dirty cottonwool clouds scudding across the Thames estuary and the City skyline unfurling behind Willy Sangster-Choate's outstretched hand promised a storm.

His thick dark hair brushed back from the brow, Willy sported weirdly unfashionable mutton-chop sideburns and his suit pants were, unbelievably, flared. He and his secretary were an eccentric pair.

He was checking his Breitling. 'We've got three minutes and counting. Sorry, love, today's a complete bummer. I'd have cancelled but you'd already left and since Charlie Villiers is my old bass guitarist, I'm listening . . .'

Holly began to detail the McIlvuddy Probate, but Willy broke in almost immediately.

'You do realise, Ms Ho, that neither Hamish McIlvuddy nor the McIlvuddy Probate are of the slightest concern of the Trust.'

'I don't quite understand,' Holly said politely.

Willy revealed a perfect set of ivories. 'The family and the family business, so to speak, have been entirely separate entities for half a century or more. And if you know anything about that family you'll understand the reason why.' He chuckled. 'I'd be out of a job, the Aborigines would have their Dreamland, and the bookies would be hysterical.'

Holly must have looked mystified for Willy explained patiently, 'Ms Ho, the cornerstone of the Trust's founding charter is "The Pursuit of Maximum Profit with Absolute Probity". The McIlvuddy's are compulsive gamblers, liars and spendthrifts, not to mention completely bonkers.'

'So what is at stake in the probate, exactly? Just the title – Lord of the Isles of That Ilk whatnot?'

Willy replied succinctly, 'The title, the right to reside in the ancestral home, a seat on the board with casting vote, a modest annual stipend derived from the working estate, and a dividend from the Trust which is shared between the siblings. And now, love, I really have to fly.'

He stood up and came round from behind his desk. 'Let me see you to the lift.'

'Thank you for your time,' said Holly as Willy walked her to the elevator door, hand on her elbow.

'Not at all, we must have a drink someday. Call Natash,' he indicated the secretary sitting at her desk. The lift arrived.

'You've been most helpful. It was your father who defended Lord McIlvuddy in the Operation Rachel Trial, wasn't it?'

'Sam – dear old Papa, yes it was. Attorney to the rockistoc-racy. A real sixties' figurehead,' said Willy, smiling. 'Yes, I know what you're thinking: I've been fixated on the period ever since my childhood. Good Lord! You don't think me and Natash wear these clothes by chance, do you? It's fashion, baby, and bloody good for business.'

The doors slid shut and she plummeted silently earthward.

★ ★ ★

On the other side of town, Hamish McIlvuddy's London residence was a basement flat off Queen's Gate near the Lyçée Français.

The morning had now turned squally with sudden showers gusting in from the sea, and feeling her joints ache from the *dojo* last night, Holly-Jean climbed stiffly from the Yammie, her beloved steed who gave her the city. Made it hers to do with what she willed. Hah!

From a phone box stinking of urine she placed a call to the Queen's Gate residence.

'McIlvuddy here.'

Pinching her nose, Holly squeaked in awful stage cockney, 'You don't know me, Your Honourable Lordship, sir, but my calling is in the profession some considers the oldest. If you get my drift.'

'Who is this? Haven't got all day,' McIlvuddy barked.

'As I was saying, Your Honour, sir, I'm in that profession, top end of course. No mucky jobs for me, strickly upper-class gents like yerself, sir.'

'Would you get to the point!' snapped Hamish.

'Yes, sir, I'm just getting there. In the course of my duties I recently overheard a conversation that might be of interest to you. That is, if you was willing to make it worth me while.'

'In connection with what exactly?' demanded Hamish.

'Well, sir, I'm only willing to say at this juncture that it concerns the Chinese billionaire Sher thingummy wot was in the papers.'

There was silence at the other end. Gonads shrinking, Hamish? Thought Holly, stifling a giggle.

'I'm listening,' said McIlvuddy in a sepuchral tone.

'They knows about you and 'im. That's all I'm sayin',

'And "they" are precisely whom?'

She'd give him credit, he was keeping his cool. So far.

'Sir, if you was willing to meet me, for a consideration I will reveal all.'

'How much, where and when?' demanded Hamish.

'The Mall of the South, sir.'

'Never heard of it!'

101

'It's just outside Croydon railway station. A big shopping centre, you can't miss it.'

McIlvuddy muttered something very offensive.

'There's a Burger King there on the second floor. I'll be there in two hours from now. That's one-thirty p.m. exactly.'

'Gawd! Burger King, you say, one-thirty. And this is going to cost me how much?'

'Only five hundred quid, sir. A mere bagatelle to the likes of yourself.'

'Five hundred punds! A mere bagatelle!' McIlvuddy exploded.

'Sir, they knows all about you and Shih Yang-fu.' Holly pronounced the Mandarin perfectly.

There was a silence on the other end punctuated by the ferocious snorting of what Holly guessed would come from special snuff box.

'Oh, very fucking well.'

She cut the line.

Holly-Jean had decided to stir it up.

As forecast from her recent lofty meteorological observations in the City, the morning had turned squally, with showers gusting in from the sea to fire up her aching joints from last night's bout. She'd phoned earlier to check on her opponent's condition. Nothing more than a sore neck and dislocated shoulder. He'd be all right. Her reputation might not.

Having found a dry spot under a still-leafy plane tree, Holly was just angling the Yamaha's rear-end out of the way of passing traffic when she spotted Hamish trotting up the stone steps from his flat to pavement level, furled umbrella in place of the deer-stalker's stick.

Holly observed from a lurk behind the plane-tree. On the street McIlvuddy stopped and sniffed the air, reached for his snuffbox and expertly blasted a couple of whacks of spice.

Then, with a noisy flourish of his brown-stained handkerchief, he set off at a brisk pace, coming directly down the pavement towards Holly.

With her black helmet on he surely wouldn't spot her, but even so she ducked down and fiddled with her spark-plug caps as he passed by whistling 'Annie Laurie'.

She turned to watch as he hailed a cab some twenty metres down the road.

She had a couple of hours at least.

Using her expensive state-of-the-art-lock-picks, ordered over the Internet from a Security Equipment company operating out of Seattle, Holly breezed through McIlvuddy's ancient loose-hinged wooden front door and let herself into his flat. The smells of pipe-smoke, snuff and whisky permeated the gloom.

She passed through the hallway and into a small kitchen. A perusal revealed nothing of interest, except a pile of unpaid bills tacked to the side of the fridge by a giant magnet. The fridge was empty except for two bottles of Krug, six bottles of India Pale Ale, and half a whole Stilton with a tiny silver scoop left inside the cheese.

Holly moved on to the small living room, which contained a marvellous walnut bureau stuffed with paperwork and half-smoked pipes. She sat down and looked at her watch. She could take her time. She picked up a bulging cardboard loose-leaf binder at random and began to peruse its contents – but all it contained was private correspondence between Hamish and what seemed to be a succession of females all addressed *My Dear Darling Maude, Elspeth, Katrina* . . . After getting through three exactly worded declarations of passion *for your cushionary lobes*, Holly balked at reading further. As the librarian at the clippings morgue had said of his father, Holly concluded Hamish was also an 'utter dog' but not without some charm. Thirty minutes later she still had nothing.

She moved to the single bedroom. A striped African rug covered the bed. The mirrored mahogany wardrobe revealed some gorgeous tweeds but little else. Hamish so far had given her nary a morsel worth the effort.

Holly returned to the hallway and was about to call it a day when she noticed the small recessed wall closet. Inside the mess of Wellington boots, Barbour jackets, mops, brooms and a Hoover she spotted a recycling bag full of discarded paper. Nothing there, she thought, but discipline forbade her to ignore it. Delving inside, Holly pulled out nothing but old copies of the *Telegraph* and masses of unopened junk mail. Holding a handful she sighed, 'Frock this for a laugh,' when she noted the printed name on one of the envelopes: *Flower of the East Health Produce.*

Now that *was* interesting.

But it was all she found. Ten minutes later, making sure she left the place as she'd found it, Holly let herself out.

Paul Carless called at two-thirty in the afternoon.

'Followed him to the Mall of the South as you said. He waited twenty minutes then left looking fit to detonate!'

Holly giggled. 'Any more?'

'He used his cellphone, looked even more agitated and practically ran back to Croydon station.'

'You followed?'

'Yeah, dumped the car and jumped on the train. He took the first Brighton slow coach and got off at Crawley and took a cab. I followed him out of town a few miles to where I am now. It's a big old stone manor house, and as far as I can tell, he's still in there. Right now, I'm standing in a cricket pavilion on the other side of a cricket pitch across from the front gates and it's pissing with frigging rain.'

'Right, wait for me. What's the name of this house?'

'Ah . . . Pyrland Hall, about five miles outside Crawley on the B245.'

'Got it. I'll come and see it for myself, find out who owns the joint. If anything develops, call me on the mobile, copacetic?'

'Mindoro.'

At the commuter car park outside Crawley station, the sun came out late-autumn harsh-bright. Holly hailed a Ford Mondeo mini-cab. 'Pyrland Hall, know it?'

'Know it? Do I look like a Paki? Born and bred in Crawley, me, Miss!'

The taxi soon left town and took to narrow, high-hedged country lanes. Holly noted her driver had tied a black mourning ribbon to his giant radio aerial as the road twisted and turned like a stuck snake through the autumn-gold woodland. The black ribbon was sold in aid of charity following the death of a universally-loved one, and was the latest symptom of the planet's masses' desperate yearning for a spiritual focus. Sixty million blooms had been cut to staunch the grief.

Holly-Jean had stood back from it all. She merely noted that as the millennium turned, the old faiths were failing and a paranoid superstition was in the ascent. Lost, directionless, the people were turning to charlatans, purveyors of the old religions. Like the unsettling experience with neat piles of sea salt on her window bay that morning. *Feng-shui*. Dangerous games. In the vespertine gloom of the millennial cusp, the Age of Unknowing had returned.

In the back of the lurching mini-cab, Holly-Jean reflected that with history dead, its place taken by live satellite transmission, the organised religions had to be living on borrowed time. In the global TV age, the people selected their saints from the evidence of their own eyes. Or that evidence presented to them by the media moguls.

And thus, concluded Holly-Jean with a wry inner grin, the empirical immediacy of sense-perception had replaced the slow-burning interior flame of meditative revelation.

But would Chelsea win the Cup?

They had stopped some distance from a pair of tall black wrought-iron ornamental gates through which could be seen the long gravel drive and the ancient cedars of a walled country estate. Crowning a sweep of immaculate English lawn were the stone parapets of an ancient structure. On either side of stone-globe pillars, mounted cameras monitored the entrance.

'Pyrland Hall,' noted Holly's driver. 'You got business 'ere then?'

'No, said Holly, casually spilling her cover story. 'I'm a publisher. Got to meet a writer who's surveying the Village Cricket Greens of England for a book. Should be here about now.'

'Village cricket, eh? Well, you're looking at the first eleven's opening fast bowler, yours truly!'

'Wow,' said Holly dutifully. She listened to the cabbie's cricketing stories for a few minutes, then asked, 'How about the big house – it's a real beauty, isn't it? Really old.'

The cabbie nodded. 'Too true. Been in the same family ever since the Norman Conquest – the De Burlingberrys they was called. Yeah, in the Doomsday Book or summink but that was till a coupla years ago when young Fergy Burlingberry went bankrupt and 'ung 'imself from a flagpole on Shaftesbury Avenue. Some Chink billionaire got the place cheap. Oops, sorry, Miss.'

Holly smiled sweetly and asked with a casual, 'That's OK. By the way, what's the name of this Chinese chappie?'

'You got me there, Miss. 'Ow did it go now? Cho Nayku. That make sense?'

Holly said it did. 'Sounds authentic Chinese.'

The cabbie beamed. 'Tell you what I'll do, even better. I'll just call in – my boss prides himself on knowing everybody on the electoral roll.' A few minutes later he had the correct spelling of the owner of Pyrland Hall: Chiu Nei-ku. Looking out of the window, he said suddenly: ''Ere's your writer bloke, if I'm not mistaken.' Sure enough, Paul Carless was sauntering across the village cricket green under the steady raindrops.

'Thanks, you've been a great help,' said Holly. 'Listen, can you wait for me?'

'Sure, Miss. Be glad to.'

Holly climbed out of the cab and stood stretching her legs and back. The sky was full of black-laden clouds, and a harsh wind was gusting, sending the autumn leaves into the oblivion of the ancient cycle. Paul Carless approached her, skirting a rippled duckpond on which a pair of swans glided.

'Nippy weather.' He produced a hip-flask of whisky and a couple of Mars bars, for which Holly was grateful. She listened to his report. Hamish was still inside.

'Any word of Minty?' asked Paul.

'Not so far. Look, I've got to call someone. Just wait a minute.'

Holly called Mr Plum Blossom's code. They stood chatting idly, stamping their feet in the chill. Plum Blossom called back. Holly said, 'Chiu Nei-ku.'

Plum Blossom replied, 'We need to talk. How soon can you be in Chinatown?'

106

Holly looked at her watch. 'I'll be there by five o'clock.'

'The Tea House, as usual.'

Holly snapped shut the Nokia and turned to Paul. 'Sorry, guy, I have to fly. Listen, Paul, no point in sticking it out here. Let's go back to Town – I need you to chase up Minty. The boy's got me worried.'

The cab's wheels scattered gravel as they spun away, eliciting an angry flapping of the male swan's wings.

Holly met Plum Blossom at the Inn of the Eighth Happiness Tea House, a rooftop garden and greenhouse above Chinatown unknown to roundeyes. Plum Blossom was dressed immaculately as usual, from his starched shot cuffs to his gleaming wingtips. He was chewing betel nut, carefully depositing the red spit in the confines of a silver-lidded spittoon, and wiping his lips on spotless linen.

Holly sat down and ordered Oolong. 'We needed to talk I think were your words.'

Plum Blossom smiled. 'Chiu Nei-ku – this man interests us greatly. What is your reason for asking about him?'

Holly explained about the McIlvuddy Probate in a few succinct words, then how she had followed him to Chiu's residence, Pyrland Hall.

'*One* of Chiu's residences,' corrected Plum Blossom. 'He has great wealth, many houses, many homes; he is the father of at least three families, a man of much power.'

'Why does he interest your people?'

Plum Blossom hesitated before answering. 'Chiu is a senior officer with the Four Seas Society. They are our Society's oldest enemy. Occasionally we work in cooperation on mutual projects, such as the recent rigged bidding for a Channel Tunnel extension line station and car park which you might have read about.' He looked at Holly unblinking, a hint of a smile hovering.

Holly nodded back and shrugged. 'Triads will be Triads, I suppose.'

Plum Blossom continued, 'Unfortunately more often we find ourselves in opposing positions. Chiu has recently been very active in North European gambling, traditionally our sphere of influence. You must keep me fully informed of all your interaction with this man, understood?'

'All right,' said Holly. 'That is, if you spill the beans to me.'

'What do you need to know?'

'Primarily, what's the connection between Chiu Nei-ku, Shih Yang-fu and McIlvuddy? I know there's some bad history brewing up to a present-day froth, but what exactly I haven't a clue.'

Plum Blossom tapped his finger and a fresh pot of Oolong arrived. Outside the greenhouse walls, the London sky was streaked with purple and slate, the bamboos in their pots bent to the wind. The well-ventilated heating prevented condensation but occasional squalls threw droplets to run in trickles down the glass.

Holly shivered and held her cup of Oolong to her nose, inhaling the sweet scents of the high-altitude dawn pickings.

Plum Blossom sat back and said, 'I mentioned to you in response to your original query last week, that McIlvuddy used to work closely with Shih Yang-fu back in the Cold War days in Hong Kong until they fell out.'

'Right, I knew that much,' butted in Holly-Jean. 'But why exactly did they fall out?'

'The details are faded with time,' replied Plum Blossom, 'but as far as I have been able to ascertain, McIlvuddy borrowed money from Shih to balance his account at the Royal Hong Kong Jockey Club.'

'So?'

'Unfortunately he did so without Shih's knowledge.'

'Ah-ah,' said Holly, shaking her head. 'The ponies, the ponies, Hamish's fatal weakness. But surely from what I understood, Shih needed McIlvuddy as his compradore, his *guanchi* with the round eyes, with the *wai-guo ren*. Wasn't McIlvuddy crucial to Shih's trade with Communist China?'

'I gather the amounts borrowed were considerable and besides, there were other white men prepared to do business with the likes of Shih.'

'So how about the Shih-Chiu problem?'

Plum Blossom discreetly disposed of a mouthful of red betel. 'During the early days, the time of which we speak, Chiu and Shih were both rising stars in the Secret Societies' firmament. Understand there was no deadly rivalry between

108

the two men, more a mutual respect as might be found, say, among the hooded cobra. That polite wariness continued through the years until one day some time in the early 1970s, during the occasion of a society wedding party at a Bamboo Union house high on the Peak on Hong Kong island, Chiu Nei-ku's fifth son forced himself on Shih Yang-fu's favourite niece. Since that day, it has been understood by all that the two men are sworn enemies. That McIlvuddy should be somehow connected to Chiu makes the situation volatile. At this time in our current business plan we have no room for such volatility. Hence our concern.'

Holly scratched her head. 'Wait a minute. I understood Shih's a member of the *Tien Tao Meng*, The Gate to the Paradise Way Society, not your Bamboo Union. But what do I know?'

Plum Blossom raised an eyebrow. 'You are well informed as ever, Extremely Unmarried Miss Ho; the *Tien Tao Meng* operate under the protection of the Bamboo Union. They carry out, shall we say, less salubrious tasks on our behalf, mostly in Taiwan and the Far East.'

'Oh, that explains it,' said Holly. 'So McIlvuddy originally was Shih's best boy, until they fell out over Hamish's gambling. We know now that Shih has set his sights on the McIlvuddy estate, particularly the land in Australia. The heir gets a seat on the board with casting vote. McIlvuddy is set to inherit unless any of his brother's progeny come forth, and meanwhile he is in some kind of cahoots with Shih's deadliest enemy, Chiu Nei-ku.'

Plum Blossom looked grim. 'An unstable condition of potentially excessive volatility which is of concern to all parties.'

'What you might call a loose barrel of uranium on deck during a typhoon.'

'Poetically put,' said Plum Blossom. 'We need to know Chiu and McIlvuddy's strategy.'

Holly theorised, 'McIlvuddy is scared shitless of Shih, has been for years, that's a given: he knows Shih is after the estate, so has enlisted Chiu's protection to advance his claim to inherit. But for what trade-off? Chiu, himself, as a rival of Shih's, would relish the chance of a takeover himself, right?

Then where would that leave Hamish? Maybe it's just a question of his vote being bought by the highest bidder.'

'Maybe he has his own foolish designs.'

'Like playing the two off against each other? They'd gobble him up and spit him out like that betel nut. Talk about fatal delusions of grandeur . . . no, even Hamish wouldn't be that insane.'

'Let us hope not.'

Holly said with chagrin, 'Which leaves little old me. Why would Chiu and Hamish choose me to fulfil the terms of the will?'

Plum Blossom smiled. 'Oh, that's easy. Using your enemy's friends against them is a historically admired tactic. By recruiting you, Shih's recent ally in his great public triumph in court at the Old Bailey, whether you are a witting or unwitting co-conspirator, the loss of face engineered is so much more acute, the pleasure of delivering this insult so much more sublime.'

He sighed. 'Old hatreds are like festering boils of evil. They must be lanced before they finally kill their hosts. But by all the gods you must watch out when they burst open and spill their fetid contents.'

Holly snorted. 'Why do I get the feeling that a load of men are dumping on me again!' She slammed down her cup. 'Of course, all parties involved must be supremely confident that I'm not about to dig up a real heir. Oh, no way, not that little woman.' Her eyes flashing with anger, she went on: 'The thing is, that contrary to anecdote, rumour and signed affidavit, it seems that Jonny, Lord McIlvuddy of That Ilk, might just have been a fertile little sperm donor after all.'

Plum Blossom raised his eyebrows. '*Gen-dr ma?* You don't say. Well, if it's true you'd better get out there and dig up the little lost heirs, or they might well become little lost corpses – if they aren't already. These men, you understand, are not playing ping-pong.'

Holly looked at him. 'Can I rely on your full support, and the resources of your Society should they be required?'

'Of course.'

Holly rose to leave, but was struck by a sudden thought.

110

'One more thing. Have you heard of Flower of the East Health Produce?'

Plum Blossom smiled mirthlessly. 'A Four Seasons Society operation, perfectly legitimate of course. The CEO is your man, Chiu Nei-ku.'

Holly returned to the office and was chatting with Ma when Paul Carless called.

'He found Minty yet?' demanded Ma.

Holly shushed her and listened to Paul. 'Tried a few mutual pals in and around Kentish Town. No luck. Eventually reached our good old mate Regan, he's from Pontypridd like Minty. Regan said Minty'd made a very drunken phone call asking for dope last Monday night. That would be after the show, right?'

'Right,' said Holly.

'Regan set up a meet in Camden but Minty never showed up. Regan told me to try Pykey the Photographer's place in Hastings – same idea as your mum. Smart old bird, that one.'

Holly quoted with a smile, ' "She's the Dragon that's smarter than a fox", as they say in Taipei.'

Paul laughed and went on, 'Anyway, I called Pykey. Got the answer-machine and left a message. Thing is I'm getting really nervous about Minty. So I'm on my way now.'

Holly glanced at the clock on the wall. 'Tonight? Hastings? Too late, mate. Swing by the office in the morning, 8.00 a.m. sharp. I'm coming with you.'

'Look, Boss-lady, I don't want to freak you out, but time's wasting, and Minty should have called in by now . . . Can't I slip down tonight, and you come tomorrow by train?'

'Look, Paul,' said Holly, patiently, 'I'm just as concerned as you are by the old cocktail-head's no-show, but I've got stuff to do tonight that can't be put off, and besides you wouldn't get down there till the pubs had kicked out and then what would you do apart from get a few uncomfortable hours of sleep in the back of the car. So first thing tomorrow, *capice*?'

'Dar Es Salaam.'

Holly knew she had put off one vital chore for too long.

She called Devon and Minty's wife, Jane. Asked first if Jane had heard from Minty. She hadn't. So Holly explained as calmly as possible that Minty had probably gone on a post-painting show binge, and that if Jane should hear anything to please call the office immediately. Jane's voice betrayed her worry. 'He's not uh "working" for you again, is he? He promised after the last time to give up all that cloak-and-dagger shit.'

Holly hesitated, 'Well, he's certainly aware of what's going on here, you know he just loves all the juicier bits of office stuff . . . Don't worry, he's probably off with his mates somewhere drinking and smoking up a hurricane.'

She rang off feeling guilty. If anything had happened to Minty . . .

Holly spent the rest of the night on the e-mail and international phone and sorting office drudgery. She went out late and slurped noodles in Chinatown before returning home to succumb to exhaustion and blessedly welcome shut-eye.

Chapter 14

Paul turned up at the – for him – ungodly hour of 8.00 a.m. yawning and bleary-eyed. Holly, already fortified with a couple of jolts of espresso, was raring to go. She handed Paul a mug of steaming black froth.

'Cast off, Haddock!'

'Early mornings are against my religion,' muttered Carless, pulling away from Number 40.

They sped through the traffic and reached the South Coast mid-morning. The wintry sun cast a harsh gleam on the sea, and the wind was brisk and invigoratingly chilly. The whitetops danced and Paul was singing along with Steely Dan.

But in the passenger seat Holly couldn't stifle rising anxiety.

Minty had been gone too long without a word, and her imagination had begun to conjure up all sorts of unpleasant scenarios.

'OK, boss, where do we start?' asked Paul.

'You mentioned Pykey the Photographer. Why don't you give him a bell?'

Paul punched the cellphone, but only got the answer-machine.

'Keep trying, Carless. Meanwhile,' said Holly, 'our best bets will be the pubs.'

Paul pointed out, 'Yeah, but they don't get busy till late afternoon.'

'So until then we'll just have to trawl the town. Unless you've got any other leads?'

Paul chuckled, 'Some famous topers live in Hastings.'

'Then let's look 'em up.'

Hastings waterfront stretches for miles along the shore of the English Channel and varies from authentic turn-of-the-century wooden fishing huts to gutted once-magnificent Edwardian and Victorian hotels and guesthouses, nowadays stuffed with inner-city refugees, dole artists, crackheads, English language schools and the odd, forlorn department store outpost.

They spent the winter's day searching for any sign of Minty. On the outskirts of St Leonard's, just along the coast, they had a pub lunch of prawn salad and Grolsch beer. By mid-afternoon they had covered the town from every angle, and had encountered along the way a motley selection of colourful characters of Paul's acquaintance. But as yet there was no sign of their friend.

By now Holly had had enough of peeling her eyes for that familiar head of corkscrew curls among the odd groups of seaside trippers. Yet her fears had grown with every passing minute of the frustrating day's quest.

'It's about time to hit the pubs, I reckon,' she said. 'Park up.'

'We'll start at the Nelson,' said Paul, locking the Explorer in the pay-and-display car park by Old Town, the preserved section of Hastings just a few streets below Pykey's clifftop studio and the stalled Victorian funicular. He went on: 'Regan told me they often come down here for the weekend from London during the winter. The idea is they get completely obliterated on whatever they can stuff down their throats and watch the rugby on the pub TV. He mentioned the Nelson as a good bet.'

'Can't wait,' said Holly, stepping over a comatose form of indistinct species clutching a Royal National Lifeboat Institution collecting-boat crusted with dried vomit.

The Nelson was out of its head. Gay old sea-dogs and cockney fuck-ups stood three deep at the bar. Holly lingered back and let Paul buy the drinks and make enquiries, watching as the bartender leaned forward to catch his words, then said something and pointed out of the window towards the Promenade.

Carless returned smiling, Holly's Pernod and iced water in one hand, his pint of snakebite – half draught bitter/half dry cider – in the other.

'Good news – Pykey was in earlier. Apparently he's gone to play pool down the road at the Man O' War. So sup up and we'll get going.' Paul upturned his glass, and with three languid pumps of his bony Adam's apple, ingested the brown foamy liquid.

'Uh-righ-teous pint!' he actually three-belched the sentiment.

'Wow,' said Holly, swallowing her anise.

The Promenade was flowing with elegant foreign-language students, distinguishable by their expensive back-pack fashion items and stylish accessories, interspersed with desultory groups of indigenous youth, pierced, studded, tattooed and mangy.

The Man O' War was situated on the road opposite the entrance to Hastings Pier, a rusting perpendicular Victorian structure violating the blue velvet English Channel like a scabrous prick. This pub was quieter than the Nelson; naval battle depictions and battleship-crew photos adorned the smoke-stained walls. Players hung around the two snooker tables, drinking pints and smoking roll-your-owns.

Pykey the Photographer was in there. Shaven-skulled, gaunt and pallid, wearing a grey demob suit and black spit 'n' polished Doc Martens, he was bent over the pool table, lining up a difficult shot. This man, to Holly's knowledge, was one of the most successful portrait photographers of his generation.

'How's biz, Pykey?' said Paul after Pykey had got his shot, won his game and pocketed the fifty-pound-note wager.

Pykey turned and spotted Paul. 'Carless, my man. Bizzy, man. Wicked bizzy.' They exchanged ribald greetings. Shaking hands with Holly who'd met Pykey once or twice before but briefly in similar pub situations, he said, 'We know we, right?'

'Right,' she smiled.

'See the shutterbug's still keeping you well cosy,' said Carless, returning with drinks.

'Fucken tired, though. Just flown back from shooting the Dalai Lama.' Pykey sipped his black and cream-top pint of draught Guinness. 'And I'm off later to Monte Carlo. Back tomorrow, any luck.'

'Monte Carlo? Le friggin' chic: nice work if you can get it.'

'Yep. Too true. Prince Rainier's annual snap.'

'Have you seen anything of Minty?' asked Holly politely, but anxious now to see her old friend. 'He's apparently meant to be down here somewhere.'

Pykey looked at Holly and snapped his fingers. 'Now I got you. You're the famous private investigator he adores.' He cocked his head and stared at Holly, his eyes travelling carefully up and down her body. 'I'd like to photograph you if you have the time.'

'I'd love it,' said Holly, genuinely flattered. 'But right now Minty's the thing.'

'It's slightly fucking urgent,' added Paul.

'We're worried that Minty's gone on one of his benders,' explained Holly. 'He's getting too old. Last time it was a stomach pump at the Royal Free.'

'You follow the drift?' said Paul.

'I know the exact drift,' said Pykey, smiling radiantly. 'And you, his dearest mates, you've come all the way down to Hastings to find him. Touching, very touching.' He chugged his pint. 'Set your minds at rest, pilgrims. Our hero, the artist, though somewhat raggedy-edged, is alive and approximately well.'

'Brilliant!' exclaimed Holly. 'Where is the dear loon?'

'Our colossal-brained creator is due to meet me at the amusement arcade on the end of our world-renowned Hastings pier just as soon as he's finished smoking the fucken huge spliff I constructed for him at his pleading behest not more than ten minutes ago.'

Fairground pipe-organ music, perfumes of toffee apples, candyfloss, hotdogs and lard-frying onions, the screams of seagulls and wind-flung fish 'n' chips wrappers redolent of malt vinegar, acrid diesel exhaust and the shake, rattle and roll of the Bumpers and Waltzers whisked Holly-Jean back to her childhood with Dad and Ma, striped deck-chairs, bucket

116

and spade, getting all the looks at Minehead Beach. ('Your mum foreign or summink?')

The flashing coloured light-bulbs of the Gaiety Pavilion announced Little and Large and FABBA the Clones Matinée Today.

'Look! There's our wandering boy. See him at the far end?' pointed Pykey.

Sure enough, at the distant end of the half-mile-long pier, still some 150 metres away, the unmistakable halo-frizz outline of Minty could be seen leaning back over the railings, face to the weak rays of sunlight.

'Min-tee!' yelled Carless, cupping his hands around his mouth.

But the wind carried the sound off to Cape Finisterre, and as the three of them marched on quicker now across the warped and sea-stained wooden planks, Holly stopped in her tracks, said one word: 'Look.'

A group of dark-clothed men had approached Minty.

'Don't like the look of that at all. Hastings is full of rough trade. Let's go!' Pykey was off at a sprint.

All eyes straining to see, their legs pumping and slapping the wooden boards of the pier, their shouts seemingly unheard, ignored, there unfolded a surreal tableau at the end of the pier. Shoving, shouts on the wind. Now a kind of scuffle had broken out.

'Leave him be, you bastards!' yelled Carless, closing, but not fast enough.

Minty was upended, red-and-white striped socks flashing visible for a second, then dropped over the side of the pier into the sea.

'Stop them!' Holly screamed at a group of old-age pensioners wrapped up tight against the wind. The old folk looked confused, frightened and huddled closer together as Holly pounded by, her legs like pistons. But it was already over.

Twenty seconds later, Holly, Paul and Pykey reached the detested pier-end railings. No sign of life. In the choppy sea directly below no sign of anything. Gasping for breath, wheezing, and in Paul's case regurgitating his snakebite, they looked around desperately at the empty wooden boardwalk.

But it had all been too quick. The dark-clothed men had already disappeared into the maze of video arcades running down the middle of the pier.

'He's a strong swimmer – perhaps he's escaped under the pier.'

'Bloody dangerous!'

Notorious for riptides and the lethally sharp barnacles and razor-clams clinging to the antique stanchions, there were signs everywhere forbidding swimming or diving anywhere off the end of the pier.

Still winded, the three of them leaned out over the pier railings shouting Minty's name. From beneath the boardwalk came a sudden deafening high-pitched roar as a twin-engined speedboat burst into view and within seconds was skimming at high speed across the white-tops eastwards in the direction of St Leonards-on-Sea. The Medusa-curled skull of their friend was clearly visible between the bulk of two large men in the back well of the bouncing twin-hull.

'Min-tee!' screamed Holly, as the twin wakes of the propellers lured two white snakes across the ocean blue.

'They'll be in Brighton Marina within fifteen minutes – you've got no chance of reaching him,' said a familiar female voice.

Holly whirled round. There stood the towering big-boobed blonde, Shirley Jacquet, hefting a camcorder.

'Don't worry – I got the whole thing on video,' she said, punching her cellphone. 'I'll alert the police.'

'Just what are you doing here, Shirley?' demanded Holly angrily.

'Bait like that, hack like me, what the hell did you expect?' expostulated Shirley Jacquet the reporter, as she, Holly-Jean, Carless and Pykey hurried back through the Promenade throngs to the Old Town pay-and-display car park and the rental Explorer. 'Like I wouldn't set up a short-wave monitor of your office telephone, *duh*?'

'What bait and what monitor?' asked Holly as they hustled their way through the foreign-language students idling by the seaside. 'No, don't tell me. I don't want to know.'

Holly-Jean had already placed a message through to Chief Superintendent Mick Coulson and was awaiting his return call. In addition she'd just let the others get ahead a few paces while she punched out the calling code for one of Mr Plum Blossom's minions, leaving her cellphone number, Ma's number at the Earlham office and the Mandarin name he liked to call her, Extremely Unmarried Miss Ho.

'You really don't know why I'm here, chasing a story?'

'Pappa-frocking-rrazzi!' snapped Holly.

Quick-marching along beside her, Shirley Jacquet ticked off her fingers one by one. 'First off, we've got your starring role in the Old Bailey fraud case in aid of your tycoon Triad godfather billionaire pal, Shih Yang-fu whatsit and the missing EU billions. Next we've got the McIlvuddy Probate – by no means a simple affair and also sloshing insane dosh. With me so far?'

Holly-Jean uttered, 'Wrong on that one. Just a title and rent-free pile.' She pushed rudely through the slow crowds; beside her, a perfumed behemoth in Gucci, Shirley held her ground.

'OK. Maybe the McIlvuddy Probate's not really big money – *maybe*,' she puffed, 'but it's still got to be the key. Because now we get to the murky connection between the two star players: Hamish McIlvuddy used to work in the Hong Kong trade; last year, Shih Yang-fu failed in a hostile takeover bid for the McIlvuddy Empire. To cap that, we've also got you following Hamish to some other Chinese squillionaire's castle!'

'To hell with chasing a story, Shirley!' Holly was angry. 'All bets are off. Find Minty, that's all.'

Undaunted, Shirley trotted gamely on, crimson-cheeked. 'Don't you see, we'll only find Minty if we can get to the bottom of this Chinese puzzle,' she gasped. 'See, girl, I didn't mention, did I, the charming group of Triad gangbangers who just happened to bust up Minty's show. No connection there, I suppose. Oh, and it slipped my mind, kiddo, I forgot the cherry on top of the Knickerbocker Glory.'

She stopped abruptly, causing Holly to bump into her soft protuberances. 'Look – you also asked me to check out some faded photograph from the seventies of the recently deceased Lord McIlvuddy, his girlfriend Moonbeam and diverse hippy types including the tambourine-player from the Incredible

String Band, who just happened to be Chinese!'

'Yowza!' noted Pykey, passing Paul a joint on the run like a relay-baton.

'With friends like you, who needs friends?' said Holly, letting aggression sublimate terrible thoughts of Minty's fate.

By common assent they slowed to a walk.

Holly turned on Shirley. 'What did you mean by a telephone bug, a monitor?'

'In a van parked opposite your place in Earlham Street.'

'Listen to me. The McIlvuddy Probate's totally irrelevant. Routine drudge.'

'You seriously expect me to believe there's no link?' snorted Shirley.

'Those guys in the boat looked Oriental to me,' put in Pykey.

Holly let the others get ahead of her, came to a halt as the Promenade crowds flowed round her. Shivered and felt goose-pimples popping on her forearms. *Pi-chi*. That old chicken-skin, as the Chinese call it.

Too much going on. Too many different strands. Worse: *feng-shui*. Roaming backstage. Pervading the arena like a malevolent swamp-fart.

Shirley Jacquet marched back, blonde hair flying in the wind, perfume and mascara suddenly too close.

'Anyway, what's the problem here, Holly-Jean?' she barked over the sudden detonating bass of a passing boom-box Beetle. 'We're all on the same side, aren't we? We're all friends, remember? Times like these you need me and my rag to help you.'

She waved her silver-painted nails. 'You think the local police would take us seriously, some loose-strung nonsense about Minty's being kidnapped off the end of Hastings' Pier? We'd be lucky not to be locked in the slammer for drunk and disorderly. Positive no street, kid. You just thank your lucky stars I can have the London office badger the law for updates and status quotes.'

Holly-Jean knew Shirley was right. The kidnapping of Minty was too weird to be believable. She'd take all the help she could get – and Shirley's tabloid was armed and dangerous.

120

They'd reached the Explorer. Holly nodded at Shirley. 'All right, get in.'

'We media have the power,' smiled Shirley.

Pykey the Photographer took his leave. Sheepishly. 'I'd stick around but I've got a taxi coming to take me to the airport in an hour.'

'We understand,' said Holly. 'Paul will keep you posted. Hope you take some good pics in Monte Carlo.'

'Thanks. Look, I really hope it works out OK for Minty.' He looked guilty. 'Awful leaving you blokes in the lurch.'

'We'll find him, don't worry,' said Holly. 'Let me tell you what my dad used to say: "If the worth of a thing is defined by its rarity, then a true and loyal friend is the most precious thing on this planet." That's our Minty.'

'Good one,' said Shirley. 'I can use that.'

'Spit on the gods and go for it!' called Pykey as the Explorer pulled away.

'Zamboanga.'

On the way across the chalk downs to Brighton, Chief Superintendent Milk Coulson returned Holly's call.

''S up?' Holly reported Minty's abduction. Coulson swore. He and Minty got on well. At Twickenham they had occasionally drowned their opposing loyalties in booze and dope.

The senior lawman commiserated with Holly then said he would get on to Brighton Marina Police and find out the latest. He was not optimistic. Seemed he shared Shirley Jacquet's assessment that the kidnappers, whoever they were, would be long gone.

'Oriental-looking, you say? So, what's it all about, Holly? Chinese the other night in Soho, now this. Don't you dare hold out on me. Oldest rule, right?'

'I haven't a clue, Mick. And we're just working some boring probate.'

'The McIlvuddy Probate,' said Mick drily. 'Millions in assets and land. *Really* boring.'

Know-all.

At Brighton Marina Police HQ the officers were polite but clueless. There were literally thousands of speedboats just like the one on Shirley's blurry video moored around the various jetties. However, two officers had already been despatched down to the Marina, and people were being questioned. The news item had been broken. Witnesses had been appealed for on local radio. So far, nothing.

It soon appeared that no one down at the Marina had reported seeing anything of a suspicious nature. It was early days, of course. Something would turn up. Ma'am was told that regrettably, the only remaining course of action must thus be to await further developments. An avuncular officer in plainclothes handed Holly a name-card.

She gave him one of hers.

Apparently Mick Coulson's call had got through. What good it would do.

Outside the Marina nick, Holly argued for a reconnaissance of the seafront. The others reluctantly agreed, but it was pointless. There were hundreds of identical-looking speedboats, and after a fruitless and depressing hour of searching it was accepted that they should give up.

What else could they do? Holly felt impotent – a state that went against every grain of her nature.

'This really frocks me off,' she announced, slamming the door of the Explorer with a loud bang.

'Only to be expected of a Hakka Tiger,' noted Shirley from the back seat.

Chapter 15

On the M23 back to London, Holly questioned, Shirley talked. First, the photograph. Shirley hadn't brought it with her. Said she hadn't finished with it yet, but assured Holly she had panned some interesting historical residue.

Holly said, 'That was the hippy girlfriend, Moonbeam, in the middle?'

'Right,' conceded Shirley.

'She'd just made them laugh or shocked them or something, don't you think?' said Holly.

Shirley agreed. 'Yes. By the way their faces are angled, she must have cracked a good one.'

'So what was the occasion and the location?' asked Holly.

'As far as I, Lowly Woman of Hack, can discover,' said the champagne-blonde investigative journalist, trying to lighten the mood, 'that particular picture was taken in Tangiers, which was the first known stop-over after McIlvuddy fled England and broke his bail bond from the Operation Rachel court case.'

Tangiers; once notorious sleaze-hole on the hippy trail.

'But who *was* Moonbeam – do we know?' asked Holly. 'I mean, flesh on the bones of myth, how about her real name for starters?'

'More. I've got her real life,' said Shirley triumphantly. 'Her name was Monica Matthews. Born 1949, Ringwood, Hampshire. A country doctor's daughter, solidly middle-class. St Brandon's Boarding School for Girls. Pony Club. Gymkhanas. Warwick University to read Sociology. Normally normal. But then along came the Summers of Love. Monica dutifully tuned in, turned on, dropped out. Hit the road, Jill. The Katmandu-Bali orbital. Resurfaces in London – a

Notting Hill Gate squat. Sometime along the way Moon-beam teams up with the aristo-freak Lord McIlvuddy. Stays at the commune in Wales. No evidence of involvement in the acid still. Next thing bang, disaster, the party's busted. Operation Rachel, Shropshire Magistrate's Court and then it was Band on the Run. In a nutshell.'

'Present whereabouts?' asked Holly.

'Not known. Parents both died in a car-wreck a few years back. No siblings. No one at the funeral answering to her description. As you know, after they sailed off from St Mawes following the granting of bail there are few definites.' She shrugged. 'Tangiers was one, obviously – that photo. Vague sightings here and there. Goa. Kovalam. Bali. Then the big zero. Stone-gone, as they said at the time. Out of sight. Out of mind.'

'And somewhere along the line she ditched His Lordship,' said Holly-Jean.

'Wouldn't you?' said Shirley. 'When they got to Manila and his nibs discovered the female delights therein, it would've been high time to bail out.'

'And you have nothing more after that?'

Shirley continued at her own pace. 'Nothing for a very long time. But by chance Monica Mathews was heard of in New York City in the early eighties. Seemed she bought a crumbling brownstone in the Lower East Side for a song when it was still a no-go war-zone. A few years later the building was gutted in a fire, and a small piece appeared in the *East Village Free Press*.'

'That's it?' queried Holly.

'Don't worry. I'm following up through my New York bureau. Got them working to track down the property-tax filings, and the Lower Manhattan District Property Appraiser's will have a current status update. Should hear pretty soon what happened to the house.'

'Beside the house, nothing of Monica since?'

'Nada. Nein. Nyet. Nope,' said Shirley, taking out her compact and applying fresh crimson lipstick.

Holly waited. The look on the journalist's face told her there was something more. She already knew what it was – the reason why she'd taken the photo from Baltasound Castle in the first place.

Shirley Jacquet snapped her compact shut. 'Meanwhile, back at the photograph. The really, really, interesting thing . . . you obviously noticed, right?'

'Pregnant,' observed Holly-Jean. An heir for the probate. 'Or one heck of a beer-belly for a pot-smoking hippy.'

Mr Plum Blossom reached Holly as the Explorer was passing under the M25 traffic jam. The connection was not good, but Holly carefully enunciated the events on Hastings Pier. The Secret Society officer listened without comment and called off.

From the back seat Shirley Jacquet continued her perorations. 'Second thing for your delectation, Little Orchid Ho – all right if I call you that?'

Holly smiled. To paraphrase LBJ, she would rather have Shirley squatting inside the tent pissing out, than outside pissing in.

'Listen to the most excellent juice which I discovered from the *South China Morning Post* database. In 1994, Shih Yang-fu publicly and officially disowned any business or personal relationship with Hamish McIlvuddy.'

'They were connected?' asked Holly innocently.

'Don't fuck with me, Holly-Jean,' said Shirley. 'Shih Yang-fu was one of the first Hong Kong traders to develop connections with Communist China in the chaotic fifties. Indeed, he made his early fortunes supplying the Shanghai Mayor's office and the City Party cadres with the fruits of capitalist enterprise. Throughout the Cold War isolation years he had a fleet of junks plying the China coast. In exchange he got his hands on raw materials like cotton and timber for his Hong Kong factories. But how to sell to the Westerners? Hamish was his compradore, his middleman, his go-between the races.'

'Get to the point,' said Holly, impatient now to hear what, if anything new, Shirley had dug up.

'Yes, you sold me a right old saccharine fairytale the other day, Holly-Jean, when I interviewed you for the inside story on Shih Yang-fu. Of course, I figured that.' She laughed. 'Which is why I went to the Hong Kong office for access to their database.'

125

Holly waited.

'Hamish stole money from Shih and was drummed out of Honkers. Thence to return to Blighty and nurse his grievance till it turned into a nice little vicious vendetta!' Her voice brayed in triumph.

'What you've got is conjecture, pure and simple,' remarked Holly.

'You think so?' snorted Shirley.

'Thick plottened-heimer,' said Paul Carless, steering off Neal Street and home.

Chapter 16

Paul Carless had been dismissed with grateful thanks and had gone off to get inebriated with his and Minty's mutual friend Regal in the heavy Cockney pubs of London's East End. He'd report back in the morning – foully hungover, no doubt. Meanwhile, Holly had finally managed to get rid of Shirley Jacquet after more than a couple of Pernods in the Lamb and Flag around the corner, having extracted with great difficulty a promise from the journalist not to break the story until at the very least they'd heard from the kidnappers.

'You scoop-pooper!' quipped Shirley, pointing as green-lacquered fingernail. 'Imagine my tape of Hastings' Pier on *News at Ten*!'

'For the lad's sake, just wait, Jacquet. It's still your exclusive,' said Holly. 'Minty's safety first, right? We wait till we hear from them.'

'Holly-Jean, if it breaks elsewhere all bets are off.'

'Of course.'

Alone at last, Holly hurried back to Earlham Street and opened the old spice-shop door. No one at the front desk. She made Oolong *cha*, sat and pondered.

The obvious deduction: the scene at the end of Hastings Pier, like a bad take from a faded *film noir*, was aimed at her for not dropping the McIlvuddy Probate. But why grab Minty, not her? What in the world would anyone want with that whacky Peter Pan who harmed no one and put brightly coloured marks onto canvas by means of a paintbrush?

She heard a noise. 'Ma?' she called. She had deliberately not told her aged parent on the phone about Minty's

127

abduction. She wasn't sure that the old lady's ticker really needed the extra stress.

'That you, *Shao-lan?*' Her mother appeared from the bathroom, dwarfed by the empty fish-tank bubbling away. In its green aura the old lady looked shaken, her eyes teary and her normally proud frame hunched.

'*Wo-dr tyan!* My God, what's happened, Ma?' Not more bad news, thought Holly.

I've had it up to my eyebrows this week. Her mother was gesticulating and groaning. Appeared short of breath, unable to bring out her words.

'What's wrong, Ma? Are you sick? You look awful.'

But the Mandarin invective now pouring lustily from Ma's lips, with its freeform references to the slow shrinking of scrotal sacs indicated to Holly that her fears were premature and that Ma was in fact suffering nothing more than an attack of unbridled rage. Indeed, her mother's language was so horrible that Holly half-expected flames to emerge from the little old dragon's mouth.

After calming Ma down and asking some straightforward questions, it transpired that the Inland Revenue had dropped round for afternoon tea and ransack.

'Don't worry,' snarled Ma. 'Those gnat-penises didn't find our stash!' This referred to Ma's secret cashbox of any money she could keep off the books – an object of mystery, kept hidden, separate from the office safe and which Holly didn't want to know about but was reputed to hold the half-mill Ma said was the barest necessity for 'running cash'. For example, Shih Yang-fu's auspicious red-beribboned cardboard box full of crisp fifties.

When Ma asked in Mandarin, 'You eaten yet?' Holly knew she was finally calmed down.

'Stomach full, thanks. You?' The ritual response.

'Haven't eaten yet.'

'Well, hang on a minute, let me just check the files, see what those bullies have been up to. Then you go eat.'

Holly stepped into her office and fired up the computer, dug through her disks, surveyed the disorder. It was immediately obvious that some disks were missing. Since nobody besides Ma would dare mess around with her desk, it appeared the taxmen had sequestered some files.

'Did they take anything with them when they left?' called Holly, punching her keyboards.

'Some disks, some paperwork, stuff,' Ma spat with venom. 'There's a receipt there somewhere. Thieving sewer-slime.' Taxmen came very low down on Ma's list of existential worth. Somewhere between the cockroach and damp mould.

A quick inventory revealed that missing from the disk, library were ones labelled *Accounts past/present, Payments due,* also the client database with records of former payments, and the files of expense accounts for each member of staff. All were gone. An official receipt had been left on her desk with Ma's scrawled signature across it.

Holly cussed the I.R. for the sheer vindictiveness of the raid. Coulson had warned her at the art gallery the night of Minty's show. The raid was revenge for the massive loss of face suffered by the Serious Fraud Office following Shih Yang-fu's acquittal – though realistically what part Holly's testimony had actually played in the trial's outcome was highly moot. And the taxmen, like playground bullies every-where, had lashed out at the softest and safest target to hand.

She was not seriously worried. Her accounts were in fairly good shape. If anything, the tax appraisal was inconvenient, but not alarming.

Like all Chinese companies, Holly, with Ma's expert cook-ery, kept three books. The skinny one for the taxman. The fat one for the customer. The real one for themselves.

The files, deep in the hard disk, were accessible only by password, chosen by Ma with the help of the Book of Oracles, *I Ching*. None of that obvious birthday nonsense, said Ma.

Only one file was kept on soft disks. The one taken by the Inland Revenue. The one that was pure gastronomy.

'Listen, Ma, it's late now. You go off and eat dinner. I'll close up.' Holly helped Ma into her favourite Burberry mackintosh, and hustled the old lady out of the office and away in the direction of Chinatown and some soothing noodle soup.

Then she locked up the shop, turned down the dimmer switch and gratefully alone in the rear office, sat at her

129

desk, with pencil and pad and began to take stock of the McIlvuddy Probate. Writing down the list of characters who had till now appeared in the job, she realised she hadn't yet called Sadie Kaiserman to tell her about Minty. She took a deep breath before punching the number. Coping with Minty's Brooklynite agent was not going to be fun.

Reaching her at the Soho Gallery, Sadie Kaiserman pretended not to be worried, but Holly could hear the waver in her voice.

'Lunkhead's more trouble than he's worth.'

Holly explained to her that they could do nothing for the time being, and must wait patiently till they heard from the kidnappers. She told Sadie that it was her presumption that the kidnappers would contact Holly herself first. But in the event that they chose to communicate with Sadie – who was, after all, Minty's agent – then it was to be clearly understood that no spontaneous independent action of any kind was to be taken.

'Just sit tight and stay by the phone.'

Sadie agreed to do thuswise and to let Holly know immediately if or as soon as she heard anything at all.

Holly added one last rider: Sadie was to keep her answer-machine on automatic record mode from now. And say her prayers for Minty's safekeeping.

'Miserable foolish pisspot!' was Sadie's final comment.

It was nearly midnight. Holly was still engrossed in her thoughts, trying to keep her mind off Minty when Mick Coulson called.

'Hear anything yet?' asked the senior Scotland Yard officer.

'*Mei-you*,' replied Holly. 'Your end?'

'Brighton Marina think they might have IDed the speedboat. One answering the description had been reported stolen a couple of days ago by the Sultan of Brunei's UK office. Nothing more they can do at the moment, apparently.'

Holly detected a highly stressed undercurrent in the tones of her policeman pal. Mick Coulson took the cares of the world on his shoulders, a good man. Hard to find these days, cliché but true. Worse, Minty was a close friend and Mick was obviously desperately worried, as she was, by the abduction. Even so Holly couldn't stem her own tide of panic and her voice cracked as she blurted out, 'But for frock's sake, we've got to do something, Mick! It's Minty! Our zany boy. Surely you haven't forgotten?'

'That's not fair, Holly-Jean and you know it,' said Mick, exhaling loudly. 'The fact is in these cases the S.O.P. is do nothing until you hear from the kidnappers. It's bloody difficult for me too, y'know, but really there's not much alternative.' He paused. 'Couple of other things, Holly. First, the good news: remember the tofu corpse?'

'How could I forget,' said Holly drily, momentarily letting drop her panic over Minty. 'Haven't eaten the stuff since. Put me right off.'

'Well, kiddo, you were spot-on. She was a Filipina, and her name was Marybel Lacsina, late of Manila. And guess what?'

'What, Mick? I'm all agog,' said Holly, humouring him.

'Marybel is the mother of one Raymond Jun-jun Lacsina . . . Ring any bells?'

'Should it?' It did actually, but Holly was too frazzled to concentrate, her thoughts were of Minty only.

'Raymond Jun-jun is only the boy named in the paternity suit filed in Manila claiming Lord McIlvuddy as father.'

Holly swore loudly in Mandarin. '*Tamada!* Are you sure?'

'What am I – chopped liver?' said Mick. 'I'm a senior cop, Holly' as a breed we don't jest about these things.'

The implications of this bombshell were too heavy for Holly to calibrate right away. Her mind whirling, she babbled, 'That really takes the frocking cake. The McIlvuddy boy's mother – the tofu corpse . . . So what does it all mean? One thing for sure, Mick, this is really getting to be one frocking Chinese puzzle. What was she doing in London, by the way, and how did you make the ID?'

Mick sighed. 'Nobody knows nothing so far. As for the ID, we found a left luggage ticket for Victoria Station in her pocket. A small hand-carry bag containing personal items and some letters were later retrieved.' Holly was lost in thought when Mick continued, 'And now for the bad news, Holly-Jean. Brace yourself. It's not good.' Coulson's next words crashed through Holly's tired mind and made it. Single

131

stark phrases filtered through: *Shetland. Baltasound Castle. Morag-Rose. Intensive care. Life support. Multiple rape and battery. Critical condition. Holding four men. Chinese factory ship.*

She put the phone down and clasped her arms tight around her. Then stood up and began to pace. Classic Oriental strategy. To scare her off, they were hurting the people around her. Which meant all-out war.

Which was when all hell broke loose outside the shop windows on Earlham Street. Someone was screaming for real. A voice she knew. Ma. *What now?*

Holly raced through the office and tore her middle fingernail unlocking the front door. Spotlit by the glow of the boutique display lights across the way, Ho Ma-ma was jumping up and down outside the shop on the cobbled street, screeching, her arms flailing at something hanging from the architrave, above the double arched windowframes.

Holly reached out and hugged her mother close with all her strength, shushing and soothing, glancing up at the object of her dread.

Turning slowly in the night breeze, just above the old lady's reach, suspended by a red thread and poking out of an elaborate container of some kind, was a two-foot long, three-inch thick, smoking joss-stick.

She managed to get Ma back inside the office, she sat her down and poured Oolong *cha*. Her mother pushed aside the tiny proffered cup and choked out, '*Kaoliang!*' Holly reached for the bottle of fiery sorghum spirit kept under the front desk for Oriental visitors.

Ma grabbed the bottle and swigged. She went into convulsions of coughing and spluttering, but it seemed the alcohol had done the trick. Accepting the wad of tissue papers, her mother looked dazed but calmer.

'You're all right, Ma?'

'Just get that fornicating piece of devilry down from there bloody quick, Daughter, and destroy it! Go!'

Holly nodded and went outside. But her steps were somewhat tentative on the cobbles. All right, she wasn't a believer. In fact, she pooh-poohed the whole *schmeer*. Yet the Chinese part of her couldn't help but feel apprehensive as she approached the suspended object.

The joss-stick was nearly burned down and taking a deep breath, she tugged it free and crushed it out under her heel. The elaborate container was easily parted from the red thread. Holly clutched it in her left hand and reached up with her right hand. She pulled down the remaining thread, balled it up and flicked it nervously away. Telling herself to grow up, she wiped her hand on her jacket vigorously, as if to rid herself of sorcery, spells, witchcraft, black magic, bad vibes.

Now she recalled the pyramid of sea-salt which had been arranged in the same place that morning. Someone was up to tricks of Wind and Water. But why on earth she knew not.

Holly became aware of the weight in her other hand. She stalked across the street to the Karl Lagerfeld boutique and in the bright flood of light, examined the heavy metal object. It was a nonahedron composed of nine antique Ching Dynasty perforated coins – the ones used in throwing the *I Ching* oracle – intricately tied together with red thread knots.

It was an elaborate arrangement and Holly was awed. Rolled the thing in her palm. Felt the residual heat from the joss-stick in the worn brass of the ancient coins. Imagined the countless hands that had been here before her. Smelled the perfumed scent of the unburnt joss, mingling with the charred sourness of the spent ash.

A scent of Chinese funerals. Of Eastern death.

Whatever else was going on in this strange game of ritual, someone had consumed serious time in this exacting construction of perfect symmetry and balance. It was a work of consummate skill and artistry. And it frightened the living shit out of her.

Holly raced up to Seven Dials and, breaking the threads, flung the unravelled coin construct into a litter bin on the far side of the roundabout.

Upstairs on the fifth floor of the Kaoliang bottle was near empty.

Outside the wind was howling. A storm from Norway had brought lashing rain and a freezing edge to the blast. Holly had double-fastened all the windows and secured the sliding door out onto the conservatory of the tiny floor rooftop. She and Ho Ma-ma were settling down for bed.

Holly-Jean had finally told a stoic Ma about Minty's disappearance, Shirley's discoveries and the rivalry between Shih Yang-fu and Chiu Nei-ku. Ma was quiet, lost in thought. Neither mentioned the ju-ju outside the office window.

Shaken the old dear to her bones, thought Holly. And frankly the look of her was worrying. At her age did Ma really need all this? Shouldn't she be in some quiet country garden tending her lotus-pond? Holly had to smile at the preposterous idea. *Ma*. Her awkward bundle. Retired? Not a hope.

Meanwhile, Holly was keeping the lid on the heartbreaking report from Shetland. Ma didn't know Morag-Rose and surely didn't need to hear more bad news. Leaving Ma tucked up in bed, Holly upended herself against the wall in a *Sirshasana* headstand. Let blood flood her skull. Swim in the red stuff. Meditate on Morag-Rose and the magic that had for once deserted that fairy-girl.

The next morning, Holly-Jean had phoned the Lerwick General Infirmary.

At first, Dr Williamson the duty houseman had refused to talk to her, so Holly had hauled Mick Coulson out of a meeting by his beeper, and made him call the local law and have them reach the doctor to personally vouch for her. The news when it came was not good, but it was better than Holly had initially feared following Coulson's first call.

'The patient has sustained serious internal organ damage, critical loss of blood and a broken pelvis, in addition to severe lacerations and extensive bruising all over her body,' said Dr Williamson.

'But she's going to be all right?' Couldn't bear the unavoidable thought that Morag had been harmed through association with her.

'She is no longer on the immediate danger list, but Morag is still in semi-critical status and will definitely remain in the IC unit for the time being.' The doctor assured Holly that given the excellent care being currently provided for her, Morag-Rose should recover. In time.

He also answered Holly's next question. 'No, there is no

way of saying what her chances of procreation in the future might be. The biggest worry, naturally, will be the psychological effect of such trauma on the wee lass. Aye, it's a dreadful shame.'

Holly had thanked the doctor and rung off, feeling somewhat relieved but hung with guilt. In her core she knew that if she hadn't gone up there muddling around, the attack wouldn't have happened; if the vagaries of the McIlvuddy Probate hadn't singled Morag-Rose out from the motley crowd and drawn the spotlight down on her for whoever was watching.

Holly wished she hadn't even sung damn karaoke with the Shanghainese lads, the alleged attackers. Now that thought returned.

Holly recognised that she had a problem with that one. The idea of those friendly wide-eyed young fishing fleet boys from the comparatively strait-laced rigours of Mainland life committing such a brutal act seemed totally out of kilter to her. And though she knew nothing of the details of the case against them yet, it was her intuitive feeling that it would be far easier for the local authorities to find a scapegoat among the foreign fishing fleet. Lot less trouble than stirring up a hornet's nest among the tight-knit, interbred locals.

Once again she called Coulson out of his meeting.

'Relentless tigress you, Ho.' But he listened to what she had to say without further comment. When she'd finished he merely pointed out that Shetland was about as far as you could get from his jurisdiction.

'I thought the MPCCLC was the official body to deal with Chinese affairs throughout the community.' Holly was referring to the Metropolitan Chinese Community Liaison Committee on which they both sat.

'Only for the Greater London conurbation and environs,' replied Mick. 'They've got others up north – Manchester, Leeds and in Scotland.' He hesitated; Holly could hear background discussion – male. 'Look, Holly, I'll put the heavy word out, OK? But frankly, I'm too damn swamped under down here to give much thought to what goes on in our northernmost extremities. I'm sorry, but that's the way it is. Press enter.'

135

'Thanks for *Thought for the Day*,' Holly snapped.

Coulson flared back. 'Now look here, Holly-Jean, you drag me away from a serious meeting on some gender-based intuitive impulse, possibly hormonal-driven, proclaiming the sudden innocence of a bunch of Shanghai seamen accused of rape and battery in some far-north outpost and expect me to drop everything! Which reminds me, didn't you recently tell me that Shanghai had reverted to a cesspool?'

'These were naive kids, Mick. Trust me on this one. You owe me.'

There was long pause filled with high-pitched shrieks. The strippers must have arrived.

'All right, Holly-Jean,' he sighed. 'I'll go in to bat for you. But now you owe *me*.'

While Ma enjoyed the comedy on the box, and with no word yet from Minty's abductors, Holly dug out her notebook once more and went over it all from beginning to end, starting with Shih's first approach via Mr Plum Blossom for her to give evidence on his behalf in the Old Bailey trial . . . Going step by step through the McIlvuddy Probate and what she had since discovered, she pondered on the bad history of the triangle of unlikely lads; Hamish, Shih Yang-fu and Chiu Nei-ku. The source: Hong Kong and Taiwan. The warfare: Minty's abduction, the attack on Morag.

It suddenly struck her that in the wild course of recent events, she'd nearly forgotten Coulson's bombshell: the positive ID, of the tofu-vat murder victim as Marybel Lacsina, of Manila, the mother of the boy named in the McIlvuddy paternity suit.

Holly looked out of the window at the persistent rain. It was obvious the boy in Manila was in mortal danger. She knew the Philippines too damn well. The value of human life there was a pittance – especially if it stood in the way of a fortune of unimaginable vastness.

She walked into the kitchen and inspected the freezer. Extracted a container of frozen *ma-lah ho-guo*. Damnitall, it was time to move! She'd go to Manila as soon as Minty had been found. If necessary, have Sangster-Choate fix the legalities: get herself appointed power of attorney, the boy pronounced a ward of court, so that in Manila he could brought in from the cold and placed under Consular protection. She dumped the frozen hot-pot in a saucepan.

The money was just too big. Or was it? Holly thought about that. After all, following the visit to Sangster-Choate it had become clear that the inheritance was not actually the great fortune originally hinted at. There was a title, a modest stipend, a seat on the board, and various rent-free accommodations. Jolly swish and all – but worth killing for? In the Philippines a thousand bucks'd suffice. But to billionaires like Shih? Hardly.

Which left the question: why the warfare? Why the lethal battle over who became the heir? Was it all just about two old Chinese men trying to gain face?

Something was tickling away at the edge of her mind. She roamed around the fifth-floor flat, her mind racing. Thought about taking a bike-ride up to the dojo for a late-morning work-out, but with the rain and wind rattling the window-panes, she decided she couldn't face the weather conditions. Nor the other adepts, after her disgraceful loss of control the other night.

She looked at Ma hunched over in front of the box. She'd been putting off the inevitable. It was time to talk. Time to disinter long-buried bones.

The comedy had finished so Holly switched off the box, poured the last of the Kaoliang and stirred the pot of *ma-lah ho-guo*. The red-hot spice would cheer them up.

She sat down opposite Ma and began to skirt gingerly around the subject of *feng-shui*, wondering neutrally if there really *was* a link between this arcane, ancient cosmology and modern-day, Stephen Hawking-style 'real' metaphysics and epistemology. At first Ma made absolutely no response, other than muttered, *Ai-yo*'s. Undaunted, Holly went on, casually observing that apparently many educated, successful and wealthy people did take the whole thing seriously. And not just Chinese. Why, she told Ma, she'd heard that there were quite a handful of practitioners already set up shop on Wall Street and raking it in.

'But why would anyone of sane educated mind believe that there really were such forces beyond human comprehension,

137

emanating from the Earth Dragon, for pity's sake,' mused Holly. 'Forces that steer our lives for good.'

'Or evil,' muttered Ma.

Holly waited, but her mother didn't speak again for a long while. The only sound was the unrhythmic bubbling of the 'numbingly spicy hot-pot', the room slowly filling with the mouth-watering scent. Holly sat patiently. It would come.

When she finally broke the silence, Ho Ma-ma's voice was low, her tones shaky like a worn reed. She spoke with a fragility Holly hardly recognised.

'I have never spoken of these matters to you, Little Orchid, but in Taipei after the war, when the KMT first arrived from the Mainland and the White Terror against the local Taiwanese power structure began, something happened. Something so evil that I have never talked about it to this day. You see, My Only Daughter, *Shao-lan*, it's not a good story.' She broke into a fit of coughing and her frame seemed to shudder with the recalling.

'When I was young I had a dear friend, a Taiwanese girl, my age, from the same township in the Miaoli Mountains south of Taipei. She was my best friend from first day at school right up to graduation.'

'Hang on, Ma, I want to check the pot.'

Ma paused while Holly turned down the *ma-lah ho-guo* bubbling on the stove.

'My friend was from a wealthy, powerful Taiwanese clan. She married a soldier, dutifully got pregnant. The day she gave birth to her first daughter was the day her family's bank was forcibly taken over by the KMT Finance Ministry, and in the ensuing riot many of her male relatives were jailed or shot. The baby was taken from her by the surviving family before she had even suckled it, and would have been smothered there and then but that my friend begged and begged for its life, swearing to kill herself, and so the child was passed on for adoption. She never saw her daughter again.'

'But why on earth?' demanded Holly. 'Chinese love children above all else.'

Ho Ma-ma looked very old. 'The baby had made the near-fatal mistake of being born at the exact wrong time, of pushing out of her mother's womb to claim the world just as news of the family's tragedy reached Miaoli from Taipei. Her arrival presaged the evilly-auspicious moment.'

Ho Ma-ma paused, her eyes far away, in another time, another place. To Holly she appeared oddly vulnerable, frail. Incredible Shrinking Ma. But Ma's voice had gathered strength: a force dug up from long-buried rage.

'Some dangerous fool,' she uttered. 'A jealous spinster-aunt, who knows, must have dragged in the geomancer and he decreed, judged, apportioned blame.'

'Madness!' cried Holly, involuntarily.

'Yes, a madness,' said Ma, collapsing inwardly once more, her voice filled with infinite sadness. 'The poor little babe took the blame for the family catastrophe. She was considered ill-omened, a harbinger of evil, bad *feng-shui*. Such a malign force had to be extirpated.'

'I don't believe it.' Holly was outraged. To tear apart a mother and child for the sake of some superstitious claptrap! The Chinese baffled her, and she was half-Han. Did they actually have beating hearts like the rest of us?

Ma said, 'Daughter, it is my deepest sorrow to say so, but the story is true. Such a lifetime ago, as though upon a different world. But I'm telling you as sure as I am sitting here with you tonight, that innocent newborn was cast out like a diseased bolus.'

Ma and Holly lapsed into silence, sipping cups of fresh Oolong.

'Now I begin to understand why you've got this thing about *feng-shui*,' said Holly finally.

'Daughter, I hate it with all my soul,' Ma replied, her eyes wide, lips quivering. 'And I'm frightened of it.' She looked at Holly. 'Whether you believe or not in the mystery of the Earth Dragon, treat it as a metaphor or literally, are a practitioner or not, and whether the family of my dear friend believed or not at the time, the result in the end was the same.'

She spread her palms and then clenched them into fists. 'The child was taken and never seen again. For the grieving mother it was a stillbirth. For her the baby was destroyed. *Feng-shui* had prevailed over biology and the soul: a mother's love.'

139

'The power those geomancers wield,' murmured Holly. 'What if it got in the wrong hands?'

The phone rang.

'You will take no further action in the McIlvuddy Probate. Is that perfectly understood?'

'Who is this? Where's Minty?' demanded Holly.

The voice intoned neutrally, 'Should you ignore these instructions, the next time it will be your body which we, ah, modify. And now time is wasting. We suggest you take an immediate look at your mailbox. We will call back in five minutes exactly.'

Holly raced downstairs three at a time, ignoring the creaky elevator. Burst into her office and ran to the front door. There below the large mail-slot was a bulky sealed-air package. She tore it open with shaky fingers. Extracted a styrofoam tube the size of a cucumber. Unhinged the cap releasing the smoke of dry ice and pulled out an object wrapped in clingfilm.

In the dim light of the office she could hardly make it out, hoping her eyes were deceiving her. She walked over to the front desk and flicked the lamp-switch. In her hand was a human thumb.

The phone trilled.

'We suggest you pack the contents of the package in ice from your freezer, get on your motorcycle and proceed at haste to St Thomas's Hospital. They may yet be able to save your friend's painting hand.'

'You *frocking* monsters!'

But the phone had already gone dead.

The Emergency staff at St Thomas's took one look at Holly's grisly package and rushed off to operate on Minty. She used her credit card to ensure that a private room was found for post-operative recovery and then used her cellphone to call Jane, Minty's wife in Devon. She was raw edgy and her words tumbled out. 'Jane? It's me, Holly. Minty's showed up and he's OK, sort of, um, but he's in hospital – here at St Thomas's, in London, Westminster Bridge opposite the House of Commons, and Big Ben, lovely view . . .'

140

'What's happened to him, Holly-Jean?' asked Jane with icy tones.

Holly elucidated as briefly and as neutrally as she could.

Jane berated her angrily. 'I thought you promised not to let Minty get involved in your work! It's bloody dangerous and now this, he's lost a thumb, how will he ever paint again?' Her voice cracked into a howling sob on the other end of the phone and Holly broke it to calm her down with pragmatic advice.

'Look, Jane, Minty needs you up here ASAP. Can you get the girls to a baby-sitter or a neighbour? You can? Then I suggest you do that and then drive up straightaway; it would be great for him to have you here when he comes out of the post-op funk. He'll want to see your face.'

Jane immediately agreed and rang off, promising to be up as soon as possible.

Four hours later, Holly was allowed to look in on the patient, unconscious and still under general anaesthetic. Out of the window, across the Thames, was an uninterrupted view of the Houses of Parliament, lit and fairy-like against the gloomy sky.

Holly leaned close to her friend's ear, and whispered, 'Don't know if you can hear me, Minty, but I think we can safely say you're off the case. Due a long holiday somewhere nice with the family. Anywhere you like – my tab. Get well, boyo.'

But he didn't reply.

Holly hunted down the harassed doctor who had performed the surgery to re-attach the severed thumb.

'Look, Miss Ho, we've done all we can. Now we just have to wait and see, and pray . . .' The young man drew a shaking hand through tousled hair. Check-in baggage under his eyes. Heavy beard shadow and exhaustion writ plain.

'Thanks, Doctor, I know you've done your best.'

'Actually it was rather *thanks* to you and your prompt action that your friend will have some kind of right hand. But face it: it's a matter of time now to see if the nerves will heal enough for the thumb to be of any use other than cosmetic.'

'We appreciate it, Doctor,' said Holly, but couldn't help

asking, 'Will he be able to paint?'

'What's a thumb got to do with painting?' said the young medic. 'His mind is intact. If I know artists, this event will only trigger further work. Even if the thumb is useless, he will relearn brush-strokes with the rest of the hand. If the nerves refuse to cooperate, it only means he has a static clutch mechanism. He'll adapt. Don't worry. He's always got the other one.' His beeper trilled and the young doctor raced off down the bustling corridors.

Holly only hoped to the gods that he was right. The thought that Minty's life should be blighted as a result of his friendship with her was more than she could bear. The only outlet for a Tiger was rage.

Chapter 17

Holly held a council of war the next morning.

Sadie Kaiserman had been informed of Minty's plight and was organising a post-op recuperation package for him. She and her assistant would be on permanent hand at the hospital and afterward. Minty's wife had arrived from Devon and was staying in a hotel in Covent Garden. Mick Coulson had posted a uniformed officer outside the private ward at St Thomas's just in case. But all agreed that Minty's role was over.

The next likely target had to be Holly herself.

'Why not just drop the bloody case? Walk away, Holls, for Chrissake,' Coulson had yelled at her down the telephone. 'You want to get yourself killed for some hereditary peer? It's arrant nonsense!'

Without giving away too much, Holly replied, 'Too late now. Wouldn't make any difference. These rich old Chinese men don't forgive. This has to be resolved one way or the other.'

Coulson had rung off with a curse.

Meanwhile, Barrance T. Wong was to remain as usual on full-time duty at Earlham Street. He would act as switchboard and electronic clearing-house for all inter-communication. Ma would stay with him to manage the shop. The old lady was subdued this morning, the shocks of the previous two days were obviously still lingering. Holly hugged her quickly and planted a rare kiss on her mother's papery brow.

Which left Carless.

'Carlotti, my man.' Holly grabbed the trucker's arm, dug out a snuff-smeared name-card. Tried Carless-speak.

'Tag Hamish McIlvuddy today. If you're driving that Incontinental of yours, parallel-park, it's all Residents Pee-ing only down there. So better watch out for the Houston Boot-ers. If you're going on the Underground, then it's Gloucester Road tube. Here's his *Min-Pyan*.'

Carless nodded happily, glanced at the proffered name-card and slipped it in his pocket.

Holly said, 'Snuffy-Nose lives at Basement Flat, 102 Queen's Gate. Just down from the French School, know it?'

Carless did. 'What's the poop with this McIlvuddy joker, boss-woman? He the one hurt my friend Minty?'

Holly explained. 'I don't know what *precisamente* his exact role is, but he's involved all right – up to his deerstalker's hat. Stick with him like a clam, for as long as you can manage. Feasible?'

'Quexacoatl.'

Holly made plane reservations then collared Shirley Jacquet at her newspaper. By the sound of it, Shirley was slap bang in the middle of breaking the story of Minty's kidnap. She couldn't stop her now. So she gave her the full story of the thumb and Minty's room number at St Thomas's for exclusive interview after recovery. Tonight the sensational events caught on video would be buffing the jaded palates of the box-watching populace.

Into Shirley's ear she said simply, 'We need to talk. *Now.*'

The two women sat in front of glasses of chilled Alsace Gewürztraminer from Hugel in a corner of the Soho Brasserie, still quiet this early in the day. Holly had a few hours before her evening flight to the Tropics.

'I want to know precisely what else your research people have come up with on the fate of Monica Mathews, aka Moonbeam,' she said.

Affecting the current trend, Shirley had just lit up a cigar and was savouring the first puffs with evident satisfaction.

'Cuban?' Holly coughed.

'Philippine. Flor Fina, a panatella from Tabacalera. Half as cheap as Havana and not too shabby tastewise,' she declared, behind blue billowing. ''Course, dreadfully uncool.'

144

Holly waved the smoke away. 'So, what did you hear from your bureau in New York? Yesterday we got as far as a fire in Moonbeam's Lower East Side brownstone.'

Shirley shrugged. 'It's not so pretty. The building changed hands after the fire. It was sold to a private company based in New Canaan upstate New York called SeedWorld. Some kind of multimedia outfit. My New York office Research Assistant, a great woman, called Fred, is tracking them down. Monica Mathews, meanwhile, moved to the Shri Rajneesh Ashram in Oregon and there contracted AIDS.' Shirley looked at Holly. 'She died in a Seattle homeless refuge five years ago.'

Holly felt her body still. Stared at her wineglass. Thought of the laughing girl in the faded photograph. Back then, in that still-life hung for eternity, she'd had all the ingredients for happiness: faith, hope, love and a laugh. And possibly a child on the way. What more could you ask of life? Surely not that it should turn and bite with deadly venom.

Reaching for the bottle with one hand, Holly drained her glass with the other and thought of all the waste.

'Yeah, tough break on the kid,' remarked Shirley after a quiet time.

Holly poured more wine. 'And the major question?'

Shirley smiled, drawing it out.

'Spill the frocking beans!' Holly urged.

'You mean was Moonbeam really pregnant in that photograph or just stone-munchied fat?' Shirley gloated.

Holly waited.

'She gave birth to a girl – Nellie Millicent Mathews. The kid attended the District of Lower Manhattan Second Avenue Elementary school first and second grade. Last public record we can find. That was before the fire, and the move to Oregon.'

'Brill, Shirl!' exclaimed Holly. 'So we have at least one definite heir – a girl for the McIlvuddy lineage. Which, as I always thought, means the Manila claim is most likely valid.'

Holly drank some more, suddenly feeling a whole lot better. A gleam of sunshine was piercing the violent gloom of bad family histories and bad *feng-shui*. It was important too, that Moonbeam had not died barren. Because now she was not alone in the cosmos. Someone was there to care for her after her passing. (Or at least someone who could be taught now, if she didn't already know.) Someone down here to give comfort and care in her afterlife, to provide the regular offerings of favourite goodies and otherworld barter stuff like fags and booze.

Which thoughts were very Chinese of her. Odd, that.

She raised her glass. 'Cheers to Nellie! And to Moonbeam grant rest eternal and may light perpetual shine upon her!'

They simultaneously swigged down the delicious wine. Thereafter lunch proceeded in somewhat drenched fashion, Shirley's cellphone trilling constantly throughout, with oaths and commands. Pleadings and insults. The Minty story was coming to life.

'Turning into a ruddy wake, all of a sudden,' announced Shirley woozily.

'Part wake, part rebirth,' retorted Holly.

'Yeah, rock on, Nellie!'

'You know, Nellie would be grown-up by now, in her mid-twenties,' Holly remarked whimsically. 'I wonder where she is right now? Maybe she's in London, maybe she's sitting at that table over there – look, the one with the tattoo. No, on second thoughts, not a tattoo. Our Nellie wouldn't be such a fashion victim.'

Shirley laughed. 'As your reporter, I advise you to take it easy on the vino, kiddo. Bit early for carousing, I'd say.'

Holly ignored her. 'So what's the story after the Ashram? Did Nellie end up in Seattle too, heaven forbid?' Visions appeared of the dying destitute woman and at her side in the gutter, a young girl with begging bowl and hollow eyes.

Shirley said, 'The Second Avenue Elementary School is all we know officially, so far. Fred has been up all night in New York and as I said is working the trace even as we speak.' She stopped. 'Now what are you up to?'

'Shh!' snapped Holly. 'I have to check something.' She was tearing through her address book. She found a number, flipped her cellphone and connected.

'Good morning. Oh, is it? Good afternoon, then . . . Well, personal actually. Um, well, I was wondering if I might make a specific enquiry on a point of progeniture? . . . Ah, no, I

146

mean right now. This is a yes or no . . . Would you? That is so kind. Right then. Something along these lines: if a female is the only living descendant, can she inherit the family title? Or does it follow patrilineal descent – men only nonsense? Ah, this would be . . . well, for example, how about in the case of an ancient Scots Earldom? Lord of the Isles, sort of thing? It depends, does it? . . . I see . . . OK, fine. Right away. Thank you so much. Goodbye then.'

'Burke's Peerage?'

'Something like that,' nodded Holly. She checked her watch. 'Look, I've got to go. Now listen, Shirl, I'm about to be a bit busy. So how about our Nellie? I'm relying on your New York office to come up with something damn soon. We've got to find her – you do realise that, don't you?'

Holly-Jean forebore to point out that there were men out there who had already killed and tortured in connection with the McIlvuddy Probate. She had to use Shirley and all her journo resources, but at the same time keep her on a very tight leash.

Shirley shook her head. 'Don't get your panti-liner in a twist, Madam Ho. To be honest, the people Fred had talked to so far have been very negative. It seems that whole Oregon time and place was like a black hole records-wise. The problem is the Ashram was philosophically anti-family, the kids all lived jumbled together, the parents in "non-exclusive groupings".'

Holly said, 'If I recall, the Ashram closed down back in the early eighties.'

Shirley nodded. 'Baggy upped and died on 'em. Murder and mayhem ensued. Big money involved.'

'I remember reading in *Private Eye* at the time that the Bhagsodosh had forty-eight Rolls-Royces in mint condition,' Holly noted.

'Hence *après le deluge* he did the mortal coil-shuffle.'

'Death and money,' Holly remarked grimly. 'Another legacy doing no one any good.'

Shirley continued, 'Anyway, when the US Attorney-General's office finally brought charges against a couple of the senior Sanyasin, the local Sheriff's Department got the chance they'd been waiting for since the day the first Orange

147

person showed up on the range.' She twirled imaginary six-guns and blew smoke from their barrels. 'He and his good ole boys goddam ran those durn hippies outtatown.'

'What happened to the Rajneesh movement after the Ashram?' said Holly.

Shirley thanked the waiter and sloshed wine in their clinking glasses. 'The Orange People drifted apart to go their myriad ways. Some returned to the original Ashram in Poona, which is these millennial days having some sort of revival. But we're not looking there yet – that would be our absolute last resort. Indian Bureaucracy is a nightmare we don't need.'

Holly sighed. 'You find Nellie McIlvuddy, Jacquet, and you'll be my friend for life.'

'I'm mortified I ain't already. Meanwhile, you'll just have to sit tight on your tush.'

'Genetic impossibility,' Holly pointed out. 'I've got a job to do on Hamish. The McIlvuddy inheritance belongs to Nellie and/or the Manila kid.'

'So what's the actual big deal with this inheritance?' asked Shirley. 'I thought you said the McIlvuddy Probate was just about a rent-free pad and a few quid pay-off every year. You hiding something from me?'

'Not at all. That's what been puzzling me, too,' Holly admitted. 'The key is there, but I just haven't turned it yet.'

'It's the Shih-Hamish connection that's got you fired up, isn't it?' said Shirley. 'Seems obvious to me that following his failure to take-over the McIlvuddy Trust last year, Shih Yang-fu must have figured having some family connection like Hamish was to his advantage. Though why, exactly?' She put down her empty glass. 'Don't forget they were old acquaintances and China Trade oppos from the Cold War days in Hong Kong.'

Holly's face betrayed nothing. It wasn't the right time yet to let Shirley know about the Chiu-Shih rivalry and Hamish's murky role in apparently playing off one Triad warlord against the other. Besides, she reckoned Shirley's research people would discover the identity of the owner of the Crawley mansion any time now.

The food came and was consumed. Deep-fried breaded

goat's cheese with gooseberry jelly and crisp-fried parsley. The second Alsace cut the richness perfectly.

'Before I forget, here's something from Oz that may interest you.' Shirley had dug out a newspaper cutting from her red leather Gucci tote-bag. 'Seems the Aboriginal claim ownership of certain tracts of McIlvuddy land near the Kimberley Range, just round about where the geologists say there ought to be diamonds. The natives have been getting restless – in fact, they've been sitting-in on their Dreamlands.'

'It's not just about diamonds,' said Holly, rapid-scanning the article. 'Charlie Villiers, a City-whizz, reliably informed me that the McIlvuddy assets Down Under are absolutely mind-boggling as far as untapped potential goes. Vast stretches of unspoiled coastline just waiting for Asian tourist development, deepwater harbours, oil terminals, the lot . . . while undisturbed beneath the interior possessions there's proven deposits, certified geological evidence of all sorts of precious metals and rare minerals. Not just diamonds, Jacquet, but platinum, uranium – the real treasure-trove.' Holly forked the last wedge of melted cheese into her mouth. 'It's all about land. Lots of land,' she mumbled. 'That's the prize. I know it.'

She spread her palms. 'You see, after all, with the Chinese you dwell among the billions, you get this anthill mentality. You crave land. It's an elemental thing.' Oh yes indeedy, she added to herself. Shih Yang-fu really wants that big piece of the planet and Chiu Nei-ku really wants that piece of Shih's arse.

Shirley was meanwhile feigning innocent speculation. 'A man like Shih Yang-fu could surely just snap his fingers to have the elder brother murdered in Manila – and then Hamish inherits the title?'

She looked at Holly, expectant. But her friend was gazing unfocused at the middle distance. Her eyes, twin dark pools, were glittering with a sudden intense charge. Then she threw her head back with a loud examination.

'That's it!' She slammed her palm down on the table, bouncing Shirley's cellphone off to clatter on the tiled floor of the restaurant. 'You beaut, Shirl! You raw prawn! It's been nagging me ever since I spoke to Willy Sangster-Choate – something I'd missed. I knew it was there but I was too stupid to see it staring me in the face.'

'Hold on there, Holls, you've lost me,' said Shirley, checking her cellphone.

Holly snatched it out of her hand. 'Don't you see,' she exclaimed. 'It's *not* about the title at all! It's about the seat with casting vote on the McIlvuddy Trust Board!'

It was obvious. The key to the whole probate was the casting vote on the board. She worked it through in her mind: Shih had failed in his hostile takeover bid last year. But he still had his dander up. In fact, he has slavering over the thought of the McIlvuddy Trust . . . Having lost face over the bid, he had become utterly obsessed.

His deadly enemy Chiu had discovered this, either by Hamish's instigation or his own intelligence sources. Chiu realises that if he can have the rightful McIlvuddy heir offed in Manila, then have his stooge Hamish inherit the title . . . he will have Hamish's vote on the board – and he will win the next buy-out attempt! Thereby getting his hands on the McIlvuddy estate, and what's more delicious, snatching it right from under Shih's nose!

A brilliant business coup and massive loss of face to his enemy!

On the other hand, it had to be in Shih's interest to turn up a tame heir of his own and thwart McIlvuddy of the estate.

Holly as usual was stuck in the middle with chopsticks drawn on all sides. Meanwhile, Shirley was still trying to figure it all out, but Holly-Jean wasn't about to help her and have that private war between old Chinese villains spread all over the tabloid press.

The journalist was theorising. 'Goes something like this: the seat on the board will go to Hamish, so that on the next buy-out attempt, Shih is successful. I can quote you on this?'

'No, you frocking well can't,' enunciated Holly, 'because it's not that simple. Worse, it could be wrong – and wrong hereabouts can get you severely compromised in the continuing to breathe stakes.' She looked at her friend. 'Shirl, I promise you when the time is right you will be the first to know. But more important,' Holly spoke in low tones, 'and trust me on this – you'd be better off forgetting everything I've said. *Especially* the name Shih Yang-fu.'

'Oh yeah? Why, pray tell?'

'Because Chinese business is a ravenous shark-reef. And you, my girl, really, really don't want to go paddling your backside in that little stretch of ocean. Copasetic?'

Shirley shrugged. Holly leaned close. 'Shih ever gets to find out you're meddling with his private stuff, you're beancurd.'

'So he really is a gangster,' said Shirley.

Holly ignored her and paid the bill. Time to sweat that Dr Manny Devesfrunto in Manila.

'I bet that Manila doctor knows where the axe is buried,' muttered Shirley with excellent journalistic instinct.

'Yeah,' said Holly, burping Alsace. 'Right between the shoulder-blades.' She marched out into Old Compton Street and hailed a cab. 'I'm going gadabout.'

'But where in the hell?' called Shirley Jacquet, anxiously hopping up and down on her purple Dolce & Gabbana six-inch stilettos. 'Damnitall, just let me put the Minty story to bed, and I'll join you.'

Holly shook her head. 'Sorry, kiddo, I fly solo, doncha know!'

'At least tell me which country!'

'Forget it,' called Holly from the cab window. 'And by the way, Shirl – and you can quote me verbatim – this entire conversation has all been pure speculation.'

Five minutes later Holly-Jean met for a hurried interview with the woman from the London Institute of Heraldry, a fancy name for what Holly guessed at an Alsace-soaked glance was a scam specialising in tracing ancestry and designing fake coats-of-arms for Texas oil millionaires. The company operated out of a tiny fifth-floor walk-up flat halfway down Longacre. Mrs Daphne D'Aubigny-ffrig was the name on the gold embossed name-card. Holly checked twice.

'Ho? That would be . . .' From deep within folds of greasepaint Mrs D.D.-ffrig peered at Holly speculatively.

'That would be the Chinese Ho's,' said Holly helpfully. 'Couple of million of us.'

Mrs D.D.-ffrig blushed and giggled. Her lemon horn-rim specs as thick as bottled glass twinkled prettily, her russet bouffant wig wobbled precariously, the twin coloured-glass

151

replicas of the *Golden Hind* hanging from her earlobes chimed charmingly, and when she clapped her hands as if to say, 'Down to business!' her cherry-varnished fingernails click-clacked while the corset beneath the orange floral print ballgown creaked alarmingly. Holly tried not to gape.

'You're the dear lady called on the phone earlier,' trilled Daphne. 'About the Scots title and the matter of patrilineal descent and female succession, wasn't it?' The cherry nails darted into a shiny black handbag, an atomiser flashed and a sweet mist dappled her powdered chins.

'Unh, *yes*,' Mrs D.D.-ffrig sighed in ecstasy. 'Opium.'

'An Earldom,' said Holly, clenching her nostrils. For a madcap moment, she decided the woman was equally inspired as she. Swimming in Alsace at lunchtime was confusing.

'I want to know what happens if there's a daughter of the dynastic heir. Does she inherit the title before the second son?' She stifled a goat's-cheesy hic. 'Salic Law, I've been informed.'

Mrs D.D.-ffrig affectionately patted a pile of leather-bound tomes stacked on the desk in front of her, accompanied once again by the symphony of her accoutrements.

'Salic Law dates from the Merovingian Age,' she confided knowledgeably. 'The Merovingians were a Frankish dynasty founded by the legendary tribal warrior-chief, Clovis.'

'The originator of sliced brown.'

Mrs D.D.-ffrig smiled sympathetically. 'Originally Germanic, the Franks conquered Gaul in the sixth century,' she went on. 'Charlemagne the Great was a descendant and his era is usually referred to as the Carolingian Age. Salic Law refers to their written laws excluding females from the dynastic succession which was later adopted by the French and other European monarchies.'

'But not the Windsors or the English Dukes and all?' said Holly.

'No, and as far as your Scots chieftains are concerned it's inapplicable. The clans each have their individual ritualised traditions about these things, most of them unwritten. Anyway, dearie, following your phone call I did a bit of research.'

She held up one of the heavy volumes accusingly, as if

Holly had demanded proof. Then she slapped it down with a loud crash, causing her pendulous mammaries to keel violently. 'Lords of the Isles aren't exactly thick on the ground, honeypie.'

'I imagine not,' said Holly.

Mrs D.D.-ffrig chuckled and touched her nose with her tongue. 'I hazard you're talking about the McIlvuddy title. I'm right, aren't I, darling?' Either the woman was rehearsing for panto, or Barry Humphries' identity problems were worse than he was letting on.

Holly stifled a giggle. 'Excuse me, but your beauty spot has smudged.'

Mrs D.D.-ffrig opened her handbag and snapped her compact. With a hanky and spit she erased the blemish. 'Better, dearheart?'

'Perfect. About the McIlvuddy title . . .'

'The *Ilk*, sweety, or I should say,' – another spray of Opium enveloped them both, '*That* Ilk. The girls get it.'

The reek of Bangkok knock-off stayed with Holly for the rest of the day.

Holly was running late. She raced home to pack a bag and grab her passport. Called and confirmed her ticket was ready for collection at the airline desk at Heathrow.

She was just pulling away from the office on her Yamaha, hand-carry shoulder-bag ahoist, when she noticed a woman walking down from Seven Dials towards her. She noticed her because the woman looked vaguely familiar. Drawing alongside, Holly slowed up.

No, she'd been mistaken. She didn't know this person.

The loud rev as she pulled away caused the woman to look up, startled. Their eyes met and for that fleeting moment some kind of exchange took place. Holly wobbled a bit on the cobbles then drove on, her mind resolutely on other things. But she did glance in her wing-mirror at where the woman had stopped and had turned round.

An arm was raised; it beckoned.

Holly just gestured airily without turning and flew on.

As predicted, the TV news carried footage of Shirley Jacquet's

153

sensational video of Minty being tossed off the end of Hastings Pier. When the story came on the box, Holly was sipping iced Perrier in the departure lounge at Heathrow. The gaggle of bevying lads at the bar punctuated the report with shouts and whoops. 'Fackin touchdown!'

Holly thought of Minty's thumb and prayed the digit would reattach itself. She reckoned her old mate would stay out of the picture for a while after this, but not for ever. If she knew that boy, he'd be back. He'd miss the rush.

They called her flight, and Holly, alone, made her way to the gate.

Chapter 18

Manila was, as ever, Manila.

Mabuhay.

The usual inadequately air-conditioned cab with the broken meter, the usual dead pig floating in the black sludge Pasig River, the usual seven-year-old hollow-eyed waif with naked fly-crusted baby at her waist knocking on the cab window at the traffic-lights on Roxas Boulevard, the usual petro-chem-faeces stench pervading the sauna air.

Holly checked in at the Westin Plaza, figuring it was Lord Snuffy's treat, and called the Lacsina woman's lawyer, Noring Estrella. He would call back in five minutes, they told her.

Holly carried the phone out to her balcony and took in the sights of the misty China Sea. Built by Imelda during her glory days on reclaimed mud far enough out in Manila Bay to waft in a semblance of fresh air, the Plaza was as removed from the squalor of Manila as an orbiting moon.

Giant, menacing, the aircraft carrier USS *Invincible* loomed high on the Bay. The landscaped swimming-pool six floors below her was noisy with crew-cut beefcakes drinking heavily. The Sixth Fleet was in town after seven months at sea.

Manila's infamous Ermita sleaze-hole had long been closed down by Mayor Lim, a Chinese Mestizo running for President who was reputed to be Triad-connected. However, the sleazostory had simply moved to Pasay City, another jurisdiction just across Roxas Boulevard ringing the Bay. Vixens, Firehouse, Misty's and Hula Hut would be hammered tonight, thought Holly. So would the young girls. It's what is called a courtesy visit.

Noring Estrella phoned. Holly explained her business, adding, 'I want to see the Lacsina child as soon as possible.'

155

'*Walang problema.* You got to see Dr Manny Devesfrunto – Jonny Mac's personal physician, you understand? He handles all the details. You got his cellphone number?'

Holly took it down. She knew everyone in the Philippines had a cellphone; the PDLT just couldn't hack the country's geography of 12,000 islands.

She said, 'as the *abogado* you'll need to be present for any interview with the boy. Is that a problem?'

'*Hindi.* Sure thing. So you want me to set up a meet with the Doc?'

'It must be today.'

'*Walang problema*, but hey! This is Philippines, *maintindihan*? Understand me?'

Holly fully understood. She'd be lucky. 'How *is* the boy?'

'The boy? Oh great, fantastic. *Mabuti.* Last time I saw him.'

'And when was that?'

'A month or two back. Cute kid, they're keeping him good and fat. Well, they wouldn, wouldn't they? Lot riding on that little boy.'

They? This Estrella sounded slick as two eels. 'It's important I see him today. *Maintindihan?*'

'*O-o ba!* Def'nily!'

Holly waited till the Semper Fi mob had dispersed into the afternoon bars of Pasay City and went down to the pool. She had a swim, ate a green papaya salad and read with half a mind her battered paperback copy of *Lord of the Rings*. She'd begun re-reading the thing in the summer when she'd spent a few days hiking round Connemara, sitting under standing stones breathing the sweet air. It was an extremely violent book. Battle after ambush after vicious attack. Not a whiff of peace, love and vegetarian cigarette papers, yet the hippies worshipped it and recently it had been voted the Book of the Century by the British reading public. Hmmm, very intellesting, Plofessoh Fleud . . .

Estrella broke her reverie. Holly was to be at Devesfrunto's clinic in the upscale section of town, Makati, at five.

The traffic was abominable, and the hotel taxi's air-con

couldn't cope. Holly was drenched in sweat by the time she reached the place. The ornate surveilled gate with armed guard admitted her through frangipani and bougainvillaea to a Spanish-colonial-style mansion. A huge slavering hound of some kind flopped all over her, trailing spume onto her ankles. She punted the dog aside with a discreet tae kwon do drop-kick. With a howl it ran off, looking back at her in terror.

She pushed open the carved mahogany double doors and thanked the gods for air-conditioning. A drop-dead gorgeous Miss Universe greeted her and asked her to wait a moment.

The mansion was laden with ugly hardwood furniture, the walls adorned with golfing trophies and photos of a handsome man playing golf with various local celebrities; Holly recognised the movie star presidential aspirant.

She was ushered into another room by Miss Philippines, who introduced herself as Bing-Bing. 'The Doctor will see you now.'

'Thanks, Bing-Bing.'

The returning smile skimmed the net and won matchpoint. Holly flushed with instant monsoon pleasure and turned to face the greasy-pompadoured Devesfrunto.

'Miss Ho, it's a pleasure to meet you,' came the cultured voice belying the pencil moustache, bulging silk shirt and gold rings. The Doc had definitely filled out since the golfing photos in Reception were taken.

Holly briefly took the outstretched hand. 'Mr Estrella probably explained that I'm acting in the matter of the McIlvuddy Probate, and since you are on record as the late Lord McIlvuddy's personal physician I wondered if you might expedite certain matters.'

'It would be my honour,' said Dr Devesfrunto, waiting till Holly had found a chair before sitting behind his huge rosewood desk. 'By the way, what did you think of my sweetheart? A damn fine animal, right?'

Holly thought that a bit much. 'Bing-Bing is certainly an exquisite-looking girl.'

The doctor looked puzzled. 'Bing-Bing? I'm talking about the Emperor Bonking, my Rhodesian ridgeback-dachsund cross. I love that dog with all my heart. Did you know

157

that Cardinal Bad personally christened him in Quiapo Cathedral?'

'Oh,' said Holly. 'Nice doggie.'

Devesfrunto leaned back, hands behind head. 'So what can I do for you, apart from dinner later tonight after a round of golf this evening?'

Holly's smile set. 'I presume you are aware of the untimely death in London of Marybel Lacsina whose son is the subject of the pending paternity challenge to the McIlvuddy Probate?'

'Aware and shocked, immensely shocked by this mystifying tragedy.' The doctor's grin was composed of several chunks of gold.

'Really, Doctor?' said Holly. 'Hardly mystifying given the huge amounts of money involved,' adding pleasantly, 'I understand that the current rate to have a person killed hereabouts is less than five hundred US dollars.'

Devesfrunto's grin widened. 'I see you know the Philippines! *Perfecto Ganap!*' His face became suddenly serious. 'But Miss Ho, this tragic event happened in London. What connection is there with the court action here?'

Holly's smile was icy. 'I'll let you figure that one out for yourself, Doctor. Meanwhile, current status of the paternity suit in the local courts, if you please.'

'These things are so slow here in my country.' Devesfrunto shrugged. 'We are still waiting for a date to be set for an initial hearing.'

Holly figured as much. 'I see from the transcripts that you are on record as declaring the deceased Lord Jonny McIlvuddy sterile. Apparently, due to a low sperm count he was unable to procreate. Is that correct?'

'*Tama!* Correct,' said Dr Manny, reptilian smile thickening, obsidian eyes glittering darkly. 'That is to say, at the time. There may now be some revision to the, ah, diagnosis.'

Surprise, surprise. 'In what way exactly, Doctor? I'd have thought either one is sterile or one is not?'

'New *evidencia*, the onward march of science,' Manny declared.

'Not to mention the fact that another heir has been discovered,' said Holly.

158

Manny's eyes narrowed to slits. 'No kiddin'?'

Holly's patience snapped. 'I am very short of time, Doctor. Now, I have good reason to believe that Lord McIlvuddy was murdered and that the child in question may also be in danger. *Abogado* Estrella informs me the Lacsina boy is in your care. Please take me to see him now.'

'Hey, Miss, slowly, slowly, *mabagal*! I reckon you better forget all loose chat-chat of murder and what you call danger to the child; you appear to got an over-anxious imagination.' The doctor's excellent English slipped as agitation set in.

'Oh, so you intend to ignore the fact that the child's mother has also been killed?' Holly stood and leaned across the desk.

'May she rest in peace.' The doctor crossed himself and touched his lips piously. 'But don't you worry your pretty head about the Lacsina kid. Jonny Mac – all his friends called him that – died of natural causes, certified, clean as a pipe, Department of Health warranty.'

Holly listened without comment.

Devesfrunto continued, 'And one more thing. Jonny Mac appointed me Medical Physician to all the GRO's more than twenty years already. I'm well used to being responsible for the health of all their babies – so *relacs*! Take it easy, *walang problema*!'

'GROs?' echoed Holly.

'Guest Relations Officers.'

'Oh, right.' Flip euphemism for whore. She stood up. 'Time's running out, Doctor. I am empowered to collect affidavits, sworn testimony, from any and all potential witnesses to the paternity claim. When can I see the child? I presume also that exhumation is pending in the matter of collecting DNA samples from the deceased Lord McIlvuddy.'

Devesfrunto grinned affably, pressed a button on his desk. He stood up and from a golf-bag leaning against the wall, extracted a gold-plated iron and began to swing. 'Custom-made in Taiwan to my personal specification. You see, gold-plate, 24 carat. I love three things above all else. The Emperor Bonking, my golf-bag and clubs from which I am never parted – I sleep with both, unless . . . and well, I'll

159

allow you to speculate on my third great love.'

Holly endured this without expression. 'The Lacsina child, Doctor. I have jurisdiction.'

'Applicable in my country?' said Devesfrunto, smiling. 'I doubt it.'

'Enough with the *bula-bula*,' Holly snapped. 'I intend to see the child either today or tomorrow. And now bring me up to date on the exhumation process.'

Devesfrunto's smile widened. 'See how you are? Such a rush. *Mamiya!* We Filipinos like to take it slow, Miss Ho . . . *Exhumation*, eh? He looked at her shrewdly. 'Oh, I should think the exhumation is going to prove *very* difficult.'

'How's that?' asked Holly, standing watching the doctor practise his golf like some pissed-off umbrella girl.

He paused in mid-swing. 'Well, you see, His Lordship, Jonny Mac, is buried in the courtyard of the Dawn of Life Health Club, his main place of business. The current owner is the former company accountant, one of Jonny Mac's favourite girlfriends. She had the place in her name from the beginning – you know foreigners aren't allowed to own premises in our country. The last thing that lady wants is to have the Lacsina boy proved to be Jonny Mac's kid.'

Devesfrunto swung powerfully, shouted, 'Fore!' and burst into boyish giggles. 'Between you and me, if there's ever a cash handout, you can bet your golf-club membership that a whole army of little brown McIlvuddys will come marching out of the *barrios*.' He continued to chuckle. 'You'd better figure Jonny Mac's staying put under that bordello fountain.'

'So sampling the DNA will be impossible?' said Holly.

'Maybe, maybe not.' His eyes twinkled. 'As his personal physician I am happy to say that I am currently *still* intimate with Jonny Mac's physical dimensions.'

Holly nodded. Of course he'd managed to save some tissue from Lord McIlvuddy's body.

'So you kept his foreskin on ice,' said Holly, 'just for that rainy day, huh?'

'A non-malignant tumour, if you want to know, also fully certified by the Department of Health, all records legit and complete,' Mammy beamed. 'And of course, locked away

160

safely where no one can get to it.'

'I imagine it would be,' said Holly.

'You know, I really like you, Miss Ho, you're my kind of girl. Let's have dinner. I can show you the town, paint it red, tango till dawn.'

Holly didn't return the invitational display of gold-capped incisors. 'The prospect is overwhelming, but I confess to jet-lag. Doctor. Meanwhile, and this is for the record, I formally request to see the boy.'

Manny walked round from behind his desk and placed a very warm hand on Holly's hip. 'Then how about just the evening round of golf instead, one of my other *serious* passions?' he murmured.

She reached down and pinched the secret meridian point at the wrist above the artery.

The doctor blanched, gasped and buckled to his knees. 'Surprisingly strong grip you got there, Miss Ho,' he croaked, rubbing his hand. He was just clambering painfully to his knees, face inches from Holly's crotch when the door opened and Bing-Bing marched in with cups of coffee. She took in the scene and broke into rapid-fire, obviously incensed Tagalog.

When Manny had temporarily placated the irate receptionist, Holly jammed the Plaza hotel card with her room number in Manny's jacket pocket, announcing, 'I expect to have access to the child within twenty-four hours. I have been appointed his legal guardian with power of attorney by the British legal system. The boy himself has been declared a Ward of Court in the UK and the British Ambassador here in Manila has been informed. As has the Deputy Minister of Justice, Gloria Magbuhos, who is a personal friend of mine.'

With these rather hopeful lies, Holly left the clinic, aiming a jolly kick in the direction of a cowering Emperor Bonking, took the third taxi to slow down and reached the hotel at seven.

As she walked to the elevator and the mouth-watering prospect of a cold shower, the lawyer Estrella emerged from behind a large potted palm.

'You encounter some difficulty reaching the boy, right?' he said. 'I can help.' Hello, someone just worked out which side his bread's buttered.

The lawyer drove a BMW and Holly was madly grateful for the efficiency of the Bavarian Motorwork's air-conditioning. They moved through lessening traffic across the city in the now firework-lit night. The *barrios* were spilling out crowds, music blared, people danced in the slow lanes. Fiesta time.

'What's the occasion?' she asked.

'All Saints' Day tomorrow,' said Estrella, manoeuvring through throngs of pedestrians spilling out of a *barrios* onto the main drag.

'All Saints,' mused Holly. 'The Christian Day of Reverence for the Dead, hijacked by American big business to become the global macabre fancy-dress day called Hallowe'en. So here in Philippines it's still a special day in genuine religious terms?'

'All Saints?' said Estrella, steering through the crowds. 'You betcha! This is Asia's *Catholic* country. Just you wait and see what's coming. Won't believe your eyes!'

They left the brightly lit cross-town thoroughfare of Epifania De Los Santos Avenue and headed into a miserable part of town on the east side of the Pasig River – Estrella named it Santa Mesa.

'Bad place, very poor, a very low threshold of human existence,' he sighed. Then brightened. 'But for tonight, at least, for the fiesta, everyone is happy.'

The BMW wound down ever narrower alleyways, its progress hampered by the wild-eyed tango-dancers and half-naked crazies brandishing their bottles of cheap hooch.

'This is Santa Mesa,' said Estrella, with a touch of reverential fear. They were deep in the heart of the teeming Metro Manila swamp.

Estrella parked the car near the gates to a big old crumbling American edifice, an oasis of architecture amid the chaos of cardboard shanty.

'This is the local Mayor's home,' he explained. 'His grandmama still lives there.'

'And where does the Mayor live?' asked Holly, flinching as

a firecracker detonated a few feet away. A gang of kids ran screaming by.

Her companion snorted. 'Way outside Santa Mesa, in Forbes Park – a rich man's paradise a few k's from here.' He paid the two armed doormen lounging outside the building with a bottle of Tanduay rum and a hundred pesos to keep an eye on the BMW, promising a further fee on safe return.

They set off into the crowded fiesta alleyways. After a few twists and turns they left Tarmac and vague street-lighting, and entered the ill-lit warren of the squatters' *barrio*. Rockets, Roman Candles and thunderflashes punctuated the cordite-laden air. Finally they reached a railway line passing through the dense habitation and began to walk alongside the tracks.

'From here on it is all the poorest of the poor, squatters using the no-man's land along the railway line, so you stick close to me. Keep your head down, just say "*Mabuti*" to anyone who speaks. *Maintindihan?*'

Holly personally resented any threads of panic Third World urban squalor might induce. On the other hand, she didn't know any of the answers either. Still, she was frocked if she was going to act like some shit-struck visitor from the fat.

As they picked their way along the edge of the railway, deafening dance music blasting from each cardboard shanty, side-stepping the fetid pools and the smell of excrement, Holly kept her head high and exchanged smiles with the many inhabitants who smiled back, dignity intact in the unfairness of their dealt hands. In bitter contrast to the squalor at ground-level, the sky was filled with shower-bursts of colour and the naked pot-bellied children squealed in delight.

After about eighty metres of railway line they passed through thickening crowds into some kind of cement clearing, a basketball court now overflowing with deafening karaoke machines blasting out the latest Tagalog and international hits. As they pushed through the throng, they reached the central attraction.

In a loosely formed space, a dozen or so half-naked men and one or two women, blood streaming from their backs, flagellated themselves with split bamboo whips. Here the deafening loudspeakers relayed the moaning of funereal chants as the penitents laid into themselves with transcendent abandon.

'All Saints' Day!' shouted Estrella into Holly's ear. 'Self-chastisement, to honour the dead, begging their intercession in the harsh world and hoping by self-mutilation to get forgiveness of sins and a better tomorrow!'

'The dead really like this sort of thing?' remarked Holly. At least the Chinese stopped at strip-shows for the dead. But who knew? Maybe decadence was a future trend for the after-life.

On the basketball court the atmosphere was lusty not pious; the air filled with sexual charge, the eyes of the onlookers crazed with alcohol-soused leers. Holly suddenly felt the overwhelming communal body-heat envelop her. She shoved Estrella on. 'Let's get the frock out of here!'

Estrella grinned over his shoulder as a woman with an enormous goitre on her forehead stumbled and fell against Holly. 'We're nearly there. Don't panic!'

Panic was one thing Holly the Tigress never did. On the other hand when she wanted out of some place, she was outta there. Like a hot knife through butter. She parted the last lines of onlookers and stepped out of the crowd on the other side of the basketball court.

Estrella arrived sweating and dishevelled five minutes later. He led the way ahead, further into the *barrio*, through almost pitch-dark into some kind of cement-block construction where kerosene lamps revealed a jeepney up on a ramp. In the corner a group of men had quit the fiesta and were sitting round a couple of bottles of local ginebra and a couple more flickering spirit flames.

Holly stepped through the gloom, aware of the sudden silence and the stark unfriendly stares. Estrella murmured some Tagalog; the men appeared to relax. He gestured up and mounted some flimsy wooden stairs at the rear. Holly followed.

The floor above was constructed of tacked-together cardboard, styrofoam, plastic bags and the odd sheet of corrugated iron. A narrow corridor was lined with doorways. Holly glimpsed an impossibly high number of tiny children, too young to be out but apparently untended, stuffed inside the tiny spaces within. The air was stifling and humid; the smell of greasy cooking oil, rotting fish and ordure enough to make you gag.

Holly swallowed, emptied her mind with *chi* technique and stepped on. At last they reached the end of the narrow space and Estrella knocked on a wooden door. It opened an inch.

Estrella spoke quietly, the door opened further and Holly was scrutinised. The door finally yielded and they entered. A young girl was tending a fat little toddler. He had pale skin and thick eyebrows.

'So this is Jonny's son,' said Holly.

'That's him,' Estralla nodded. 'Raymond Jun-jun McIlvuddy – cute little tyke, don't you think?'

The girl proffered the boy, but one glance at Holly was enough to unleash a roar of terror from the infant and she backed off. Estrella and the girl began to converse.

Holly glanced around. The space within consisted of two home-made plank bunk-beds, a fridge and a sink with a bucket of water standing nearby. There was a massive music centre with karaoke dominating one wall and some posters of Leonardo Di Caprio. Holly knew from previous experience that entertainment first, sustenance second, could be the slogan of the Filipino poor.

'Can't we get him out of here to somewhere nicer?' she said, when there was a break in their conversation.

Estrella shook his head. 'Believe me, he's safer here. No one who matters knows his whereabouts. Devesfrunto doesn't even know exactly – not that he'd ever dream of setting foot in Santa Mesa, let alone this *barrio*. Let's keep it like that.'

Holly shrugged and nodded. For the time being, what with the fraught atmosphere of fiesta outside, she guessed it made sense.

Estrella said, 'But if you wouldn't mind, a cash donation would be very welcome.'

Holly pulled out all the pesos she had in her pocket and handed them to the girl, who simply stared at her with huge eyes.

'I'll be back with more,' Holly said helplessly.

'*Salamat*,' intoned the girl with a sweet smile, pocketing the cash.

Estrella continued to speak in Tagalog for a few minutes. Then he turned to Holly. 'OK, let's go. We don't want to draw undue attention to ourselves and endanger the boy.'

'What about those guys downstairs?' Holly worried. 'They saw us come in.'

'Those men are related to the Lacsina family and they will protect Raymond Jun-jun to the death. Especially since there could be money in it for them if it all works out to plan. Frankly, Miss Ho, despite the squalor, I think it's best the boy stay here till this thing is resolved one way or the other. I guess you realise now that Dr Devesfrunto has the exhumation, and thus the eventual outcome of the case, under his control.'

'I guess so,' said Holly.

Estrella added, 'However, in my country, nothing is ever definite, especially in matters of legality. There are always ways and means.'

Bet there are, thought Holly, wondering if the Lacsina family would ever see any of the McIlvuddy money.

'Why did you decide to help me?' she asked as they made their way back to the car.

'Leverage,' he told her. 'I like to level the playing-field. The good Dr is exceedingly wily, especially when it comes to money – and golf, I might add. Besides,' he stopped and looked at Holly with earnest eyes, 'I do care about little Raymond Jun-jun as if he were my own son. You have to believe me.'

Holly didn't comment. Estrella was only a fraction less unlikely an angel of mercy than Doc Manny himself. Anyway, as was par for the Philippines, she would trust no one unless proved otherwise. The republic of Telling Lies might be a more accurate title for the flawed paradise.

By-passing the basketball court, which hummed and blared a few alleys over, they eventually reached the car without incident and Estrella tipped the men. Just as they were pulling away, Holly heard the squeal of burning rubber. A shiny black utility vehicle perched on massive tyres hurtled round the corner and swerved off in the direction of the railway line.

'Bit fancy for around here,' remarked Holly. 'Do you think—'

'*Walang problema!*' said Estrella. 'Drug dealers, most likely. Santa Mesa is a huge market for *shabu*, what you call ice, crystal methamphetamine? Tonight's All Saints' Eve. Those guys with the whips are going to keep it up for two days without sleep. And the rest of them don't intend to go to bed.'

With beds like that to go to, who could blame them for letting rip, thought Holly.

The lawyer started the BMW. 'The dealers love those big-tyred RVs. Don't worry. They're just making a fiesta drop for their *barrio* customers.'

Which about said it all for Manila, thought Holly, looking back as they pulled away. There was no sight of the big boys' car.

By the time they had crossed the sprawling metropolis to Manila Bay and reached the Out-of-Manila experience called the Westin Philippine Plaza Hotel, jet-lag had set in and Holly declined Estrella's offer of a drink. Her mind was consumed entirely by the thought of a shower, food and an air-conditioned bed.

Estrella said he'd call for her tomorrow at nine o'clock to accompany her to Devesfrunto's clinic to serve official papers. Holly thanked him and, stifling a yawn, said good night.

In her icy room she ordered smoked salmon on wholemeal bread with dill mustard, a tomato, onion and olive salad and a bottle of chilled Vina Sol from room service. Resolutely banishing guilty thoughts of the *barrio*, she stripped off her sweaty clothes.

She was showered and dressed in a luxurious silk-cotton towel-robe courtesy of housekeeping, when the waiter rolled in with the tray of food. Holly looked up as on the box Philippine TV News Patrol declared in melodramatic tones punctuated by blaring disco music the latest election assassinations, drought starvation casualties, kidnappings, incestuous rapes and numerous fires caused by the All Saints' fiesta fireworks, including many which complete razed entire squatter shanties.

Her appetite was gone.

Holly surfed the cables till she found palatable images, a BBC World documentary on Beatrix Potter and the Lake District, and after a while ate her supper in desultory fashion.

Jet-lag overtook her halfway through the third glass.

Chapter 19

Estrella was waiting when she arrived in the lobby at 8.45, refreshed from a good sleep, an early morning swim, workout and massage, followed by a healthy breakfast of fresh tropical fruits and excellent Oolong *cha*.

They crawled through the traffic to Devesfrunto's clinic in Makati, witnessing one rear-ender which ended with guns drawn and everyone ducking low beneath the nearest cover.

'Manila,' shrugged Estrella with a sheepish grin.

They arrived at the ornate Spanish mansion just before ten o'clock. Already an hour late. 'Precisely punctual in Pinoy time!' announced Estrella as they walked through the unguarded gates to the clinic.

'Where's the security?' asked Holly, breaking into a trot.

'Probably having a bite to eat,' shouted Estrella. 'Hey! Slow down!'

But Holly was already pushing open the unlocked mahogany front door. No sign of Bing-Bing. A rich smell of yeasty bread reached her nostrils. A curious buzzsawing registered in her ears. She tiptoed to Devesfrunto's office, gently inched the door open. It was a far from uplifting sight.

Handcuffed on all fours to the big armchair was the good doctor's naked body, his head lolling down over the high back. His ripped neck was the flie's fiesta, the buzzing their appreciation of congealed blood. A similar winged-insect bacchanal was taking place at the neck of The Emperor Bonking, whose front paws were secured tight to a rope looped round the chair.

His penis was as yet in *coitus uninterruptus* with His Master's Anus.

Estrella took one look and threw up. Holly led him outside

and told him to stay put. 'You going to call the police?' she demanded.

'No, not yet,' coughed Estrella, wiping his mouth on his sleeve. 'The police in my country are what I think you call an oxymoron, a contradiction in terms. As far as I'm concerned they will be informed only well after we have left the premises, and after we have ensured there are no evidential connections to either of us. Trust me on this one.'

Holly shrugged and said, 'It's your country. Now I've got to find that DNA sample or at least the tissue/cell portion that the Doc kept behind from Lord Jonny's remains.' A pleasant task for a stinking hot humid Manila day, enough to get you singing the Overture to *Oklahoma*, I don't think!

Holly gritted her teeth, and went back into the house. She located a sink, drenched a towel in water and held it to her nose. The whole place was a shambles, and someone had spray-painted Tagalog obscenities, Holly noting the words, *Bing-Bing* and hoping the poor girl hadn't stumbled into something she shouldn't have . . . Holly returned to the office and took a careful look around. The place had been systematically searched and trashed. The golfing photos were strewn about and had been torn from their frames. A wall-safe hung open and empty. The carpets had been ripped up, floorboards prised apart. The gold golf-clubs had been bent and buckled. The other rooms in the mansion were similarly desecrated. Holly reckoned there must have been a whole gang of them. They probably paid off the guards and told Bing-Bing to scat.

On the desk was a blood-smeared card. She picked it up. It was the Plaza Hotel card with her room number. Great! Holly wondered if Devesfrunto had told them what they'd wanted before he died. Was it the whereabouts of Raymond Jun-jun Lacsina McIlvuddy? Or of the pre-cancerous tumour which could provide the DNA evidence? Holly reckoned both.

She ran outside, grabbed Estrella. 'We've got to get to Santa Mesa! Maybe he told them where Raymond is!'

'I told you not to worry – Devesfrunto didn't know exactly where Raymond was hidden, only the cellphone of the relatives,' said Estrella. He paused at the gates. 'Besides, I don't think he told them where the body sample was.'

'Oh?' said Holly. 'And what makes you so sure?'

He thumbed back toward the big house. 'That back there's Chinese torture. Our local gangs are affiliated and subservient to the Triads. The Chinese teach our guys the worst stuff. And that was pretty bad: using his dog to defile his manhood. Ultimate humiliation. We Filipinos are *muy macho*.'

Holly looked at him. 'Exactly. So why do you say he would endure and not tell? Frankly speaking, Mr Estrella, between you and me, the money isn't that big. And the good doctor looked to be pretty well off already.' She gestured at the mansion. 'So why *do* you think he didn't tell?'

'Two reasons,' said Estrella. 'You see, we go back aways. I knew Manny very well. Better than anyone, in fact.'

'Make your point, we've got to get to Raymond Jun-jun,' said Holly.

He shrugged. 'Dr Devesfrunto was a self-prescribing heroin addict. He hasn't felt pain since a brief posting in the Vietnam War.'

'And the second reason?' asked Holly, pushing Estrella out of the gates.

The lawyer looked embarrassed. 'He slept with The Emperor Bonking every night, including those nights when he had female company. Seems the doctor liked to involve all of his partners in the most intimate fashion.'

Holly stopped in her tracks. 'Two and the dog makes three?' she said incredulously.

Estrella was sheepish. 'These things slip out. Rumours. He had an unnatural love for that dog. In fact, you could say my old friend died as he would have most liked. In numb ecstasy.'

'With his best friend up his bum,' said Holly.

A few blocks away Holly grabbed Estrella's free arm as he was about to use his cellphone and report the murder. 'Do a U-turn. We've got to go back!'

Estrella swung the steering-wheel and with a squeal of burnt rubber they crossed five lanes of enraged honkers. Back at the mansion Holly raced through the gates and into the clinic. The golf-bag was under the desk. She dragged it out and upended it. Nothing fell out. Empty. So her hunch had been wrong.

A side pocket revealed books of cards, little pencils, golf-tees and spare gloves. Another pocket was stuffed with golf-balls.

Puffing, Estrella arrived behind her. 'What you find?'

'Nothing,' she said. 'Come on, let's get to Santa Mesa. It was just an idea – something you said about sleeping with the dog. You see, the Doctor told me he also slept with his golf-bag. A peculiar man. Anyway, nothing here. I was wrong. Go! Let's burn more rubber!' She thought about fingerprints and decided to keep the golf-bag with her.

They reached the house at the edge of the *barrio* twenty minutes later. Holly knew from her last extended sojourn in the Philippines – a delicate negotiation in Muslim Mindanao – that there are never enough fire-engines to put out all the fires caused by the fireworks at fiesta times. Moreover, water distribution is always a problem. In the Metro-Manila *barriopolis* it is simply absent. Sometimes urban fires are brought under control by the efforts of trained men, fire-engines, pumps in working order and organised effective action. These fires usually occur in the big international hotels, foreign-owned factories or the fortress-like private housing developments.

Other fires are just left to burn out owing to the lack of equipment, personnel and inaccessibility by fire-engine.

Unfortunately, the shanty *barrio* in the heart of Santa Mesa was one of the latter. As Holly and Estrella jogged towards the railway line, all they could see were the blackened, still smouldering shells of the hovels of the poor. Holly broke into a fast run and raced across the basketball court, crowded now not with revellers or penitents but with destitute families sitting on pathetic piles of salvaged belongings. Her heart was pounding by the time she reached the burnt-out jeepney still up on its ramp.

The entire upper story of the flimsy habitat had gone. All that was left was a stinking mountain of charred wood, ash and melted plastic. A sooty fragment of Leonardo Di Caprio's face fluttered on the breeze.

Estrella found someone to talk to. Holly waited till the Tagalog had finished.

'They came with petrol-bombs,' he reported. 'There is no sign of Raymond Jun-jun, but in the panic everyone scrambled and dispersed. He may yet show up. They've found three bodies so far, but they were baby girls. We will just have to pray the babysitter got Raymond out in time.'

'I see nobody official doing anything,' said Holly angrily. 'Where's the bloody Mayor?'

Estrella smiled mirthlessly. 'Him? Probably in the provinces for the holiday.'

'But who's in charge of the rescue operation?' persisted Holly.

The lawyer looked sad. 'What rescue operation? These people organised their own bucket-chain from the Pasig River. The authorities will do nothing for the time being. It's a public holiday, All Saints' Day. Besides, these fires happen every fiesta. And anyway, the people here are squatters, *Maintindihan?* Some land-owners will be pleased that the fire razed the shanty.'

'But we have to do *something*,' said Holly, feeling desperate. 'Can't we organise a search-party or something? I've brought pesos.'

Estrella spoke to the men standing nearby. He turned back to Holly. 'These people have also lost relatives. Everyone is searching for someone. They are of course concerned to locate Raymond Jun-jun, but it's not a priority. They will accept your pesos as a gift for their children's food and medicine. They thank you. But any search will take time. Meanwhile, these men told me the squatters' association is already organising food distribution at the basketball. The charity people are kicking in. The is the Filipino way, Miss Ho. You have to try to understand. This fire is not an unusual occurrence.'

'And a big thank you to All the Saints,' muttered Holly, turning to go.

Back at the Plaza she called London. Spoke at some length and in some detail to Mr Plum Blossom and then reached Shirley Jacquet.

'Any more news on Nellie?'

'Yep,' said Shirley. 'But first you tell me where the heck you've been. And where are you calling from anyhow?'

'Manila,' said Holly.

'Bugger me!' squawked Shirley. 'Of course, I should've guessed: Dr Devesfrunto and the paternity suit. So how'd it go?'

'Not so great,' said Holly. 'Look, I'm on my way back to Town today, so let's hear what you've got on Nellie.'

Shirley filled Holly in. SeedWorld, the company which had bought Moonbeam's Lower East Side townhouse, had been revealed by Fred, the newspaper's New York bureau's research wizard, to be an independent film company owned solely by Nellie McIlvuddy.

Shirley laughed. 'Took her dad's name did Our Nellie, and as it turns out, she's a freelance documentary-maker, whose last effort – about an AIDS hospice in a Chicago housing project – only friggin' well won a prize at the Banff Film Festival! How about that?'

'Good old Nellie, grew up all right despite it all!' cheered Holly. 'Go on.'

'According to Fred's source at SeedWorld, serendipitously an old acquaintance of hers, Nellie has been in China a couple of times in the last year trying to make underground films of ethnic dissidents.'

I don't *believe* this, thought Holly. Not *China*.

'Anyway,' said Shirley, 'her first attempts apparently hadn't been too successful and she recently flew back to New York depressed after failing to meet anyone real in Tibet. All her contacts turned out to be chancers, cowboys, con-men or overinquisitive security types.'

'So where is she now – back in New York?' said Holly. 'If so, then I'm flying direct from here.'

But Shirley advised against it. 'Her exact whereabouts are presently unknown.'

'How so?' demanded Holly.

'Well, as recently as two weeks ago and against the communal advice of the handful of freelancers part-timing at Seed-World, Nellie returned to China in a state of great excitement about some new contact in a place called Sinkiang Province, if I've pronounced it right. She was going to meet some guy who apparently works with the Uighur ethnic resistance.'

'Sinkiang!' exploded Holly. 'Uighur resistance? Oh, for frock's sake she'll get herself a bullet in the back of the neck!'

Sinkiang. Where she and Ma had been granted ownership of the Health Tea Company! Talk about weird coincidence – which Holly, when it came to anything remotely connected to the Chinese, never did. *Feng-shui*. . . The gods are such playful frockers.

'What's the very latest you've got?' she said.

Shirley replied, 'About a week ago she called the Seed-World office from some place called Urumchi, to say she was off to meet the contact in the Far West of the province. Here I quote, "in the foothills of the Tian-shan Mountains that straddle the borders with the Republics of Kazakhstan and Kirgizstan". Of course I called the hotel she was staying in.' Shirley paused.

'Come on, come on,' urged Holly.

'It ain't good,' said Shirley. 'Nellie McIlvuddy, twenty-four-year-old heir to the Chieftain of the Clan McIlvuddy of That Ilk checked out of the Urumchi Holiday Inn the morning of October the seventeenth and has not been heard of since.'

October the seventeenth – more than two weeks ago. Urumchi . . .

Oh, my sainted frock.

Holly made plane reservations and called Ma in Earlham Street. Everything was apparently calm there. She told her mother a heavily diluted version of events in Manila, leaving out the violence and the fire.

'How's life in Earlham Street? No more *feng-shui* voodoo crap, Ma?'

'Hush! Don't mention it, OK? Listen, *Shao-lan*, when are you coming home?'

'A little while yet, Ma. I'm going to China.'

There was a slight pause. 'Whereabouts?'

'Would you believe Sinkiang?' said Holly, laughing breezily. 'Might as well check out our new enterprise while I'm in the vicinity. Remember: the herbal tea company?'

'*Sinkiang!*' Ma exploded into barking Hakka. 'Only Daughter, you must be out of your mind! I told you the Far West was full of tribals and Turkmen, the mongrel descendants of Genghis Khan!'

'That's Mongol.'

'I meant mongrel! Anyway, no place for a young lady! You'll get arrested and thrown into a Labour Camp digging bunkers in the salt desert for the Lop Nur nuclear testing site! Clitoro-cloacal copulating chthonicites!' (Nearest equivalent translation of ancient Hakka: Ma's was a lengthy sentence referring to the unsavoury sexual practices of the denizens of the underworld, those unpeaceful dead who have yet to be laid to rest in the hereafter.)

Holly laid Ma herself to rest and made a final call – to Mr Plum Blossom. The latter sounded vaguely irritated, though for a man of his impeccable manners you could never really tell.

'Extremely Unmarried Miss Ho,' he said pleasantly, 'it is always a pleasure to hear from you, even at such an unusual frequency. Perhaps you disapprove of my card-playing and are making a habit of calling me from my game at every crucial bid.'

'Sorry, Plum Blossom. Look, I need you to get word to Shih. Looks like Chiu Nei-ku has begun upping the ante.' She told him about the fire-bombing and the torture of Dr Devesfrunto. Plum Blossom made no comment.

Holly said, 'Get word to Shih that Nellie McIlvuddy is in grave danger. Explain that he needs her alive – she is the rightful heir to the seat on the McIlvuddy Trust Board. If he proves her protector, I guarantee her vote will be his on the next buy-out attempt.'

'So you have found her?' Plum Blossom said tight-voiced.

'That's actually rather the problem.' Holly-Jean knew she could trust Plum Blossom but this was uncharted territory. She hesitated. By openly calling for Shih's help she was leaving herself beholden. And worse, she was most likely lowering herself by the anklesocks into a cauldron of malice such as the ordinary citizen of Planet Earth would simply not believe. But then what choice did she really have? As her ancestors would say: *Use the Dragon to Trap the Tiger.* She only

176

hoped she had on spotless underwear when the time came.

She took a deep breath. 'All right, PB, here goes: Nellie McIlvuddy may currently be in mainland China. Sinkiang. Exact whereabouts unknown.'

'Sinkiang?' He muttered a neat Mandarin oath recommending the universally beneficent effect of having all the penises in Sinkiang placed in rat cages. This was some night for cursing.

Holly cleared her throat. 'Worse. She may be involved with the dissident underground.' She could hear the sharp intake of Plum Blossom's breath all the way over the spinning globe.

'Dissident Sinkiang? *Tamada!*'

'Looks as though it may possibly be. It's a complete disaster, isn't it?'

'It is,' said Mr Plum Blossom.

Then there was silence at the other end until Holly got nervous. 'Mr Plum Blossom, hello? Are you still there?'

The answer crackled through the ether. 'I am thinking, Extremely Unmarried Miss Ho.'

'Well, think out loud,' said Holly. 'I'm getting antsy here.'

Plum Blossom sighed. 'The Society can help, of course. Eccentric China now is more or less a federation of PLA regimental warlords, local cliques and ethnic factions. These disparate groups look to the stability offered by our international networking. But I cannot say just how effective our *guanchi* will be in the Far West.'

'But surely the same problem applies to Chiu,' said Holly. 'And from what you told me, Shih is the better connected to the Societies.'

'Yes, of course,' agreed Plum Blossom. 'On the other hand, any intervention will cost Shih dearly. He may baulk.'

'Try him,' said Holly. 'I don't fancy going in there naked.'

'When are you leaving?'

'My plane for Shanghai leaves tomorrow at six. But the Roxas Boulevard traffic and Ninoy Aquino International Airport mayhem means I'm checking out very much in advance. Then it's a three-plane hop via Beijing and Xi'an. I don't get there till some ridiculous time like Thursday.' Today was Monday. Wasn't it?

177

Plum Blossom said, 'Your mobile phone will work in China?'

'The Ericksson people say so, but I've never had the chance to test their blond blue-eyed veracity.'

'You are a good friend of the Society, Extremely Unmarried Miss Ho. I will ensure that we do our utmost to be of assistance in your endeavour, and naturally I shall approach Shih Yang-fu to underwrite the entire proceedings . . .' He hesitated; his voice dropped to an uncharacteristic gentleness of timbre. 'But Ho Shao-lan, I am forced now to say that your proposed excursion has me deeply concerned, and indeed as your longtime friend, I would strongly counsel against it.' He went into this formal Mandarin stuff now and then.

'Don't sweat it, Bro.' But Holly was touched. He absolutely never called her *Shao-lan*.

About seven in the evening Holly-Jean checked that the mini-bar was as she'd found it so that Reception couldn't pad her bill too liberally. Her clothes for the 4 a.m. wake-up call were laid out ready and her bag packed to go, with nothing on her mind and other than a taxi-ride to Hobbit House on Mabini to hear some good music and a few drinks before an early bed, when the phone rang. It was the concierge.

'Your guests are on the way up, Miss Ho,' said a chirpy female.

'Guests?'

'Yes, the three gentlemen with an appointment and your name-card.'

'Right you are.' She grabbed her bag and dashed out of the room. Made it to the emergency stairwell just as the lift dinged. Crouching, she peered through the crack in the fire doors to see two tough-looking Filipinos in business suits and dark glasses and a little Chinese in a flowery shirt come barrelling out of the elevator doors and turn at a clip in the direction of her room.

She raced down the stairs and looked for somewhere to hide in the hotel's vast split-level lobby. A Palm Court orchestra was playing at one end of the mezzanine but there was no cover there. She glanced to her left. One of the elevators was flashing on the descent. She looked around desperately. A sign across the way said *Business Centre*.

She burst through the doors, smiling and gesticulating at the female in charge and dumped herself down in a partitioned mini-office. This late in the day the place was empty apart from the two of them.

The girl spoke with a welcoming smile. 'May I be of assistance, Miss?'

Holly took a gamble. 'I don't know. Look, er, Miss . . . I am avoiding the unwelcome attentions of some male admirers – I'm sure you understand. Is it all right if I hide out here till they've gone? So persistent. Ardent, one might say.'

The girl laughed. 'Of course – stay as long as you like. But perhaps I can help? If you tell me what they look like, I'll see if they've gone.'

Holly described the group and the girl stepped outside. She returned a few minutes later with a worried expression. 'Those three men look like very bad people.'

'Actually, they *are* very bad people,' admitted Holly. 'Um, Miss, look – you don't know me, but I am a guest of the hotel and I really don't have anyone else to turn to. Please, I need help.'

She improvised wildly but on a locally favoured theme. 'Those men have been employed by my former fiancé. I met him on one of my many business trips here and foolishly accepted his offer of marriage. It was a dreadful mistake, as I soon learned not long afterwards, when he got drunk one night and beat me. I called off the engagement and told him I never wanted to see him again. Unfortunately, he will not accept our romance is over. He has become deranged with thwarted love. Somehow he discovered my schedule on this trip and was waiting at the airport upon my arrival. I managed to convince him I was needed at an important meeting, but ever since then he has been bothering me – sending flowers, telephoning constantly. He has had his henchmen shadow me since my arrival. I fear that he might even try to kidnap me.'

'*Kidnap!*' The most feared word in the Philippines' middle-class lexicon did the trick.

'What can I do? Shall I call Security? I'm Rio, by the way,

179

Miss.' She held out her beautifully manicured fingernails.

'And I'm Holly. Rio, you're so great to help me just like this. I can't thank you enough. But don't call Security. Too messy, I think. I just need to slip away and hole up for the night. I'm leaving early tomorrow as it is.'

She thought for a second. 'What I need to do is check out of the hotel and get to the airport without his friends knowing I've left. They'll wait all night if they think I'm still somewhere in the hotel having a swim or a sauna.'

Rio smiled happily. '*Walang problema.* We have automatic check-out through the Business Centre computer. Just give me your credit-card details, then I'll put in a request for a further night's stay which I'll cancel later on, but which will show up at Reception indicating you are still in residence.'

'You'd do that for me? Brilliant!' said Holly. 'You know, I love the female gender of this country of yours.' Adding rapidly, 'Er, not being rude about your menfolk.'

Rio laughed and said, 'Don't worry. As the song says, "I second that emotion". OK, then. Now you just wait here. I'm going to ask a friend in Concierge to keep an eye on those men – I'll say they're suspected panderers. You know, introducing escorts, and the like.'

Holly said, 'I don't want them actually thrown out. They'd just be waiting outside. I'm safer here.'

'I understand – leave it to me. Wait here, I'll lock up and close the Centre, and when I come back we'll fix your check-out. Then it's about time for me to go off-duty. I think I know how we can slip you out through the Service Exit. So just sit tight and don't move, Miss.'

'Holly.'

'Holly.' Rio picked up some files and went out locking the doors of the Business Centre behind her and flipping a card which showed opening hours. She flashed Holly a V-victory sign through the glass.

Holly idly surfed the Internet on the computer in front of her until Rio returned some fifteen minutes later carrying a big black plastic bag. She reported on the men. 'Right now they are spaced around the mezzanine and lobby. One of them is sitting at the courtesy seat by Reception. Let's have your credit card and I'll sort out the bill.'

When she'd finished keying the plastic and Holly had signed, Rio fished into the plastic bag and brought out a chambermaid's uniform. 'Put this on.' She helped Holly affix the hotel's linen cap with hairgrips and stuffed her things into the plastic bag.

'Right, now hold the bag up in front of you and follow me. We'll be turning left out of the door and down a corridor to some swing doors. We pass Reception at one point so keep the bag obscuring your face. Once through the swing doors we'll be in the staff area and safe.'

'Lead on.'

They stepped out into the lobby. Head down following Rio's lovely long legs, Holly couldn't resist a glance from under a hanging flap of black plastic; she caught a glimpse of the Chinese guy on a bench near Reception speaking into his cellphone.

'Hurry!' hissed Rio. They made it through the swing doors.

In the women's changing-room Holly slipped out of the chambermaid's uniform.

Rio turned to Holly and said, 'There's a whole night before your flight. I've got a scooter – do you mind a ride to my place? You can hide out there.'

'Mind?' said Holly. 'Love it.' She placed her hands in a tight grip round Rio's slender waist as they weaved into the jeepney-knit snarl of Roxas Boulevard.

Rio's apartment was a studio flat high up above the reclaimed mud of Paranque, only a short ride from the airport.

'If your ex-fiancé is so madly in love, and I know the lengths to which Filipino men will go in pursuit of a woman,' Rio said thoughtfully, 'then he will no doubt have made contacts at the flight control desks. In this country, the peso rules. It'd be easy for him to have access to passenger lists. We just have to hope he believes you're still at the hotel.'

'Rio, I can't thank you enough,' said Holly, kissing her new friend's cheek.

Chapter 20

Pre-dawn at NAIA, Holly had a scare when through the dishevelment of her new found-and-lost freedom, she thought she heard her name being paged. Couldn't be, surely. But it was.

'Ms Holly-Jean Ho, flying on South China Airlines flight SC 533 to Beijing, report to the information counter.'

The airport was not yet sardine-packed this early in the morn so she was able to skirt around the pillars and various kiosks till she had a clear view of the information desk. Her name was paged again but there seemed to be no one else lurking in the vicinity.

Who could it be? Perhaps it was Plum Blossom with some good news. Or Shirley saying they'd found Nellie alive and well in Lewisham . . .

'I'm Holly-Jean Ho.'

'This was delivered for you by private courier.' The man indicated a package.

She peered inside a loose wrapping. And groaned. It was unmistakeably Dr Manny's golf-bag.

'This note is also for you.'

She tore the envelope. 'Thought you'd like this souvenir of your trip to Manila. Take it or get rid of it, either way don't give it back to me. *Salamat po!* Nice meeting you, Ms Ho. Till the next time. Your true friend, Noring Estrella. *Abogado.*'

Holly shrugged and took possession of the golf-bag. It was pretty much empty apart from some balls and a couple of gold-plated irons, but it still weighed her down. Holly-Jean hated check-in baggage, always travelled with hand-carry only. Quietly come, quietly go.

Then she had a brainwave: the golf-bag would provide good cover for her trip to Sinkiang. Holly-Jean Ho would be scouting out possibilities for a consortium of golf-course developers from Florida.

Her flight was called.

Should you contemplate flying to Urumchi – pronounced Oo-loo-moo-chi in Mandarin – don't.

It took Holly-Jean forty-three hours and a total of three planes before she finally arrived in the freezing black-smog-shrouded city late Thursday evening as the first flurries of sotty snow raced in from the land of the Steppenwolf.

The Holiday Inn was the only international hotel in town and charged accordingly. The tariff was two hundred bucks a night with a lousy exchange rate, but promised a hot shower which was all Holly wanted at this moment as she tipped the bag-boy with his enormous Generalissimo peaked hat and chainsawed hair. Welcome to China, The Lair of Bad Hair.

Opening the grime-sealed window of her standard single, Holly looked out onto the flickering and dim-lit city. Universally used perforated bricks of reconstituted coal-dust are China's contribution to the planet. The air, frozen by the tundra wind, was solid. Holly closed the window, coughed and blew a tissue of black snot and phlegm.

She tried out her cellphone. God a tentative line to Earlham Street in London but it went down after a few seconds of the office answer-machine tape. She showered and went downstairs.

The hotel restaurants were all shut, but she was informed by the five receptionists that the weirdly named Jolly Roger Bar – they were, after all, she recalled Barrance T. Wong's words, the furthest place from the oceans to be found anywhere on the planet – was open till late and served snacks.

One Pernod and water in the desultory company of the handful of international salesmen and engineers stopping in Urumchi this winter night was all she could handle.

On her way back to the lifts, a gaggle of flushed Taiwanese businessmen with their painted Uighur consorts and a blonde, heavily mascara-ed Kazakh girl, spilled out of the hotel's revolving doors and exaggeratedly the worse for drink, as in the Oriental manner, weaved their way to the bar.

By the time the off-key blurrings of songs boomed up from the karaoke, room service had delivered watery wonton noodle soup to Holly's room. She took a rare pill to disable jet-lag and soon fell asleep.

The next morning, the sooty snow had settled waist-high and people outside the hotel were everywhere shovelling paths to their shopfronts. Urumchi couldn't afford snow-ploughs. Holly-Jean tried again to call London on her cellphone. But once more failed to make a decent connection. At least somewhere in the static she could hear Brit tones. London's receiving!

After a cup of bad Oolong tea and a sickly-sweet biscuit, she decided on a discreet word with one of the day-time reception staff. Intuitively, she chose an ethnic girl rather than a Han. She drew her to one side and asked for information about the ancient cave paintings at Turpan.

The girl seemed only too happy to be actively engaged in some kind of meaningful existence and enthusiastically accompanied Holly to the hotel's tour centre. There she gathered a number of brochures before sitting down with Holly in a couple of armchairs in a corner of the quiet room.

After an exhaustive research of all the possible itineraries involving cave paintings, Turpan, camel-rides and horseback tours to Swan Lake in the high Tien Shan Mountains with the suitability of golf-course development an underlying theme throughout, Holly broached the subject of Nellie.

'By the way, I was hoping to meet up with another freelance consultant who I understood would be visiting here these days. Of course, one's schedule gets completely off-line once one is actually travelling in such a vast country as China, but I wonder . . .' she smiled sweetly, 'did you recently come across a guest by the name of . . . er, McIlvuddy, I think it is. A young American lady?'

Of course the girl remembered Nellie. Like Holly herself: a single female foreign tourist in winter was indeed a welcome rarity. Should she call the GM?

No, no, Holly would rather she did not call the General Manager to discuss the matter. She tapped her nose in the universal gesture and quoted the popular Mandarin phrase, 'Business whispers and creeps.'

The girl understood perfectly. Discretion would be assured.

Holly got all the scant details she could of Nellie's short stay and her subsequent check-out about twelve days or so before. For a very generous renminbi consideration, albeit reluctantly accepted at first in order to save face, the girl even took Holly to the hotel front door and pointed out the taxi driver who'd taken Nellie sight-seeing on her last day before her apparent onward flight.

Holly thanked the girl and took her name-card, but did not return the gesture – an unheard-of social gaffe which she explained away by apologising profusely for having managed to lose her entire stock on the plane from Xi'an. She then had to turn down the girl's offer of having a new batch printed up. Doing business without a name-card in China? The girl looked amazed and then vaguely suspicious. Since the whole object of the exercise was not to draw attention to herself, Holly quickly elaborated a tale of collecting a new stock of name-cards at her next port of call . . . Kashgar. The girl accepted this and wished Holly good luck.

Holly stepped outside into the freezing winter morning.

She approached the taxi driver, sitting side-saddle in his open front door and smoking a black loose wrap of tobacco leaf. He was a Uighur or some other kind of tribal. Not Han Chinese. His face was a red wrinkled walnut, with a fierce bladed proboscis and thick flowing black moustache. He wore a sheepskin jacket that ponged to high heaven and an embroidered conical trilby of some kind of soft-beaten hide which seemed to be the universal headgear for the ethnics.

Holly used the Arab salutation, 'Sala'am aleikum.' Then apologised for having to speak in Mandarin, explaining that she was an English tourist and hadn't yet been taught any local dialect.

After an initial unfriendly lack of response, the man brightened considerably when he caught the glimpse of fresh green in the dull grey morning light. For a twenty-dollar bill he confirmed his recollection of Nellie. For a fifty he promised a repeat of Nellie's itinerary that last day.

Holly bought a fake-fur parka in the hotel boutique, checked out, and as a feeble sun probed the leaden sky, climbed in the back of the cab. They crawled through the dismal city-centre traffic in one long jam of steaming, stinking buses and snowdrifts. About ten minutes into their slow progress, Holly glimpsed a sign.

Harmonious Friction Wedding Salon.

'Stop the cab!' She stepped across the brown slushy sidewalk and entered the shop.

'May I help you?' asked a young woman.

'No thanks, just looking,' said Holly, with a smile and a shrug as she turned to go. Time was awasting and unlikely ownership notwithstanding, she glanced once round the shop to which she and Ma owned the deeds.

'I'll be back. Some day. Maybe.' As she hopped across the sooty slush to the cab, she didn't notice the girl in the shop pick up the telephone.

Finally out of town, bouncing and slewing on the rutted road westward to Hining, the Uighur heartland, Holly felt exhilarated. White-knuckled but high. Sure it was all foolhardy and extremely dangerous, and sure there was an acidbath of anxious dread lining her gut as the taxi slid wildly towards the snow-draped towering pines at the side of the windy mountain road. But hey, how many girls got to get this far-out for a living?

Then she thought of Nellie and fell back to earth. Whoever Ms Nellie McIlvuddy really was in the living flesh, Holly knew one thing for sure: she was a foolhardy twit! Making a documentary of the Uighur dissidence? Holly shook her head. Why not do something safe like become a crocodile orthodontal hygienist? Frock idealists!

The world would be a whole better place if people left ideals in the hands of harmless poets and got on with the basic simple humble job of making their tiny apportioned spot of humanity and the planet, clean and workable. And why for frock's sake bother with someone else's obscure fight on the other side of the planet, when there were plenty of issues flaming away at home! A fight perched upon the tottering gyroscope that was modern China – on behalf of

Moslems who would probably enact the Sharia if they ever got independence and have Nellie stoned for wearing blue jeans in public?

Holly snorted out loud. Folks, make an underground documentary with the Chinese dissidents – and die differently! Nellie got top marks for inventing an extremely creative method of suicide.

Holly-Jean knew well that the terrified old men who owned China, finally had comprehended the fact that their supernova was terminally unstable and about to become a black hole. Consequently, their attitude to dissent was abrupt and to the point. To the back of the kneeling neck by bullet, in fact.

Holly recalled with increasing anxiety in the back of the bouncing cab that only last month following a bomb in a local cinema in Yining showing a Han movie, there'd been a mass public execution at the execution grounds outside the city. Relatives were permitted to collect the dead on payment for bullets expended. Neither BBC World News nor CNN had been able to obtain film of anything related to the brutal crackdown and had reported only word of mouth. So how could a young freelancer like Nellie hope to get away with it? She'd surely stick out like a red light in the wilds of the Moslem west of China.

Oh, *Nellie* . . .

Chapter 21

On the outskirts of Yining as evening snow fell in pale waves from the doughy sky, the taxi was ordered to stop by a PLA militia roadblock. Under cover of her parka and sinking low in the back seat of the cab, Holly flipped her cellphone and punched in London.

Nothing but static. She'd been trying all day. Was it going to be too late now? Mr Plum Blossom, where are you and your guys when I need you? She snapped the cellphone shut and hid it away in the folds of her new snow parka.

In the sudden wind-chucked flurries of snow, pairs of soldiers with huge wool-fleece mittens, bundled up with extra scarves over their uniforms, were searching the row of halted vehicles. Two officers watched from the middle of the road where a line of oil-drums blocked passageway.

While their taxi waited in a skewered line of trucks, vans and jalopies nosed into the banks of drifted snow, Holly silently rehearsed. Breathing deeply and using *chi-kung* techniques to wipe her mind clean and centre her *chi* energy, she arranged her passport and visas, tugged out some fresh green and placed her golf-bag in prominent view.

In the front seat, the taxi driver did not appear entirely jollied up by this event and was displaying extreme anxiety, agitatedly fingering his prayer beads, repeatedly pulling off his conical felt trilby and running his hands through his hair, muttering loudly enough for Holly to understand in bad Mandarin that he sorely regretted having taken her stupid money, half-foreign *female ghost* making a big trouble for him, and this his cousin's car which he had to rent at 200 renminbi per day and cover all repairs and petrol and expenses, not to mention what it was going to cost to get through this little private tax office – if, that is, they got through without ending up in jail or wearing the summary lead neck-ventilator. A line of veiled women bundled up in layers of sheepskin, and coneheaded betrilbied men were herded off a newly arrived bus whose every surface gleamed under the arc-lights with polished chrome and iridiscent panels painted with depictions of Mecca, Koranic verses and snow-capped mountains. Two soldiers finally made their way over to Holly's cab. A young man in a creased, ill-fitting uniform stamping his feet in the icy cold, his breath plumes of steam in the freezing night air, stooped down to the taxi window. He glanced briefly at the driver's passbook which he handed over his shoulder to his partner, then peered into the back of the cab at Holly. A second or two's scrutiny of her clothes and hairstyle and eyes widened, he straightened up, calling out, '*Wai-guo ren!*'

Foreigner.

The word galvanised the two officers watching the checkpoint. They despatched the young privates to work the bus lines, then trotted over, kneeboots glistening with spit'n'polish in the arc-lights.

'Passport.'

Holly-Jean handed over her passport.

'You from English?'

Holly decided to speak Mandarin. '*Shr-de. Wo shr Ying-guo ren.*'

The sound of her perfect rendition of the language of the Middle Earth, the language which many Chinese still believe only the Han can ever truly master, seemed to unsettle the two men. They hesitated, studying the passport in the beam of their flashlights, then withdrew a few paces and conferred in urgent undertones.

It was obvious that the last thing they'd expected, nor no doubt relished finding at the checkpoint this winter night on the outskirts of Yining, was a half-breed foreigner who could speak Mandarin fluently – a *shao-jyei* – a single woman travelling alone. What's that all about?

Back in the cab, whatever the import of her presence, Holly knew they'd be figuring it was going to be *ma-fan*; headache trouble.

189

Just then, angry shouting broke out by the newly arrived bus. Holly watched from the rear of the taxi as a young man in a sheepskin jacket and kilt was shoved to the ground. While one soldier placed a boot on the man's squirming neck, another reached down and pulled an ancient-looking hand-gun from the folds of the man's clothing. Other soldiers had arrived and with loud yells their rifle butts slammed down with sickening thuds upon the unfortunate victim. It was over in seconds, and the limp body dragged away at the run.

The two officers who had taken Holly's papers appeared more tense now as they shuffled back to the cab. The driver meanwhile sat immobile, his emanations of terror palpable to Holly, the bristles on the back of his neck sensing the icy steel of the muzzle.

One of the officers now leaned in towards the open rear window, snowflakes settling on his peaked cap. 'What is your purpose in Yining, Ho *Shao-jye*?'

'A very good evening to you, Officers,' said Holly in her best bright and breezy voice. 'My purpose is research into leisure potentialities; golf-course development – tourism, bringing in much-needed foreign reserves, cash, to your beautiful country.' She smiled and, as if to prove the point, lifted up her golf-bag while at the same time innocently allowing her passport holder to drop open and reveal its green lining.

'Please exit the taxi,' said one of the officers.

Holly slowly climbed out of the vehicle and walked a few paces on the packed snow to stand at a polite, unthreatening distance. She moved closer and held out her hand. 'Warm greetings to you, Officers. Terrible weather, isn't it?'

The men flinched, gloved hands on polished holsters but Holly resolutely presented her friendly palm, with fixed smile and bright eyes while her stomach churned with fear. From the direction of the bus tortured screams wafted on the night.

Holly-Jean Ho was by nature, nurture and defining charac-teristic, a tigress. But she was no deathwish glorycat. And at times like these she had to call on all her martial training to prevent panic.

Once more erasing her emotions with *chi-kung*, she deep-ened her smile at the two nervous young men. 'I won't bite, I promise you.' She cocked her eyebrows, put a little pout in her smile, kept dangling her hand.

One of the young men finally grinned and they shook hands briefly.

'But why you come all the way out here in this winter weather?' he asked. 'No golf for you in Yining.'

Holly burst with enthusiasm in the dismal night. 'To visit! To taste and see! To test the possibilities! This is a special, wonderful place. The last untouristed Shangri-la on earth: Sinkiang.' She spoke to them in soft tones punctuated by breathy clouds of condensed warmth in the falling veil of snowflakes, choosing her words of flattery with care to disarm the men's nerves – and to still the floods of adrenalin coursing through her own veins.

'I'm here in Yining and other destinations hoping to set up contacts with interested parties in the golf and tourism industry. After all, everyone knows that Sinkiang is the most beautiful unspoilt destination left in Central Asia, and Yining historically was a port of call on the Silk Route.' She paused dramatically and gestured around at the snow-draped pines and black and white mountains rising steeply from the valley to loom against the stormy cottonwool sky.

'You know, gentlemen, here in Sinkiang, you have the great names of history! Genkhis Khan, Marco Polo, Tamurlaine, Attila the Hun and, of course, Kublai Khan who built his pleasure dome here in Xanadu! Such names! Names which evoke magical images in the hearts and minds of the jaded foreign tourist. And who will come with wallets packed with US dollar bills . . .'

The men seemed startled by Holly's wildly inaccurate improvisation, until she dropped the final magic words. Then they huddled close to her, looking over their shoulders to see if anyone was watching.

Holly likewise glanced round. But no one was taking much notice of them. They were too busy kicking the cuds out of some other unfortunate ethnic. There was still a commotion at the bus line and most of the militia men were occupied with the lines of squatting passengers.

'With my deepest thanks and heartfelt compliments for assisting me in my humble endeavours here in Yining.' She bowed her head and slipped the folded currency inside one of the greatcoats. Without another word her passport was back in her hands, and she trotted over to the taxi without further ado, slammed the door shut and slapped the driver on the shoulder. '*Tso-kai!* Let's git!'

The driver started the engine on the third attempt while Holly's stomach eructed with acid. At last they lumbered on, spinning mush through the narrow gap in the oil-drums sliding at a forty-five-degree angle to the straight.

Once they were well out of sight of the roadblock and negotiating the silent streets of the outskirts of Yining, the driver exhaled with an explosion of breath.

'*Wah-sei! Ni nema li-hai, shao-jye!* Gorblimey, Miss, you're no wet girl's blouse!' or words to that effect. Damp knickers notwithstanding, thought Holly wrily.

Outside the slowly moving cab there was not a soul on the streets. The snow was settling on the impossibly dense clusters of low mudbrick structures of the ramshackle city. In the evening gloom Yining appeared whitewashed and pristine. There was little other traffic, and the only apparent inhabitants were packs of dogs that appeared out of the mist and chased the tyres of the taxi, barking insanely.

Holly asked, 'Is it curfew?'

'First sign of fear,' said the driver, his spirits restored, as they drove past a parked convoy of covered Army trucks. 'The fornicating Han turtle-eggs are getting scared.'

Across town, in what appeared to be the far outskirts on the other side, closer to the sweep of mountains, the driver stopped the car at a walled compound and pointed to an arched doorway.

'You can stay there for the night. Ring the bell.'

Holly climbed stiffly out of the cab. She looked doubtfully at the unmarked and unlit doorway. 'This is definitely the place you brought the American lady?' she said nervously. 'The *shao-jye*, Nellie?'

But he was gone with a swish of rubber on snow.

Holly breathed in the icy night air and pulled the bell. Dogs began to howl and after a long while there came a commotion of oaths and clattered bolts and the door finally

192

opened. A woman hidden in a headscarf peered out at Holly by the dull beam of a fading flashlight.

'You have a room for the night?' Holly said in careful Mandarin. 'I'm a foreigner. English. A traveller.'

The woman looked around quickly, grabbed Holly's sleeve and pulled her inside without a word.

Behind her the wooden door was bolted fast.

Chapter 22

A maestro cock was crowing somewhere a few centimetres from her eardrum. Holly-Jean woke from a deep sleep on a narrow cot under layers of mouldy sheepskin. She opened her eyes and looked around the gloom of the wood and mud structure. Saw horses' tails swishing clouds of flies. Rubbed her eyes. A tail lifted and a big dollop of manure was delivered. She was in a stable.

She'd been too blurry the night before to take much in after the sixth *gan-bei* of flamy arak. She lay back again and blinked a couple of times, cleared her throat and tasted the lingering after-burn of the sorghum distillation.

Images floated painfully to the ethanol-spill surface of her mind. She recalled dimly the endless rounds of toasts in the smoky atmosphere of the large wood-beamed and mud reception room with its heavily-shrouded curfew windows. The music from the zithers and tambourine. The sensuous belly-dancing. The bagel-style round bread, *gr-dr nan*.

An acidic wash in her stomach accompanied the memory of chewing the gooey mouthful of eyeball from the singed head of the whole roasted mutton, a non-refusable gift of honour from her host, a handsome Uighur named Tarik whose business, she learned, was horse-trekking for the fledgling travel industry. Another image filtered up.

The forcefully declined offer to purchase a very special contraband; the tragic gorgeous skin of a snow-leopard, one of the rarest and most beautiful animals on the planet.

She raised herself and threw off the heavy horsehair blankets. There was a wood-fire stove a few feet away from her, and an old lady in voluminous clothing and embroidered mirror-inlaid veil was squatting, stirring a bubbling cauldron of what smelt like mutton soup, with a hand-rolled cigar of green tobacco dangling from her lips.

The old lady grinned smokily and from another pot ladled brown liquid into a mug, reached a handful of greasy mare's butter from a muslin-covered mound and dropped it in, handing the mug to Holly.

Smiling polite thanks, Holly blew on it and sipped the steaming greasy tea. As soon as the first drop touched her gullet, her bowels erupted.

'Toilet?' she said in Mandarin. The woman didn't understand. Holly made a gesture indicating imminent deluge.

The old lady cackled and pointed to a lean-to structure past the horses at the far end of the stable.

Holly made it just in time, discreetly emptying the tea behind the horses on the way, squatting over a hole in the earthen floor. She washed with a bowl of steaming water in an outhouse across the central courtyard of the long low compound, and as the first wintry light filtered over the mountains, she strapped her golf-bag to a little pony and mounted up.

She said her goodbyes to the women of the house and took her place second to the rear of a column led off by Tarik, consisting of six men and two silent women. With her talisman golf-bag as back-support, Holly-Jean headed out towards the Tian-shan Mountains. The Mountains of Heaven.

The ride took six hours of slow climbing up the pine-forested slopes of the foothills of the Tian-shan bordering Kazakhstan. As early evening dusk settled, they reached a lake just below the timberline where sheep grazed on sparse winter grass. By the lakeshore was an encampment of felt hurts, the nomadic shepherds' white circular tents.

Her backside numb and her thighs locked in agony, Holly had to be helped down from her horse. She stumbled at first, but after a hot mug of mare's-butter tea with a slug of arak, she revived.

Following a ritual welcome by the assembled nomadic shepherds and another shared cup of arak with their headman, Aziz, a handsome devil with an elaborately waxed and

195

twisted moustache, Holly wandered off by the lakeshore in the twilight. It was way over time to make contact with Plum Blossom.

The pine-clad valley was curtained by snow-topped peaks, glowing pink in the dwindling sun. The baa-ing of the sheep reminded Holly of another less-travelled spot, Baltasound Castle. She thought of Morag. Shook her head violently. All right, Holly-Jean, enough with the lonely planet bollocks, time to get with the programme, kiddo!

Making sure she was far from anybody able to observe, she crouched down by the ripples of icy water, hitching up her full-length parka as though performing private business, flipped her cellphone and called London.

Nothing on the first two attempts.

She skimmed flat stones, ducks-and-drake style. Tried again. Nothing on the next ten attempts. Refusing to panic, she weighed her options. Stay on the trial of Nellie alone, without having made contact with the Society? She pressed redial. Or slip away at the first opportunity and hoof it back to Yining and wait for official Society contact?

Miraculously, she heard a ringing tone. Obeying the obscure ritual of electronic miasma that brought her finally to Plum Blossom, the line was amazingly clear.

'Good to hear from you, Extremely Unmarried Miss Ho.'

'Me too. But we've got no time for pleasantries.'

'I should imagine not. Now speak slowly and clearly.'

He had her describe the location as well as she could, the number of the clan group and the quality of the weaponry in evidence, which so far was nothing more to Holly's semi-tutored eye than a couple of ancient hunting rifles and the odd Kalashnikov. However, when pressed further, she had to admit to Plum Blossom that speaking none of the local dialect she had no definite information on the group other than the purely innocent one publicly presented, a horse-riding trek outfit with the shepherds of the Tian-shan.

'And the McIlvuddy girl?'

The cellphone line began to moan and fade, and Holly's voice began a delayed Doppler echo. She spoke quickly. 'Nothing yet, but I did year last night when negotiating my trek that the leader, Tarik, had taken another party of tourists trekking recently. No details were offered. The word "foreigner" was mentioned.'

'That's all you got?' Plum Blossom sounded worried.

Holly explained that she hadn't pushed the conversation despite the flowing arak. She knew she would have to win the Uighur's trust before mentioning Nellie McIlvuddy.

'That's all I know so far,' she said. 'Give me time. Look, someone's coming – I have to go.'

'Keep in touch, Extremely Unmarried Miss Ho.' The line went dead.

Still squatting at the water's edge, she turned to watch the approach of a young man. He stopped some distance away, staring at her, perhaps trying to drum up the courage to talk. Perhaps not. Had he seen her talking into the Ericksson? She decided to get rid of him. Waving frantically she shouted in Mandarin that she was having a pooh. The young man turned and fled.

Even so she decided to secrete the cellphone in her knickers. Thanking the gods for cool Swedish design, the thing was as compact and thin as a rigid panty-liner.

She stayed by the water's edge till called back some while later for food.

At the feast that night she was allowed to forego the eyeball. That epicurean delight was reserved for a distinguished-looking Han Chinese who had arrived just in time for the bonfire dinner in the company of a small group of horsemen travelling from the direction of the high mountain route to Kazakhstan, the Horgas Pass.

Thirty souls gathered round the fire as the night lit up with dancing, singing and arak under the skull-expanding immensity of the Milky Way.

Holly's attempts to converse casually with the Han Chinese visitor when the opportunity arose during the night's festivities got nowhere. The gentleman kept a polite, smiling distance. By discreet listening, Holly-Jean discerned from his occasional refined Mandarin that he was educated. But most of the time he spoke in dialect with the headman and a small group including Tarik.

That night Holly-Jean slept like a child in a toasty yurt full of women. Their arms draped round each other, their bodies mingled for warmth and comfort, Holly closed her eyes in deep peace, as in a crowded womb.

There was no sign of the Han Chinese gentleman in the morning.

There followed as promised and paid for, three days of trekking the valleys and rivers of the mountains. By now familiar with each other, she was happy on the back of her hardy little brown horse with its blonde straggly mane. At dinner the second night she officially named him *Mar-kr da Puo-luo yuendong ma*, Marco the Polo-Playing Horse, much to probably feigned amusement. Still, as far as she was concerned, they were old friends.

On the fourth day, Holly-Jean decided to break her silence. She waited till Tarik was alone on a clear stretch of grassy trail through the vaulted arches of a snow-draped pine cathedral and she cantered Marco up to walk alongside him.

'I need to talk about something, Tarik,' said Holly.

His eyes sparkled as he reined in his horse and inclined his head towards the forest.

'No, not *that*,' she said quickly. 'The taxi driver who brought me to your house in Yining from Urumchi knew that I had another purpose beyond just trekking in the mountains. I'm looking for a family friend you might have brought on the last trek. An American girl, Nellie. She probably had a small film camera with her.' Holly stopped and gazed into Tarik's eyes. 'Do you know who I mean?'

Tarik held her stare without blinking then walked his horse on ahead. Holly dug her boots into Marcos's flanks and trotted on to catch up. She spoke carefully.

'I understand that Nellie might have been involved in documenting sensitive matters. I thought it better to wait for an appropriate time to tell you of my personal interest. After three days you must know now that I have travelled alone and present no concern to you.'

'And what precisely is your "personal interest", Ho *shao-jye*?'

Holly said, 'First you tell me just how much you know about Nellie McIlvuddy.'

Tarik's eyes narrowed. He halted and dismounted. Holly did likewise. They walked the horses into the forest and looped the reins over the branch of a pine.

Squatting down, Tarik lit a black leaf cigar and Holly drank from her leather water-bag.

'If it was indeed true that I had taken some publicity-seeking American on a trek in these valleys, then the concerns of certain parties would naturally be heightened. Therefore you will speak of all these matters in complete frankness,' ordered Tarik in convuluted Mandarin.

Holly considered his request. She would have no other chance. Now or never it was time to open up.

'All right, Tarik,' she said, 'I'm going to trust you. I hope I've judged you correctly, that you are a man of Honour.'

He looked with intense black orbs into her eyes. 'You need not doubt it.'

Holly shrugged and explained briefly about her professional involvement in the McIlvuddy Probate and about Nellie's inheritance on a board-vote that was crucial to the plans of the extremely powerful *tai-kung*, Shih Yang-fu.

'The man who is currently responsible for assembling the consortium of banks, financial institutions and international expertise that were required by the Beijing leadership to implement the biggest human engineering undertaking in history: the damming of the Yellow River, the subsequent inundation of more than two hundred cities, the displacement of more than thirty million homes and the consequent re-drawing of the global map.'

Tarik's unwavering gaze never left hers.

Holly went on, 'This is a man whose *guanchi* with Beijing is of the highest order. This is the man who has charged me with locating and securing the American girl, Nellie McIlvuddy.'

Holly paused. Tarik still said nothing.

'You'd certainly agree such a man could be immensely valuable to you and your comrades' ethnic aspirations.'

Tarik hawked and launched a huge gob of tobacco-ey phlegm in a neat trajectile to land like a daub of black paint on a snow-draped branch.

'Or immediately destructive,' he finally spoke.

Holly's voice was rising despite her efforts at staying calm. 'Tarik, I've put myself in your hands with this conversation; here in this remote spot you can easily dispose of me without anyone being the wiser. But if you trust me and if you know where Nellie is, then please, I implore you, take me to her. It'll be worth your while, that I can guarantee. Cash-wise,' she added. Why not gild the lily? This was China, after all, and Shih Yang-fu could certainly afford it.

Tarik scowled at her, stood up and with a loud gushing, peed against a nearby pine tree.

Holly felt her nerves tauten: maybe she'd got it all wrong. Gone and made a complete and utter fool of herself. Worse, put herself and Nellie in lethal danger with her big mouth and talk of Beijing. Perhaps Tarik wasn't an ethnic revolutionary at all. Perhaps he was just a shrewd businessman arranging horse-treks for silly foreigners with too many romantic travel plans. Worse, perhaps he was one of the myriad informers for the Party that were part of the fabric of China's society.

But then again he had implied that he knew of Nellie, hadn't he? Holly breathed out and emptied her mind. In neutral she waited for him to finish his business. It was a bit late here and now in this lost corner of the planet to worry about such things.

On-On Tigress!

Doggedly, she addressed his turned back as he shook himself. 'You take me to Nellie, and I promise you that Shih will reward you in abundance.'

Tarik turned and untied the horse reins. 'At least one hundred thousand UK dollars,' said Holly, plucking the figure from the ether.

Tarik handed Holly Marco's leather rein and without speaking, they mounted and walked the horses back to the trail.

An hour or so later, having rejoined the column of horses, the trail through the pines diverged and Tarik led the way off to the right, down towards the valley floor. Another hour later they reached a rocky outcrop and a deep cleft in the mountain, walled in on all sides by thick evergreen forest.

As they followed the narrowing, tangled path, ducking under the lower branches, Holly gazed ahead through the foliage to where smoke was rising from the middle of a small clearing. Behind the smoke she made out the dark gaping slash of a rock cave.

Silently, from nowhere and without warning, they were joined by other horsemen. Holly's reins were taken from her and Marco was led into the gladed canyon. Dismounted, Holly was carefully searched by a woman and her bags were examined. Tarik laughed out loud. 'Go easy on her, she's worth one hundred thousand American dollars!'

Holly pursed her lips while universal laughter rang out.

A Western girl with long red hair and luminous green eyes emerged from the entrance of the cave. 'What's all the fuss about, Tarik?' she called. He pointed his cigar in Holly's direction. 'Oh!' said the girl, turned, walked over and greeted Holly with outstretched hand. 'So you're the one who's come all this way to find me.'

'Nellie McIlvuddy, I presume,' replied Holly, clasping her hand in hers.

Chapter 23

'Well, I think we should definitely move out tonight,' said Holly after they'd eaten dinner. She had taken Nellie aside from the fireplace to try to persuade her of the folly of her endeavour, and to further elucidate to the young girl, the crucial role Nellie was playing, albeit unwittingly, in the bitter rivalry between the two Chinese billionaire businessmen, Shih Yang-fu and Chiu Nei-ku.

And so far, Holly'd hit nothing but a brick wall. A young, charming, beautiful idealist brick wall.

Although she had cited the recorded deaths of Marybel Lacsina and Dr Devesfrunto, the possible connection to the brutal assault on her cousin, Morag-Rose, in Shetland, the firebombed *barrio* and the present unknown fate of Raymond Jun-jun McIlvuddy, her half-brother, and had even suggested the not-unremote possibility that her father, Lord Jonny McIlvuddy himself, had been murdered . . . Holly just couldn't seem to get Nellie to understand the mortal danger she faced from the Chiu faction.

Nor did Nellie apparently give a hoot as to the lethal consequences of this crazy involvement in Chinese politics. The girl was infuriatingly stubborn, utterly wrapped up in her documentary. Inside, Holly was torn: she secretly admired Nellie's principles while at the same time recognised that her job was to save the girl from the forces gathering against her.

'Tonight, for frock's sake,' repeated Holly doggedly, 'we go back to Yining and any kind of plane out of here.'

'Impossible,' said Nellie fiercely. 'My film isn't finished yet and I've been up here more than two weeks already waiting for the final interview. These people must have exposure; they desperately need the eyes of the West focused on their struggle.' Her teeth flashed brilliantly in the firelight. 'Besides, I've been assured of this interview, the first ever with this guy.'

'Which guy?' asked Holly. She was finding Nellie's passion a wee bit hard-going, but tolerated it as the prerogative of youth.

Nellie gushed on like a schoolgirl with a crush on the gym teacher.

Holly snorted, 'This is the real world, kid, the brutal world of Mainland Chinese dissidence.'

Nellie ignored her, saying, 'The charismatic leader of the struggle is coming here – the *Imam*, to give him his title – and I'm going to interview him on film!'

Holly grunted. 'Imam, *Shmimam*.'

Nellie ran on: 'The Imam has just escaped from a prison convoy. He was en route from one forced labour camp in the Taclamacan Desert to another in the copper mines of the Altay Mountains. He is currently the most wanted man in Sinkiang, with a price of the equivalent of fifty thousand US dollars in renminbi on his head.'

'Worth that much?' whistled Holly. Perhaps she should up the ante on Shih Yang-fu's behalf. Still, she wondered just how much of this was true, and just how much Nellie had been sold a whopper.

The girl gesticulated with her hands. 'That's an absolute fortune for these tribals, but they would rather kill themselves before giving him up. He is a true leader of men, an inspiration in this monochrome world. And these people have promised that they would grant me uncensored footage. Do you understand what that means?'

'Sure, I do,' said Holly, with grim relish. 'It means a chance to get very dead, very slowly, very unpleasantly.'

'Entirely beside the point,' snapped Nellie. 'Holly-Jean, this is a chance to make *history* – every documentary film-maker's dream.'

'Ah-ah,' said Holly. 'Do I detect the self-serving presence of the beast named ambition?'

They were walking along the edge of the clearing, the light from the fire flickering shadows onto the rock wall above

203

them, the dark mass of the pine forest impenetrable in the night.

'Scoff if you must, but this is my lifework,' said Nellie in reply. 'You see, I figured it out: *I am come to bear witness.*'

Holly said nothing.

Nellie's voice rose an octave. 'I'm telling you I won't compromise on this film. Not for you, not for some Chinese zillionaire, not even for my father's legacy! It's non-negotiable, you understand?'

'Well, couldn't you just leave your camera with one of the men you trust, along with a list of questions, and have the interview recorded and smuggled out to you over the border?' Holly suggested. 'Kazakhstan's not more than a day's ride over that mountain.'

'No way.'

Holly sighed and pointed up at the glittering night sky and the weeping stars. 'Do you think this little ethnic struggle amounts to much on Planet Dax?'

Nellie shrugged and said nothing.

Holly continued, 'Look, you don't really know that you can trust these people. We might just be hostages – who can tell?'

Nellie spun round. 'I've learned the hard way that sometimes in life you just have to make a leap of faith. It's a matter of intuition, not logic. You either hit the clear blue sea or are dashed to the jagged rocks below.'

Holly felt her skin goose-popping. *Chi pi* – chicken-skin, the Chinese say.

They returned to the campfire and found that Nellie's contact was back, with a party of new arrivals. Holly recognised the contact as the Han Chinese gentleman who had visited the shepherds' encampment by the lake three nights before.

Nellie was acting as excited as a young girl on her first date. She whispered breathlessly to Holly that the Imam was already in the camp, but that he had decided to keep his identity secret for · fear of informers among the recent recruits. The filmed interview would take place at dawn, then they would set off immediately and should cross over the Horgas Pass into Kazakhstan by the next nightfall.

'Good enough,' said Holly, vastly relieved.

A few moments later when no one was paying attention she wandered away from the camp into the darkness. Time to try to call Plum Blossom.

The moon was high above the mountains when Holly eventually laid down her head. As usual, she had secured her passport, dollar-cash, credit cards and visas in her belt-bag which was double-fastened securely round her waist. With her knees drawn up, her back up against the golf-bag and the cellphone positioned snugly in her crotch, she turned on her stomach and closed her eyes. It wasn't that she didn't trust these proud mountain warriors, but the temptation might prove too great for a tribal with a sharp knife and the stealth of a panther, to come calling silently in the deep of the night.

Nellie arrived much later and rolled her bedding beside Holly. 'Are you awake? Holly' she whispered excitedly.

'I am now,' replied Holly drily.

'It's fantastic, y'know – like, this guy's a higher being!'

'You sound a bit "high" yourself.'

'Yep,' she giggled. 'They've got some really strong Karaganda grass.'

'Enjoy the night, Nellie, but we leave tomorrow, rain or shine, got that?'

'Yeah,' she whispered, her mind awed by the dreams of others. 'But Holly-Jean, these guys . . . they're something else again, really. Far-out.'

Holly harrumped. 'Just don't sell your trust too cheaply.' Whatever that meant, knowing she sounded like a middle-aged schoolmarm.

Nellie whispered back, 'It's easy for you to say that. You talk a lot about trust, but in this life how do you know that you can trust anyone at all? Can I even trust you, for that matter?'

'Precisely, Nellie, you can't know that,' said Holly, yawning as she reached for her bag, 'but in my case, maybe this will help.' She dug into her pack and brought out the faded photograph from Morag-Rose's photo album. With her maglite she illuminated the picture of Moonbeam and McIlvuddy all those carefree years ago.

'Your mum and dad,' she said.

'*My mum and dad,*' echoed Nellie wonderingly. She looked at Holly with tears in her eyes, and then bent close to examine the old photo, the link to a past she'd never had.

Finally she said softly, 'I've seen pictures of them before. My mother kept one or two over the years, but this one I've never seen. They look so young, so happy. So *great!*' She looked again and pointed. 'Mum must have just said something to make them laugh . . . Oh, *Mummy.*' Her voice broke and Holly reached out to hug the young woman close, and began to rock her grief away.

But was that thunder rumbling in the hills?

'If that's what I think it is, we've got to get out now!' Holly yelled suddenly jumping up. Grabbing the girl, she ran helter-skelter from the encampment towards the black edge of the clearing. 'C'mon, Nellie, run for frock's sake!'

But Nellie had turned back. 'My film!' she screamed.

'Forget the film Nellie!' Holly ran back after her. But it was too late.

As she reached their bedding the night sky was suddenly rent by the deafening sound of thudding rotors swooping over the lip of the steep roc wall. Searchlights threw the canyon into instant blindingly bright light and loudspeakers mounted on the sides of the huge heli-gunships blasted out in high-pitched Mandarin, 'Lay down your weapons and place your hands in the air!'

Holly scooped up her pack and the golf bag and dove towards the safety of the dark forest amid the screams and scattering people, feeling the earth strafed by bullets around her feet.

Too close!

She stood stock-still, her arms over her head in the steady beam of the spotlight, the wind from the rotors and the clattering din cowing her. Small arms fire erupted from the clearing and the hovering spotlight was punched out.

This smattering of resistance was met with a colossal rain of maddened firepower, but the temporary dark was all Holly-Jean needed as she flung herself into the treeline and dug deep into the undergrowth, screaming all the while,

'Nellie, are you with me? Nellie!' But the young woman was nowhere in sight.

Without further warning two rockets whooshed out of the night sky and demolished the cave entrance, bringing down a pile of rubble. Oh Nellie!

By now the clearing was ignited by tracer fire and new searchlights while rockets pounded down with earth-shaking thunderclaps.

The scene was of a strange lethal splendour as tracer fire danced in and around the glade like alive feral Catherine wheels.

Holly-Jean buried herself deep in the undergrowth, and grabbing handfuls of foliage, she crowned her head with camouflage.

The firing stopped abruptly, leaving only the bittersweet smoke of cordite and the thud-thud-*roar* of the rotors. Peering out from under cover Holly counted two helicopter gunships hovering above the canyon while a small but sleek, commercially heli-jet was just touching down in the centre of the clearing.

Nobody moved. Only the snow danced madly in the whirlwind of rotor-blades. From the loudspeaker a voice in Mandarin announced, 'Listen carefully and there will be no further bloodshed! Will the two foreign guests, Miss Holly-Jean Ho and Miss Nellie McIlvuddy, please make themselves visible.'

Holly climbed to her feet. No sign as yet of Nellie. She slowly raised her arm and stood immobile.

The order was repeated, this time in English. 'The two foreigners will please stand and approach the landed helicopter. Be sure to move slowly and make no unnecessary sudden movements. This is for your own safety.'

Their names were repeated again in American English. Then the voice reverted to Mandarin. 'All other parties shall remain without any motion whatsoever. Any digression from these orders will be met with gunfire, is this understood? Now, I repeat, will the two foreign guests make themselves identifiable and approach the landed helicopter.'

Holly walked slowly out of the forest and feeling faintly ridiculous with her golf-bag on one arm and her pack on the other, she moved across the clearing to the waiting helicopter.

'Stop and identify yourself!' came the order. Two snow-suited men had jumped down from the helicopter and stood at attention with guns ready.

'Holly-Jean Ho.' She reached for her passport.

'Hand over the document.' She held out her passport to one of the snowmen.

'Let me go and get the other foreigner,' Holly said. 'She may be wounded.'

The snowmen conferred by headset. 'Go. We will accompany you. Don't try anything stupid.'

Holly made her way across the clearing, conscious of the two men behind her. She reached the entrance to the cave which under the wavering searchlights was revealed as a mound of rubble. From behind it came the moaning of wounded people and the keening of distraught women.

Ignoring the stares of the silent watchers, Holly moved closer to the rock wall. 'Nellie?' she called out. 'Are you there? We've got to go. If you're worried, bring your camera and the film. I'll take care of it, I promise. They want us, you see, just us two. They're not interested in these others. You've got to come out now or your friends will be annihilated, do you understand?'

There was some loud murmuring and the voice of female dissent. Then the clear accented English, 'Get the fuck out of here, Yankee troublemaker. Look what you've done, you stupid bitch!'

This was met with loud guffaws from the two snowmen.

A little while later, Nellie came stumbling from the darkness as though shoved from behind. Her face in Holly's mag-lite beam appeared streaming with tears and blood-streaked.

'Come on home, Nell.' Holly hoped the young girl's heart hadn't been broken into too many pieces, as she grabbed her by the hand and tugged her at a half-run back across the clearing and up into the waiting heli-jet.

'Welcome aboard Flight 714,' said the bearded American pilot, glancing back to check that Nellie and Holly were strapped safely to their luxury seats. 'Now to get this little kite over the mountains and outta this godforsaken country!'

208

Behind them, the snowmen wordlessly kept watch from the open door as the plane swooped upwards and until they were out of the valley. Leaving the gunships to head off in the opposite direction, the little heli-jet skimmed the snow-capped mountains.

Holly didn't say anything for the first few minutes of lurching flight, trying to check which direction they were indeed heading in. On the onset, Nellie kept yammering questions from the rear: 'Are they Secret Police? The PLA militia? Why is he an American pilot? Where are they taking us?'

Holly kept mum. Just patted Nellie's thighs and whispered for her to try and stay calm. But when she was sure the lights of the other gunships were disappearing fast away from their flight path, she pointed out the window.

'Look, Nellie, you see out there,' she said to console her, 'the gunships have gone off in another direction. They didn't want your friends and your friends didn't really get hurt that much. No one was killed, as far as I could see. These people are only interested in us two foreigners.'

'Who are they?' Nellie demanded angrily. 'Don't you see, we've just betrayed the others! Destroyed their cause! Now the authorities will come and kill them!'

Her voice rose in hysterics. Holly reached out and pinched Nellie's wrists at the secret meridian pressure points. Time to be brutally frank.

'Calm yourself.' She spoke loudly over the roar of the jet-rotors. 'Your part in this game is just a tiny blip. Believe me, you're simply not that important. This rescue was organised by private individuals and has no bearing on politics or local intrigue in any way.'

Nellie just waved Holly away, muttering about betrayal. Holly heard her berating herself. 'It was all my fault. How could I have been so stupid. Stupid little childish cow!'

Holly felt it best to let her be. Her reaction was understandable. But frankly, for her own part, Holly-Jean was damn relieved to be out of that beautiful Shangri-la.

When she was confident that they were flying over the pass towards Kazakhstan, she spoke to the pilot.

'This is not an official Chinese militia plane, right?'

'Call me a cunt, sis,' said the pilot, 'but does this sweetheart look like it belongs in the Chink Air Force? Pardon my French, the name's Ricky, and I fly commercial, babe, stricty-issimo.'

Holly shook his hand. 'Nice to meet you, Rick, and thanks for the ride.'

'Chill that, sweetheart. Another charter, another collar.'

'So who paid for this private charter, where and when?'

Rick studied his dials and spoke obscurely into his mouthpiece. Turning to Holly, he remarked, 'Official stuff makes me nervous. Never had much truck with authority, you get my drift? All those freakin' questions.'

'You've done a good job, anyway,' said Holly. 'So who's in charge?'

Rickly replied to a sudden squawking from his headset, spoke for a few minutes into his mouthpiece, presumably clearing himself with the nearest air-traffic control. When he'd finished, he turned to Holly and said, 'Cleared the Kazakh border control. We're outta China!'

Holly leaned back and told Nellie the news. But the girl seemed to have entered some kind of state of shock and did not respond.

Holly moved back up to the co-pilot's seat and began to chat with Ricky. After a little banter, she repeated her question, 'So who booked you on this gig?'

'C'mon, darlin', you know the score. No names, no pack drill,' reproached Ricky. After a minute or so he relented. You could say these guys are definite friendlies.'

Holly nodded. 'Mind if I use my cellphone?'

'Freakin' right, I do,' Ricky snorted. 'It'll screw up the electronics. You just wait till I put this little boat down in Alma Alta. 'Bout an hour or more flying yet.'

Holly sat quietly thinking. Alma Alta. Hey, ho. Well, whatever: she figured she would remain extremely wary of Ricky and the two silent snowmen till she knew just from which side of the various fences aroundabout their cash was being dispensed.

She tried another casual tack. 'So where did you set out from? I mean, you must have found it tricky to locate us, right?'

'Freakin' right, sis,' said Ricky. 'We been plying those valleys for two days. Hugging the ground to keep from being too public, get my drift? Then last night we got a definite set of aerial-ground site locators which was when we picked up those two heavy mothers. I thought we were in for it but then they introduced themselves as friendly spectators – some sort of local outfit.'

'PLA?' asked Holly.

Ricky chuckled. 'I don't think they were *that* official, more like cland-est-ine. Item: two state-of-the-art gunships, Heavenly Mandated Generalissimo – for the personal use of – get my drift?'

'Seems a bit far-fetched to me. You're actually saying there are unofficial gunships flying around Skiniang?' said Holly.

'Better believe it, darlin',' laughed Ricky, apparently tickled by her innocent questions. 'Since I been working for this outfit, I've seen enough freelance action over the skies of China you'd think it was a goddamn airshow some days. It's one huge mother of a country, and you've got a lot of different merchandise coming and going, every which way, round the freakin' clock.'

'But what about the official military, the PLA?'

'Hah!' Rickly glanced round at her. 'Cliques, factions and China's got this ropy old Air Force mostly. All right, some's been modernised recently, but no way they can cover all the ground, no how. Round about these Western skies, you don't get much interference at a low-level. Sure, if you was to take some kind of B52 into China's airspace, you might expect some reactive activity, maybe a little flak, but a nippy little birdie like this sweet mother: in and out, nobody's the wiser. When I was booked for this gig in fact I'd just come back from Kashgar.'

'So you're based in Alma Alta?'

'Oh no, sis,' said Ricky. 'I just come and go anywhere's in Asia. Anywhere's the job sends me.'

'So who's your boss, then? Who pays your wages?'

'Oh, baby, you got a sweet tongue. But un-hunh.'

And after that he was silent.

They landed on a quiet stretch of airport near some empty

hangars while the dawn broke in the eastern sky behind them. As Holly climbed down from the helicopter and stretched her legs on the Tarmac, a familiar voice carried across the chill sweet air.

'Extremely Unmarried Miss Ho. Good morning.'

'Mr Plum Blossom,' gasped Holly. 'How delightful to see you.'

He laughed happily. ' "Delightful" is an admirable under-statement, Ho *Shao-lan*. You are to be commended for your composure and dignity. Stylish, entry, Holly-Jean. Anyway, you got Nellie out safe and sound.'

'I did?' quipped Holly. They helped Nellie down, and with the two snowmen carrying their bags, made their way into a small office inside one of the empty hangars.

Holly was still taking it all in. 'You know you're amazing, Plum Blossom, but this one utterly and absolutely takes the cake. I mean, how did you possibly get here so soon? I only just spoke to you in London.'

'No, you didn't,' said Plum Blossom, smiling. 'You spoke to me in Alma Alta; the call was re-routed electronically to me here. I came out here on Shih's request just after your intended itinerary to Sinkiang was confirmed. The Society has been observing your every move since your arrival in China. You remember your visit to the wedding salon?'

Holly just shook her head and whistled appreciatively. She asked, 'So how come Shih's pulling all the Society strings these days then?'

'Oh no, it's not like that,' said Plum Blossom. 'He has put in certain requests, we have calculated our charges in both cash, equity in businesses acquired as a result of a successful outcome and of course, concomitant favours now owed to us. As a reasonable and honourable man, he has agreed to pay accordingly for our services.' Plum Blossom looked unchar-acteristically shy for a moment as he lowered his voice and muttered, 'I admit my personal involvement in this activity is due to my own concern for your safety, Extremely Unmarried Miss Ho.'

Holly kissed his smoothly shaven cheek. 'Thanks, *Mei Hua shenshen*. I owe you yet another one.'

'Don't mention it, Extremely Unmarried Miss Ho.

Besides, we're making a very good business out of this. So, in fact you are to be congratulated.'

'Hey, hold your horses, we aren't out of Bumfuckov, Siberia yet.'

'True, Holly-Jean, very true,' said that suave assassin.

Tea was drunk while Plum Blossom conferred on his cellphone.

'So what next?' said Holly. 'Back to London?'

'Eventually,' he nodded. 'First we take a charter out of here to New Delhi, where Shih Yang-fu has laid on his private commercial jetliner. We will decide our destination there, after it is noted what reaction if any, the Mainland authorities decide upon. Don't overlook the fact that Shih has *guanchi* at the very highest level in Beijing. Having said that,' sighed Plum Blossom as though discussing nothing of more import than the cricket score, 'Beijing is always riven by factionalism, now just as it ever was in the days of the Emperors. Shih may need time to smooth some unruffled feathers or grant requisite saving of face. He also wants us to wait and see what response from the Chiu faction is forthcoming.'

'They know of Nellie's existence, then?' asked Holly, glancing over at the ashen-faced girl, sitting listlessly at a rusting metal table, ignoring her cup of tea.

'Undoubtedly,' said Plum Blossom. 'This is China, *shao-jye*. Eyes are everywhere. It's just a matter of having the *guanchi* and of course the cash, to make those eyes give up their secrets. If we know you visited the Harmonious Friction Wedding Salon in Urumchi, no doubt others did too. Chiu's clique have plenty of business in China. It's almost definite that they've been trailing you since you left London. After all, didn't you run into some kind of trouble at your hotel in Manila?'

Holly nodded. 'Took care of it.'

'I am full of admiration for you, my dear Extremely Unmarried Miss Ho. You are a veritable Tigress and young Nellie is safe and sound.'

'Yes, well . . . talking of Nellie I think I'd better go and see to her,' said Holly. ''Fraid she's taken a few knocks, what with one thing and another. I presume we're going no further than bed tonight?'

'No. But most unfortunately, the airport hotel here is barely adequately. Transport is due anytime now to transfer us. But please don't expect much,' he said. 'We'll meet for food at six a.m. Now I have other business to attend to. Sleep well.'

'You too, Plum Blossom.'

'But of course, Extremely Unmarried Miss Ho.'

Holly got up twice in the night, ostensibly to check Nellie was sleeping well-covered from the chill frost air, but also to check their door was unlocked.

Don't ask.

Chapter 24

An hour into the flight out of New Delhi, seated in the deep-purple velvet luxury of Shih's private sixteen-seater Lear jet, Holly felt the wings bank high vertically as the plane altered course and apparently headed back in the opposite direction. Since they had been informed at the outset that London was their destination, Holly calculated that they were now heading East.

Back towards China.

She waited till the plane righted itself and went to look for Plum Blossom. He had been busy occupied with a radio-set throughout the flight so far.

'Taipei,' he muttered tersely when Holly approached him. 'With a stop in Bangkok where I am to disembark. My services are required there. You will be in Taipei under Shih's protection. It is his home base. You and Nellie will wait there pending developments.'

'Just like that?' said Holly indignantly. 'I might just have other business of my own to be taken care of back in Town.'

Mr Plum Blossom looked at Holly. 'I'm afraid that what this means is, there has been some dangerous reaction from the Chiu faction and Shih Yang-fu has chosen Taipei to secure your presence. Taipei is where he wields his greatest power.' He hesitated. 'I am not sure that I agree – I would have preferred to have you both in London under the Society's protection. But so far my counsel is not being heard. Besides, I am now wanted elsewhere. However, please rest assured that the Society is very powerful in Taiwan. Far more so than any force either Shih or Chiu could muster. However, I will not be there, at least for the time being.

Which means my *guanchi* will not be so readily at your disposal.

'Furthermore,' he shrugged, looking away from Holly in an unusually evasive manner, 'at this moment the Society is trying to maintain a more benevolent, um . . . legitimate public profile in Taiwan. Both in terms of elected representatives and enormous investment in development of licensed businesses, listed on the Taiex stock exchange and fully open to public scrutiny. This makes it a little worrisome for me. I have already contacted my best Taipei *guanchi* to ensure your safety throughout your stay there. But even so . . .'

He couldn't meet her eye. Holly's blood ran cold. Plum Blossom was *never* like this: ashamed.

'But for how long are we expected ot stay in Taipei?' she spluttered angrily. 'I've done my job as far as locating an heir to the McIlvuddy Trust. Am I now expected to hole up in Taipei for the frocking millennium?'

'Ho *Shao-lan*, I will do my best from afar to oversee your temporary stay in Taipei,' said Plum Blossom. But he looked weary as he turned back to his radio mouthpiece.

Holly returned to her seat and spent the remainder of the flight thinking.

Taipei was gleaming in the aftermath of a rainstorm and low-angled winter sunlight. Plum Blossom had disembarked at Bangkok as promised and Holly felt both a homecoming nostalgia for the ancestral home of the Ho clan and the chill of arriving naked in that cosmopolitan Chinese city where extremeness was all.

Her skin puckered up in goose-pimples and an icy chill made her frame violently shudder as the limo glided silently by the fantastic glass and steel structures that lurched skywards at every angle. Vertigo-inducing edifices of such profound ugliness that can only exist because mind-boggling money combined with an utter absence of taste had utilised criminals masquerading as architects. But it wasn't just these crimes against humanity that made Holly shiver as the limo surfed into the forecourt of the Shangri-La Plaza Hotel on plumeria-bedecked Tun hua South Road.

It was a sudden foreboding.

Chi-pi. That old chicken-skin again.

Representatives of the hotel management, both foreign and local, distinguished-looking types introduced as Shih's senior officers and their wives, and assorted beautiful people of Cosmopolitan extract, all clapped politely as flashlights popped and two uniformed beauties hung garlands of fresh frangipani round Holly's and Nellie's necks.

'Talk about low-profile,' hissed Nellie. 'What's this all about?'

'Your guess is as good as mine,' murmured Holly, feeling underdressed but all smiles as they were swept into the hotel. 'Ah-ah – that might explain it,' she said, pointing up at a huge banner hanging above the marble floor with the following words written in giant red flourishing Mandarin characters below nattily drawn English: *Welcome to our All-Honoured Foreign Friends to the Sixth Taipei French Film Week. Congratulations to all in Celebration of French Film!*

'Jolly good cover, Shih old boy,' muttered Holly, allowing herself and Nellie to be presented with yet more gouquets of fresh cut blooms and flutes of champagne as they joined a line of other foreigners shaking hands and air-kissing cheeks. After a lot of PR nonsense they were assigned a twin-bedded room to share and Nellie finally unwound enough to speak in full sentences for the first time since the Tian-shan.

'I bags the shower first! I stink worse than a skunk from all that horse-flank embrocation, not to mention the fact that recently my armpit sweat has started to smell of rancid mare's-milk butter – and that's just the upper body levels!'

'It's all yours, kiddo,' winced Holly as Nellie stripped off, left her clothes where they fell in a heap and slammed the bathroom door shut.

She looked around the tastefully appointed twin room. It was like any gilded cage for a pair of nightingales. Nice tasselled bedside lamp and all, but a cell's still a cell to a Tigress.

She opened her Ericsson cellphone and used the electronics to scroll out her address book. Looked up several entries under Ho's of Taiwan. There was one branch of the family based on An-ho Road that she recalled with fondness from her last visit a couple of years back. It was just around the corner, if memory served her well. They ran a thriving luxury in-car entertainment centre. Perhaps she could slip out later. She punched the numbers.

'*Wei?*'

'Hi, Maternal Sister-Cousin. Ho *Shao-lan* from London here – who am I speaking with?'

'*Wah-sei!* That really you, *Shao-lan?*' said a male voice. 'You're in Taipei? Where? I'll come and get you for dinner, have you eaten yet?'

Holly got through all the prelims and managed to make a date for just two of the family to meet her for a quick drink in the hotel bar at nine that night. Maternal Brother-Cousin Ho had at first insisted on calling up a whole fleet of Ho's, but Holly managed to avoid that by promising a full-scale reunion at some later date, pleading exhaustion and a hectic schedule as an excuse. She simply had to prevent the whole mob coming over and filling the Shangri-la lobby with red gobs of betel-nut spit. Besides, the less Shih's lot knew about her local allies the better. She already had a bad feeling about this Taipei trip.

Anyway, you never knew when you might need help; far better not to advertise the fact in advance that she had an entire clan at her disposal.

Holly shut the phone down with a satisfied smirk.

Awa' the Ho's!

Nellie finally vacated the bathroom and Holly had a good long soak under the power-jets. But as if to emphasise the sense of imprisonment, dinner was served in the room.

Plum Blossom called from Bangkok after the meal to enquire if everything was OK.

'Sure it's nice and all,' said Holly, 'but how long do we have to stay cooped up here? I wandered out into the corridor just now and ran instantly into a scrum of Armani suits, sunglasses and shaved heads. All smiling politely and reeking of perfume, but not keen on letting me wander. Not keen at all.'

'The muscle, I'm afraid,' said Plum Blossom. 'Look, I've already talked to Shih's people in Taipei. Just be patient and don't worry. You'll probably relocate to Shih's HQ in the mountains within a day or two at the most. It's like a fortress up there. But a beautiful location – landscapped gardens surrounded by rainforest. Waterfalls, wildlife, the works.'

'Great,' said Holly. 'Another prison cell. By the way, is Shih actually in town? Maybe I can talk to him. Surely the overriding need now is to introduce Nellie in public in London as the heir to the Trust, and then await whatever legal challenges to the legitimacy of her claim are mounted by the opposition, namely Hamish backed by Chiu Nei-ku.'

Plum Blossom agreed. 'However,' he added, 'it seems that Shih wants to keep you hidden from view for the time being. I think he may want to run tests on Nellie.'

'I assume you're referring to DNA testing,' said Holly. 'Well, surely such tests should take place in London if anywhere, from a legal point of view. Best clinics, local court-appointed pathologists, et cetera. Besides which, I thought the problem really was that all existing samples of Lord Jonny's DNA went missing along with Dr Devesfrunto's bloody demise and that of his unfortunate dog.'

'That we don't yet know,' said Plum Blossom. 'Current reports from Manila have failed to turn up any proof of the existence of the sample of Lord McIlvuddy's body that the doctor allegedly kept secure. We have your word for it, Holly-Jean, and of course, no one's doubting that, but as for actual skin tissue or the like, nothing. One thing's for sure, the other side don't have it either. They're still tearing around Manila kicking in doors and trashing every place they visit.'

Holly said, 'You know, I guess I just assumed the evidence to support the legitimacy of Nellie's claim to the inheritance would take the form of the various photographs of Nellie with Moonbeam and her father together, backed by sworn affidavits of family members such as Morag-Rose in Shetland and of course her mother's medical records. My bet is Manny Devesfrunto's taken the secrets of Lord Jonny Mac's DNA to his and his dear old faithful doggie's grave.'

Plum Blossom was suddenly abrupt. 'Are you using your cellphone? You are? Then we will stop this conversation forthwith. We are touching on delicate matters. Now listen to me, Holly-Jean – please be patient for the time being. I know it's hard for you, a young woman born in the Year of the Tiger and all that . . . but just try to keep your head down until further notice; maintain a tight hold on Nellie and don't do anything stupid or heroic! You do understand me, Extremely Unmarried Miss Ho?'

'Understood, oh bossman. Nellie's gone comatose on me anyway, so just remember to send any cheques to Ma in Earlham Street should I fail to make it back in one piece!' And she snapped shut the cellphone lid.

Later on, leaving Nellie moodily riding the remote through the surf of the cable TV, their twin-room door locked and guarded by the mobile mannequins, Holly was 'allowed' downstairs and met up as arranged with two male Ho clanners in the hotel bar. She noted the discreet scrutiny of a single one of Shih's fancy muscle and concluded by it that she was of little importance at this juncture. Nellie was the prize, and Nellie was to be protected. Holly stored this piece of information away.

She and her distant cousins drank beer, ate fancy dried mussel-fish and swapped family gossip – mainly about the Taipei clan's well-being and current prosperity in the financial storms. They also enquired at length as to Ma's health and wanted to know all about the business in Earlham Street. Of course, Holly found herself fending off perennial questions as to why she had neither married nor procreated.

Later they were joined by her old Taipei acquaintance Nick Mayo, former international banker, China Hash House Harrier extraordinaire and ex-'madam' at The Cub Pack, a boy-brothel in Angeles City, north of Manila; the brothel was owned by the notorious Andrew Mitchell, the man known as 'The Scoutmaster' to the anti-paedophile squad at Interpol.

After quite a few Taiwan Beers the two Ho's left and Nick stretched out his legs and asked, 'So what made you call me, Holly-Jean? No offence, but in my recollection you seem to be the harbinger of all sorts of nastiness with a capital nasty.'

'Oh, just passing through,' she replied airily. 'Sort of happenstance – nothing too murky.'

'What the hell is that supposed to mean?' said Nick, signalling for more beer.

'Nothing at all,' said Holly. She didn't add that actually she was renewing her Taipei *guanchi* in all its forms. Just in case. 'We're old friends, aren't we? So tell me, what's been happening with you these days?'

Nick leisurely recounted to Holly that he was in temporary retreat from the harsh world, cosily ensconced in his Taiwanese-style farmhouse perched halfway up Yang Ming shan, a mountain overlooking Taipei to one side and the Pacific Ocean on the other.

'Taking a lengthy, and may I say, rather well-earned sabbatical, dear girl,' he drawled.

'No need to work?' said Holly. 'As I recall, the last time we met . . . um, Angeles City, wasn't it? You claimed to be on your last dollar.' She twinkled her eyes and watched him squirm with embarrassment.

'Ah, yes, well, harrumph,' he coughed. 'Thought I told you at the time that was just a freak coincidence. You just happened by utter chance to find me there at all. Not my scene, y'know. Quite the contrary. Ladies' man.'

Holly smiled politely. 'It's all right. I've learned it takes all sorts . . .'

'No, no,' Nick Mayo stuttered. 'You really must understand. Holding the shop for Mitchell. Merely. Know him, don't you? China Hasher. Good man. Ah, got into a rather sticky line of work for a while back then. All finished now, of course.'

' "Sticky" line of work?' queried Holly innocently.

'Bad choice of word,' spluttered Nick. 'Look, it was a business thing, pure and simple. Can't go into all that now . . . Anyway, history, over for good. Closed subject.'

Despite his being the pure embodiment of absolute political incorrection, Holly had a soft spot for Nick. After all, it had been his timely intervention at the head of a small army of taxi-driving Hash House Harriers which had saved the day when the chips were down, way back when she'd last been in Taipei. The feeling was growing that she might be needing a friend or two this trip to Taiwan also.

'So you're living well then?' said Holly. 'Easily put your hand on a few crisp folding green ones whenever you like?'

Loosened by the beer, and edging ever closer along the pink velvet sofa they were sharing, Nick told how he was, in fact, *deeply cushioned* against the vagaries of the spinning planet's market forces by the vast sums he had somehow managed to *ferment* from the bank's recent merger with Chase Manhattan. This was just prior to his resignation.

'Golden handshakes also came through OK?' said Holly.

'Oh yes,' nodded Nick with gusto. 'Jolly golden.'

The evening passed pleasantly enough and Holly accepted a date for the next day. After lengthy negotiation with the Shih muscle's superior, it was agreed that Holly (but Holly alone, Nellie was not to be permitted to venture out of her room), and one minder would be collected by Nick at nine in the morning for a spin in his Jag up to the farmhouse and thence on to a spot of golf. Another minder would drive a separate vehicle also.

Nick chuckled with amusement as he listened into the discussion and added as he said good night, 'Lot of bollocky ballyhoo for a tourist lady, eh? Imagine if you were involved in something really murky, for fuck's sake . . . Nightynight.'

Holly found Nellie fast asleep and the air-conditioning icy. The TV showed 'yellow' porn on at least five channels.

She woke early with a sore throat and slipped out of the room leaving a guilty note for Nellie to read on waking.

Chapter 25

Holly and Nick were just finishing up at the ninth hole right next to the car park of the expensive golf club which seemed to slice its emerald way through the tropical rainforest not far from Nick's farmhouse when the minder got a call and began jabbering agitatedly in rough Taiwanese. Suddenly a gun appeared in his hand and he screamed at Holly and Nick to get back to the Jag.

When the sound of a pistol-shot rang out from the thickly forested hillside to the left, Holly grabbed Nick by the wrist and threw him to the ground behind his Jag. 'This isn't your battle, Nick. Get the frock outta here and don't look back!'

While the first minder shielded her, the other jumped into his 4WD utility tank and spun gravel. As the jeep pulled alongside, Holly clambered aboard, while the minder hung on to the doorframe with one hand, pistol brandished in the other, for all those ducking behind the clubhouse barstools to see.

Nick called out as they pulled away, 'What about your golf-bag?'

'Keep it!' screamed Holly.

They careered around the twisting mountain roads on two-wheels mercilessly torturing the rubber, climbing higher and higher into the Taiwan central massif. After a while it was obvious no one was following and they slowed.

The driver asked, 'Anyone get hit?'

Both Holly and the minder said no.

The minder conferred on his mobile phone, then said to the driver in Mandarin, 'Boss says to go straight on up to the Farm. They're bringing the girl there now. Step on it!'

It took an hour of hairpin bends and cambered corners to reach the high mountain pass and the rough stone walls of the modestly named 'Farm'. A gate swung open and Holly glimpsed armed guards standing about at regular intervals as they drove at a sedate pace through pine groves. Eventually they came to a large, low, white-painted cement-block mansion surrounded by a parapet and a moat. Many more society foot soldiers were in evidence, standing about singly or in groups, Uzis and pistols at the ready. Holly was hustled inside the building, along pink marble corridors, and locked inside a ground-floor bedroom.

Two grim-looking tomboy females with razorcuts and thick necks entered, strip-searched her and removed her cellphone. They made no response to her questioning so Holly kept silent too. When they were gone she examined the room. The Baroque wrought-iron bars across the windows were more for show than to keep out any hapless burglar foolish enough to attempt a break-in at the private headquarters of the head of a Chinese Secret Society, a ruthless billionaire to boot. She chuckled at the idea as she checked the bathroom and walk-in closet. All very nice. For a prison cell.

Holly took a long shower and put on the clothes that had been laid out in the walk-in. Black linen shirt and pants by Missoni. A knock-off but an excellent one.

For the rest of the day she was left alone, apart from tray meals brought to her door. Around midnight following a late-night supper tray of simple noodle soup with stir-fried spinach and a bottle of guava juice, the door opened and Nellie entered. When the door was locked behind her the young woman ran forward and fell into Holly's arms sobbing.

'They took my film!' she cried between sniffles.

'Your film?' Holly was amazed. 'You managed to hang onto your film? I thought you lost that back in the Tien-shan.'

'No way!' Nellie said, horrified. 'I left the camera behind but I managed to grab the film. Don't you remember when you came to get me from the cave when the little helicopter was waiting? After th-the attack? The g-guys pretended to hate me, and shouted all that bad stuff about betrayal, but one of them was busy extracting my roll of film, and I stuffed it down my pants. But now these girl-goons just found it, and some stupid fucking Chinese dyke went and exposed it! It's gone for ever! Just look!'

Holly scooped up the bundle of celluloid and rolled it neatly and secured it in her belt-bag. You never knew what computers and digital remastering could do these days. Now she had to console Nellie. She needed her sussed and ready to go, if they were to bust out of this gilded joint.

'Hey, you did damn well so far. No need to blame those women – just doing their job,' she soothed. 'Now listen carefully to me – we've got to get out of this tasteful little palace. I definitely don't approve of this lock and key set-up. In fact, it stinks. So chin up, Nellie, I need you to get your pecker throbbing hard! Figuratively speaking.'

'But my film, my work, all of it wasted!' Nellie was still too upset to hear Holly's words.

So Holly lifted Nellie up by her shoulders, held her close to her face, eyeball to eyeball, and enunciated as reasonably as she could, 'Right now, that bloody film isn't actually the frocking point here, do you understand? I'm afraid it's all a bit less romantic and a sight more dangerous than documentary film-making, but you, my dear young woman, are the object of deep affection, claiming the collective hearts of two rival Chinese gangs who have now apparently embarked upon open hostilities involving the use of bullet and automatic weapon. And we have, in fact, been brought under duress here to this fancy mountain hideaway to avoid being mown down both in cold blood *and* pure daylight upon the far from gentle streets of Taipei. Do you follow me so far?'

She realised her voice had risen. This was no good. One of them had to stay sane. She breathed slowly and deeply. Used *chi* to centre herself and step out of the panic.

She moved to the double bed and pulled Nellie softly down beside her. 'Let's just lie down and wait till morning, shall we?'

'If you say so,' sniffed Nellie, stretching out her legs on the bed and reaching her arms in a tight embrace around Holly's waist.

The bombardment started before dawn. A hole the size of a medicine ball appeared in the wall beside the now-shattered window while Nellie screamed her lungs out and more shells rained down on the Farm in deafening whines and crashes.

Nellie screamed non-stop, 'What the fuck is going on? Is this a war or what? What was that – some kind of missile? We're going to die! Help me, Holly-Jean. I don't want to die!'

Holly stayed calm and when Nellie paused for breath, she pointed out, 'This is Taiwan, honeypie, and these gangs don't play for fun. This is their own fire-zone, no one to stop them and weapons of all kinds at hand. Meanwhile, let's see if we just can't use this battle to our advantage!'

She peered out of the ground-floor window. The drop to the parapet was no more than a few feet. 'Come on,' she whispered excitedly. 'Grab some clothes from the closet – we're getting out of this bullyboys' nasty little squabble!'

They dressed in seconds, choosing black from head to toe. Then with Holly leading the way they slipped out of the crumbling windowframe and under cover of a particularly spectacular eardrum-perforating firework display somewhere to the right, they dropped silently onto the parapet, narrowly avoiding the squished remains of some unfortunate bull's-eye.

Crouching low they reached the far end of the parapet, away from the focus of the firefight and Holly was first to go over, inching herself down the parapet wall and into the murky waters of the moat. She stood waist-high and held out her arms for Nellie.

Together they waded through the gooey bed of stagnant moat-water and clambered up the reedy bank on the other side of the moat. 'Now run for it!' Holly hissed.

At a crouch they pelted across the open ground, cursing the half-moon's rays and made for the pitch-black forest and the inky mountainside. A few feet into the forest they ran up against a razor fence. Holly quickly stripped off her Missoni jacket, wound it round her wrist and negotiated passage over for both of them.

Attack dogs began howling somewhere nearby, but their keening was more like grief than anger to Holly's ear and the constant crashing of detonations and all the mad pandemonium of the surprise attack was still focused away from them, on the other side of the Farm.

'Is that a mortar attack or something?' asked Nellie as they stopped to catch their breath under cover of the forest.

'I wouldn't happen to know what precise weaponry was involved,' whispered Holly nervily. 'Look, for fuck's sake, who cares? It blew a dirty big hole in old boy Shih's fancy gaffe – is that good enough for you! We're not safe yet, Nellie, and we've got a long way to go tonight, so shut your trap and follow me. Time to move deeper into the forest cover!'

Bang!

Too late! They'd been spotted! Some flanker must have overheard their whispers and suddenly a splatter of shots rang out close by. Cursing, Holly threw Nellie down in a thick clump of fern. She spreadeagled her own body into the loamy earth and tried to slow her breathing. But even now loud voices and crashing footsteps were thundering through the undergrowth towards them. In silence Holly rolled foetally into the thick fern undergrowth close to where Nellie lay and became still. Mastered her *chi* and became one with the forest.

The voices grew louder and the footsteps slowed to within a few feet.

'You see anyone?' said a Mandarin voice.

'Must've been a snake or something,' replied a guttural Fumien-accent.

'Fucking big snake you arst me!' said the first.

'Sod that for a laugh. I hate snakes, let's go back to the others.'

Thanking Fumien for his phobia, Holly waited till she was sure they were gone before she inched up and over to where Nellie lay. She whispered her name. 'Nellie?'

No reply.

Holly reached into the thick jungle growth and touched flesh. Flesh that was sticky with warm blood and which groaned. Nellie had been hit!

Holly raised herself up carefully and peered in the dim filtered moonlight at the face of the young girl. It was ghostly pale and her lips looked dark blue. Holly sat up and listened. The sound of gunfire was less constant now, confined to bursts of angry chatter on the far side of the mansion. Fortunately none of the fire-light appeared to be heading this way, at least for the time being. But who knew what might happen next?

She dragged herself next to Nellie and gently lifted an eyelid. The girl's unseeing eyes indicated that she was only semi-conscious. At least the soft groaning when Holly probed her body meant she was still feeling pain.

Holly thought hard. Although she knew better than to move a body suffering unspecified wounding, she had no choice but to get Nellie out of this battlezone. What she had learned and heard about such Chinese Society fire-fights, this battle would go two ways: either it would be over swiftly, with a strategic retreat to lick wounds, point lethally made, insult delivered, face gained and face lost. Or it would be something else again – a crazed battle of enraged foot soldiers run *amok*, till the last man was no longer standing.

Whatever, she didn't feel like hanging around with a wounded companion just to find out which.

Holly whispered again, 'Nellie, can you hear me?' Still no response.

Holly checked the earth around Nellie's body. Her fingers came up smeared and sticky with blood. Just how much blood had the girl lost? This was no good, thought Holly. She had to move her – and now.

With all her mustered *chi*-strength she dragged Nellie further into the forest with but a vague idea of which direction to go, certain only that it was the one heading away from the bang and clatter of guns and the screaming of men. She didn't know how long she and Nellie moved like centipedes over the earth, but long after the sounds of the attack had died away into the distant silent forest night she kept on carrying the dead weight.

For long punishing hours she hauled her young friend's feverish body through the tangled jungle that at times seemed to knot itself around her and threaten to cut off the blood supply to her limbs; then she had to summon up every last bit of power in her screaming muscles and rip herself free, feeling the blood flow down in the process. Until at last Holly found herself at the top of steep incline and heard a new sound, the rushing of fierce water rising up from somewhere below. Water would be a life-saver if she could only get Nellie conscious for a short time and able to drag herself down to its source.

Holly knew that her own strength was already sapped beyond endurance. In the last of the setting moonlight she came to a break in the treeline; below them, the forest dropped away in a steep pine-dotted cliff; down to where the silvery trace of a river was carving its way to the foothills.

Nellie groaned, and Holly grabbed her by the shoulders and began to shake her violently. 'Wake up, Nellie, you've got to wake up!'

Ruthlessly, she continued to shake the limp body, urging her all the while to waken. Finally Holly let out a howl and flung herself down beside Nellie, and she lay heaving and wracked with pain and despair. So it was going to be now, on this cruel beautiful hilltop, that it would end.

Then: 'Get off my leg, you're killing me!' came a dopey voice from beneath her.

'Oh good girl, Nellie, you beauty!' Holly gasped through tears and bloody chokes. 'You see that lovely river down there? We're going to get to it and drink all that cool, refreshing water. And we're going to all right, see? But it is steep, Nellie, my dear – very steep, so you've got to hold on to me for dear life. Do you understand?' she shouted hoarsely.

Nellie moaned and rolled her eyes, nodding.

'Right, then. Let's do it!' Holly tugged and pummelled Nellie over to the moonlit edge. With a cracked yell she cried out, 'Sorry, kiddo, you go first – but hold on I'm coming!' and she rolled Nellie's limp body ahead over the precipice and into the abyss towards the water. In the same second Holly leaped out in a dive with both hands forward to grab Nellie's tumbling form and clutch it to her own.

Ripped and battered, they tumbled together in a cartwheel of flailing limbs and whipped branches. Halfway down Holly suddenly felt the earth fall away beneath her and clinging to Nellie, both of them screaming, they sailed through the air for gravity's long seconds to finally land with a dizzying, smashing bellyflopsplash into the river below.

Stunned and momentarily losing motor control, Holly-Jean felt herself dragged furiously by the raging current against

229

sharp rocks and over jagged stones. Nellie had slipped away from her on impact and she could no longer see her in the foaming turmoil of whitewater rapids.

Suddenly Holly was dunked under the surface for long seconds in a violent eddy. Accepting the river was her master she stopped struggling, relaxed her body completely, went limp and let herself be taken by the force of falling water. The river ride was fast, galloping, bucking: ten, fifteen minutes of intense, senseless, chaotic motion that threw Holly out the other end below the rapids and into a stretch of relatively calmer water a long way lower down the valley. At last with a few desperate strokes of her numb arm-muscles she beached up on a pebbly shore and lay gasping and choking, but exhilarated and alive!

Feeling herself cautiously, she found no broken bones, but discovered that there was a nasty gash on her left thigh from which blood was flowing. She cleaned the wound in the icy clean river water, and satisfied that no dirt was trapped inside, tore off a remaining strip of Missioni and fashioned a simple tourniquet to staunch the blood-loss.

Now she looked around her in the luminous starlight, reaching instinctively for her belt-bag. It was there, water-logged, no doubt, but her credit cards, passport, tickets and cash were safe. Not that there'd be much chance to use them round here in this gorgeous desolation.

She took stock. It seemed that she had washed up in a kind of natural pond where a flat section of the valley spread the river thin silver in the light of the Milky Way. Ahead of her, downstream, the pass narrowed and the white tips indicated the water flowed fast on down.

Holly-Jean gazed back up towards the steep mountain heights, then studied the flow of the river into the pond where its violent surge diminished instantly into placid calm as if by magic. Not a ripple disturbed the surface in the middle of the pond. There was no sign of Nellie. Still, it was a miracle she had made it. They must have dropped down a few thousand feet in that helter-skelter.

Nausea suddenly washed over her and she lay back shuddering as shock chemicals flooded her system. Breathing gently and deeply, concentrating all the diverse *chi-kung* techniques she'd been taught, in order to restore the last of her remaining energy and heal, she began to feel stronger. But then her mind began to jiggle about.

She heard her own voice somewhere near, speaking to her, saying: 'Holly, you've come this far, and you're really determined to make it out alive, but when you think about it, why bother? Wouldn't it be so nice to sleep for a while, hey?'

'No,' her other self replied drowsily. Because Nellie McIlvuddy is somewhere nearby and needs me.

Holly staggered to her feet. Rolled forward and dropped into the river face-down. Opened her lips and drank deeply of the clear icy water. Giggling with hysteria, she hauled herself up and staggered into the undergrowth of the forest.

Holly-Jean knew her body well and could read the signs in advance. She just made it into deep cover before the last of her energy drained away like an off-switch and with a last-ditch lunge she grabbed armfuls of fern and foliage, covered herself and, as massive shock set in, passed out.

Chapter 26

Holly-Jean reluctantly shed the skins of sleep, unwound her pearly shell and left the void. She opened her eyes and yawned cavernously. Birds sang and swooped to feed as sunlight filtered through the pines, making a ladderway of beams in which winter-winged insects gambolled. This idyllic awakening ended with a clang of anxiety as Holly remembered where she was.

Nellie! She must find the wounded girl!

She rose up weakly, her leg muscles screaming with pain, examined her thigh and found the wound was healing and a scab of dried blood already starting to form. So far, so good. She loosened the tourniquet and washed the cloth in the river, reapplied it looser as a bandage.

Fearful of being seen in the bright daylight by any hostile types who would no doubt be scouring the mountains for herself and Nellie, Holly kept to the shadows of the forest and picked her way over the rocky outcrops along the riverside heading downstream.

About one hundred metres further down there was another drop, a sweet waterfall which cascaded into a dark lagoon. Butterflies danced in and out of the shadows; a huge toad leapt off a mossy rock and dove in just for the hell of it. Holly laughed as she stood rooted on a lichen-draped rock for a few moments, drinking in the beauty of the place, vowing to return one day.

As she scanned the vision she saw something down below. She knelt to get a better look. It was a body! On the far side of the lagoon, Nellie lay face up on the pebbly bank. She was not moving.

Hopping from stone to stone, Holly clambered swiftly

down the rocky wall of the gorge and dropped to the shore of the lagoon with a rolling jump. She reached Nellie's body and bending down to examine her, feared the worst. The skin on the girl's face was grey and waterlogged.

She pulled open Nellie's eyelids but they were still. Her lips were blue. She showed no signs of a pulse. Holly laid her ear close to Nellie's breast. Was it her imagination, or was there a faint but determined heartbeat. A glimmer of life! She pinched Nellie's nose and blew deep into her throat, began to pump with both hands on her chest. One-and-two-and-one-and-two.

'Come on, breathe!' she bellowed, urging air into the girl's lungs again and again.

Suddenly, yellow mucus erupted from Nellie's gullet and she came to, spluttering and choking, gasping for air. 'Holly-Jean! It's you!'

'Holly-Jean too true, kiddo!' Holly cried, wiping puke from her eye.

They both began to laugh hysterically till Nellie began to choke again.

'You must have partially blocked the windpipe by choking on your own vomit,' Holly explained. 'You were damn lucky Miss Dyno-rod here popped up in the nick of time!'

Nellie subsided into exhaustion once more till Holly shook her awake again. 'We have to move. To stay here is to die. That wound of yours is looking angry.' With effort she managed to turn Nellie over and peel back the tattered clothing over the wound. The flesh on Nellie's lower left back was gouged out in a shallow hole the size of a fried egg. A piece of shrapnel must have nicked her, but hadn't entered her body. Even so, Nellie was damn lucky to be alive! The hours in the icy water had cleaned the wound and prevented septicaemia. For now. But the torn flesh looked greenish and Holly knew the wound had to be treated without delay. Which was easier said than done.

What to do? Risk getting caught by unfriendlies and be killed anyway, after first being gang-raped for a day or two? But then not to seek help was to die. There was no choice.

Nellie began to babble quietly to herself. Holly stood up and looked around. 'Trouble is, apart from the obvious plan to head on downstream I have no earthly clue which way to go.'

Nellie had struggled up onto her knees. She looked up at Holly and croaked, 'Go on without me. I'm going to die anyway, so save yourself.'

'Don't you dare say that, Nellie McIlvuddy of That Ilk!' said Holly angrily. 'We can still find a way out of here. But only if you pull your weight too!'

Nellie raised her head and stared at Holly, a look of wonderment in her eyes, then she took a deep breath, gazed around, then back up the mountain from whence they'd come. 'You're right. We made it this far, we'll make it all the way home.'

'That's the spirit, girl!' cried Holly. Something in the far distance caught her eye, and with a yell of joy, she pointed downstream to the valley, beyond the scrubby hillocks to where the beautiful, heart-warming glitter of the sun laid its kiss upon rice-paddy.

People!

She hauled Nellie to her feet. 'All we've got to do is cover a few clicks to those paddyfields and we'll find help.'

'I can walk with a stick.'

'Then I'll find you one and then let's get the frock outta here!'

Nellie reached out and grabbed Holly's arm. 'First, I want to thank you,' she said, her eyes alive again, bright with hope. 'You've saved my life.'

'You're very welcome,' said Holly-Jean. 'Now move your arse!'

Chapter 27

They reached the first signs of human habitation around dusk. A small girl fetching water from a well spotted them and, eyes widened in terror, ran back to the little three-sided Taiwanese farmhouse, shouting.

A red-faced peasant farmer and his family appeared and stood watching silently as Holly limped slowly down the river bank towards the village, Nellie's left arm round her shoulder and a pine-branch crutch beneath her right.

Holly began to shout in Mandarin when they were within earshot. 'Need help! My friend is very sick!'

Hearing her words, the peasants ran towards them, and with friendly arms supported the two exhausted travellers the last of the way towards the farmhouse.

'Welcome, welcome,' cried a fat lady, obviously the matriarch of the household. She just got the words out when Nellie collapsed like a crumpled rag doll.

One of the men turned to Holly and spoke in Mandarin. 'What happened to your friend?'

'Fell into the river,' Holly croaked out. 'We were in the whitewater rapids all the way down from the top of the mountain! Cut her back on rocks . . .'

'*Wah sei! Nimen shao-jye shrma il-hai!*'

But Holly's strength had finally sapped and she couldn't answer any more; she just shook her head. She let the man catch hold of her as she fell.

The two weary stragglers were laid gently down, their wounds bathed clean and dressed, hot food and drink administered and help summoned. Some time later, an ambulance arrived and they were taken to the Miaoli General Hospital – a modern medical establishment with a first-class Casualty

Department, used to dealing with the habitual road smashes on Taiwan's notorious freeways. Holly was allowed to leave after an overnight stay, but Nellie was checked into the Intensive Care Unit.

On arrival at the hospital, Holly had used the public phone to call Plum Blossom's Taipei contact number, and soon thereafter a number of well-dressed 'associates' turned up and stood lounging outside the private ward where Nellie lay. Holly guessed these were Bamboo Union members, more powerful than the men who worked for either Shiu or Chiu.

She stayed at a Society motel in the town and waited out the four days of Nellie's treatment, alternating bouts of deep sleep with waking periods of deep boredom, till the young American girl was fit to move to a Taipei clinic.

On the day of her discharge, Mr Plum Blossom himself arrived in a big Cadillac, and he gallantly helped Nellie down the steps of the hospital while Holly held the door open and the Society men stood and watched.

They stayed another week in Taipei until it was decided they should return to London. By which time Holly had garnered most of the story from Plum Blossom.

Shih Yang-fu himself had not been in Taiwan during the attack on his 'Farm', but his men had exacted such a terrible revenge on Chiu faction bars and gaming establishments throughout the island, that the government had been forced to step in. Military patrols had been beefed up, night business was curtailed and everyone complained bitterly. So a truce was ordered and now an uneasy calm prevailed over the island.

Holly asked Plum Blossom the latest on the home front. 'Meanwhile back in London?'

'Oh, all very jolly,' said PB. It transpired that Ma was well and keeping the business ticking along. Minty was recuperating. His show had been a wild success. All the publicity surrounding the sensational kidnapping had fuelled the art world's cravings for a new hit. In fact, her boy had also, apparently, made a six-figure sum from selling his story exclusively to a Sunday tabloid.

Minty had spent at least some of the money on a long retreat at a luxury ashram in Sri Lanka with wife and kids. There, under the tender tutelage of the famed Yoga teacher Louise Grime, Minty's thumb and the rest of his body were healing. As for his mind – Holly could only guess. She fervently hoped he had not been permanently scarred by the trauma of the kidnapping.

Indeed, Holly-Jean still felt terrible guilt about the whole episode. Sure, she understood that he had just been a pawn in the game of Chinese chess. But she was the cause. He'd been used to get at her, a completely innocent bystander, dragged into the maelstrom by the mere chance of being her friend.

Yet 'every cloud . . .' as they say. His paintings were hotter than hot right now. A Saatchi of some description was believed to have snapped up the bulk of his most recent works.

Of course, the matter of the McIlvuddy Probate had yet to be settled, since no trace of Dr Manny Devesfrunto's tissue/cell sample from Lord Jonny Mac's body having been discovered. The case would eventually go to arbitration on evidence including photos of Nellie with her mum and dad, her mother's medical records, blood types, et cetera. But no defining DNA.

Therefore Chiu might still want to fight it out in the courts.

In which case a long and dreary legal struggle would take place some time in the future when a free slot could be found in the Court of Probate schedules. Needless to say, only the lawyers were anticipating the event with relish. Yakety-yak-yak-yak! thought Holly as Plum Blossom sipped his tea in the Shangri-la lobby and awaited her reaction.

'So we are free to return to London, all debts paid in full, no assassins lurking in the shadows to trouble our beauty sleep ever again, and a very fat cheque in the jolly old post, hmm?'

Mr Plum Blossom looked pained. 'My dear Extremely Unmarried – no hang it all, may I call you Holly?'

'Of course.'

'You see, Holly, I will never forgive myself for allowing such terrible harm and those inexcusable indignities to befall yourself and Nellie. Be assured this kind of thing shall never happen again in London or elsewhere while I am alive. The Society has lost face. You will forever be under our protection.'

Holly loved it when he got all worked up and formal like this.

'Unless, that is, I choose to take some other job in a far-off land, on some distant shore way, way, way, beyond the reach of the Society . . . *La Mer* . . . *Somewhere beyond the sea, waiting for me* . . .' She broke into song. While Plum Blossom looked on with eyes enraptured.

'Enough!' she said briskly. 'Let's vamoose muchacha, hon-delayhondelay!'

So they collected Nellie from her clinic room and had the luggage brought from the hotel by a Society officer.

It was time to head home.

They were walking across the crowded Chiang Kai-shek International Airport mezzanine heading to the VIP lounge for first-class Cathay Pacific Air passengers when a familiar voice rang out.

'I say, Holly-Jean! Holly-Jean Ho, old girl!'

Plum Blossom and assorted Society minions immediately spun round, their hands groping for their inside jacket pockets.

'Now, now, don't get nervous, keep calm everybody, it's only me, Nick Mayo, returning young Holly's golf-bag. Managed to track you down and catch you just before you left. Good timing, eh?'

Holly stood and gaped as Nick marched towards her, golf-bag in hand.

'It's all right, Plum Blossom, he's a friend of mine,' she sighed.

Plum Blossom spoke tersely and the Society men backed off.

Holly said pleasantly, 'I really don't want the thing, Nick, but since you've come all this way, why not join us for a drink in the VIP lounge?'

'Don't mind if I do,' he said, falling in step beside her. 'Funny thing is, I've got something rather weird to show you.'

238

'Really?' said Holly politely as they entered the quiet haven of the lounge.

'Yes, really. You see, I was looking for a spare golf ball the other day and remembered your bag still had a few deep down in the side pocket.'

'That's right,' said Holly. 'I believe there were still a couple left in there. So?'

'Well, that's the odd thing,' said Nick, gratefully accepting a frosted glass of foaming Taiwan beer. 'I upended the bag to get the last of the balls out and this one appeared . . .' He produced a golf ball from his pocket with a dramatic flourish.

Plum Blossom, Nellie, Holly and a pair of Society handlers stared as one at the ordinary-looking golf ball.

'And so?' said Holly, polite smile beginning to crack.

'So bloody well this!' Nick dug his nail into the golf ball just under the slogan, twisted and with a loud pop, opened the ball into two halves. Inside one of them lay a snug glass sphere.

Nick carefully lifted this out and held it up for Holly to see. 'It's only some feller's bloody knobhead, that's all!'

He thought it was funny, he would say later, but not *that* funny.

But Holly, Nellie and Plum Blossom were still laughing when their flight was called.

Chapter 28

The dinner hosted by Mr Plum Blossom the week before Christmas in Holly-Jean's honour was a resounding success, though in her personal opinion the Chinese style of never-ending rounds of self-congratulation had bordered on the smug and sycophantist, though of course that was all part of tradition and to be endured.

To her credit, she'd tried to deflect each valediction towards her allies and co-conspirators. What the heck, it was the way things were done.

Besides, the meal, consisting of about fourteen courses in a private dining-room above Gerrard Street, had been scrumptious and the reunion of friends had overcome any awkwardness of cultural dichotomy.

The actual reason for Mr Plum Blossom's decision to host the party, besides the obvious festive time of year, remained obscure, but Holly guessed he was acting on orders from on high. Though from which precise lofty bower of power she could not say for sure. Maybe it was the Societies who were happy to have a successful and speedy conclusion to what could have been a very discordant episode in the internal affairs of Taiwan, not to mention the Far West of China.

Though their long-term plans probably found a place for anarchy in that far-flung corner of the crumbling empire, it was sure to be controlled anarchy under their own terms and at their own convenience.

No doubt the tycoon Shih Yang-fu had contributed to the evening's expenses; he could well afford it, after all. For surely he was, by now, happily anticipating the vast tracts of land soon to become his once the Probate was settled and young Nellie took her seat on the board.

Little did the old goat know that the price he would have to pay to secure her cooperation was going to be drastically high. Indeed, Nellie had already worked up quite an agenda in consultation with various aborigine tribal organisations, conservation groups and other interested parties. The way she saw it, her inheritance included a profound obligation of duty, for after all, Nellie was first and foremost an idealist. And a McIlvuddy to boot!

Her long-term plans included preservation of tribal sacred grounds, generous money grants for a whole cornucopia of diverse social welfare, cultural and art projects, and more, much more, that she just hadn't yet thought of.

Poor old Shih, thought Holly wryly, for him it really would turn out to be a bitter-sweet victory. Sure, he'd won his historic playground fight with Chiu and seen off the luckless Hamish, but in doing so, he'd bitten off far more than his rotten, mangy old gums could possibly chew. As the Chinese say, with Nellie McIlvuddy on the board, he'd invited a scorpion to ride on his back across the swollen river.

As for Nellie herself; Holly glanced at the animated girl across the table. On the surface, she seemed to be perfectly recovered from her ordeal. Savouring the new challenge presented by the board seat and vowing to continue with her career in documentary film-making. Although there was a sadness there too, Holly acknowledged. Had to be. For until now, there's been no positive word from Manila regarding the fate of her half-brother, Raymond Jun-jun.

As far as Holly had been able to discover, the boy had perished in the Santa Mesa barrio fire, the night of All Saints.

Still, until a body was positively identified, there was an iota of hope. But realistically, as she had explained to Nellie in a quiet moment before the banquet, it wouldn't be good to get hopes too high, for after all, they were dealing with Manila and its chaotic, if not to say, non-existent social system. Holly had made Nellie understand that there was little chance that her half-brother would ever re-emerge from the charred ruins of that cardboard and corrugated iron citadel of the poor.

241

In response, Nellie had declared with typical gusto, 'I won't give up on the boy, Holly-Jean. I swear to you now that, just as soon as I can get away, next week at the latest, I'm on a plane to Manila. If the authorities won't help, I'll undertake the search for Raymond Jun-jun McIlvuddy myself!'

Holly raised her glass to Nellie, 'Attagirl!'

Yes, things had panned out fairly well, considering. In fact, all in all, from the humble viewpoint of Holly-Jean Ho & Associates, Software Intellectual Property Rights Consultants, 40 Earlham Street, Covent Garden, London WC2, it was definitely what you could call a job well done.

So congrats to all, and it was indeed a very joyous and warm affair.

Ho Ma-ma, of course, sat in the seat of honour, the one with its back to the door as tradition demanded. A couple of her mah-jong oppos were seated nearby to keep her company and help devour the offerings. (And devour they did!)

The Honourable Hamish had been invited. But he declined because he had apparently already left Town, leaving only a forwarding address as P.O. Box 155679, Rio De Janeiro. Shirley Jacquet equipped that Chiu Nei-ku had bought him a one-way ticket to Rio for Christmas and told him not to come back.

One no-show was very welcome – the office till now had heard no more from the tax people, and that was just fine with Holly and Ma.

Nellie McIlvuddy sat to Ma's right and was in great form. After all, she now had the financial backing to make a great career in film.

Shih Yang-fu did not attend, but instead sent elaborate gifts of X.O. brandy and giant floral displays. He, of course, would get his piece of the planet in his Christmas stocking.

Also in attendance were Chief Super Coulson, Minty, Carless, Shirley Jacquet, Charlie Villiers, Sadie Kaiserman, a pale, ethereal Morag-Rose, recovered and *en passant* to the road East.

They'd toasted with Alsace at Holly-Jean's request – Hugel, of course – and empty cardboard wine boxes were piling up in the corridor outside. A late arrival had been Professor Janet Rae-Smith who had just finished a meeting at Number 10. She was warmly welcomed but declined the Alsace in favour of mineral water. Poor old Jan.

At one point towards the less formal end of the proceedings, well out of earshot of Morag-Rose, not wishing to expose recent wounds, Holly-Jean had asked Coulson what had happened with the Shanghai fishing boys. Mick told her that a similar case of rape and battery had occurred while the Shanghai lads were still incarcerated in Lerwick Gaol as prime suspects. Moreover, Mike told a vastly relieved Holly-Jean, the DNA tests had proved negative. They'd been released.

'I knew they were innocent. They were such babes – talk about wet behind the ears,' remarked Holly.

'Hardly,' was Coulson's arid response. 'Shetland Customs and Excise discovered ten keys of high-grade heroin in the crew's quarters of the Shanghai factory ship. Your lads are back in Lerwick Gaol awaiting transfer to Peterhead in Aberdeen.'

'Oh dear,' had been Holly's reply. But she was distracted. Time was running out. She looked at her watch. Where *was* the man? She began to fidget. He must get here soon or it would be too late!

Suddenly, with great commotion and profuse apologies for having knocked a tray of abalone soup flying from a waiter's arms, Barrance T. Wong made his dramatic entrance, brandishing what appeared to be a heavy loop of film in both hands.

'Ah, this is the film Nellie took in the Tien-shan. I digitally remastered it! Good as new! Merry Christmas!'

'Wow! You absolute sweetheart! My hero, Barrance!' screamed Nellie, jumping out of her seat to hug a painfully blushing Barrance T. Wong. While all cheered and clapped, and someone shouted, 'Pulitzer for next year, Nellie!'

It was a great Christmas party.

But eventually it was time for goodbyes and best Christmas wishes as the good company broke up for the night.

Holly and Ma had decided to walk the few blocks back to

Earlham Street. It was rowdy on the streets with the festive mob out and about, and the shop windows full of the spirit of commerce and tinsel.

Holly re-ran the tape of the evening in her head as they strolled slowly with bellies overfull and heads sloshed with wine. Minty was driving straight back to the country tonight with Carless as co-driver, both them stupid twits just asking to be breathalysed. The other guests had dispersed with much hugging and kissing. The emotional warmth of the seasonal celebration of the birth of Jesus Christ had worked its heavenly magic.

They reached Number 40 without further mishap. A light snow was falling, but as soon as it hit the cobbles it melted away.

'Home again, Ma,' yawned Holly.

'Home again, Little Orchid,' agreed Ma.

There was a handwritten envelope tacked to the door of the shop. Holly recognised the script, but wary of any ritualistic manifestations as had been experienced hereabouts of late, she stuffed the envelope surreptitiously in her pocket without opening it, before Ma got to notice and raised a fuss. Now she ushered Ma inside the apartment front door and along the narrow corridor to the tiny lift where they went straight on up to the fifth floor.

When Ma was safely ensconced in the shower and singing snatches of Taiwan opera, Holly tore open the envelope and unfolded the single sheet of paper as something fell to the floor.

The sheet was headed *Emburey Hotel, Covent Garden, WC2*. There were only two lines: *Merry Christmas. I'm waiting in Room 403*. The letter was signed *Frangipani Johns*. So the flower-lady was persistence itself.

Holly squatted down and groped on the carpet for what had fluttered out of the envelope when she had torn it open. She found the old photograph under a chair. It was a copy of one she had in her possession – the one in the gilt-frame on her desk. The one of the tall upright young British soldier and his tiny Chinese bride in white.

How the frock did the flower-lady come by a copy, thought Holly. But then something puzzling made her turn on the overhead light and look a little more carefully at the so-familiar image.

The poses were slightly different. This was not a copy. *This was another posed shot.*

Her heart now beating furiously, Holly-Jean grabbed her coat and with a shout to Ma, 'I'm off out, Ma, something's come up. I'll call!' she was gone.

The Emburey Hotel was an elegant Edwardian pile on the corner of Great Russell Street and Bloomsbury. Room 403 opened to reveal the woman who had seemed hauntingly familiar to Holly that morning on her way to Heathrow for her flight to Manila.

'You came,' she said, holding out her hand.

'Where did you get that photo?' asked Holly.

'Don't you know?' said Frangipani Johns.

'Tell me.'

'That is the only photo I have of my birth-mother and her English husband.'

'Stop!' exclaimed Holly, pacing the floor as the words sunk in. She spun round. 'You're saying my Ma is your mother?'

Frangipani smiled. 'I was adopted as a baby in Taiwan by a Hakka family who were leaving by fishing boat for Hong Kong to avoid the KMT White Terror. I was given that photo for my eleventh birthday. Merry Christmas, *mei-mei*, Little Sister.'

After a reviving drink and the exchange of unreal pleasantries, Holly had discovered that Frangipani was a successful fashion designer working out of Hong Kong and Shanghai.

Frangi, as she liked to be addressed, knew all about Holly-Jean. She'd discovered her identity and the whereabouts of Ma and herself after a year's worth of research and the expenditure of a fair amount of money. It was ironic that the P.I. Frangi had hired to track Holly and Ma down was in the same business – and when the identification was confirmed the man had declared a passing acquaintanceship with Holly.

'Old Ferdy Atherington, the rogue. How come you chose him?' asked Holly.

'London *Yellow Pages*. Letter A.'

She couldn't help herself but constantly Holly-Jean found herself staring at Frangipani, examining her features, gazing into her eyes.

'This is weird,' muttered Holly. And she realised that she had known subconsciously of the blood-tie that morning on the Yamaha in Earlham Street. There'd been a jolt of recognition which she now recalled. 'We have to go see Ma.'

'That's why I wanted you to know first. To help me break the news to her. I don't know if she ever found out that I was alive.'

'Oh, I reckon she knew all right,' said Holly quietly. Things were falling into place. 'But why did you have to scare the wits out of the old dear with all that *feng-shui* nonsense?'

'Do you know the real story about the baby birthed just as the fatal news arrived from Taipei?' asked Frangipani as she pulled on her cashmere coat.

Holly recalled the night Ma had broken her long-imposed silence; the tale she'd told of the baby being taken from the mother at birth. Of course, she had been talking about her 'dear friend' at the time.

Holly said, 'The birth occurred just as news of the family bank's demise and the subsequent slaughter of the family in Taipei reached the countryside. Some kind of geomancer, a *feng-shui* man, declared the baby an evil omen and so inauspicious as to be sacrificed there and then. Ma said that her dear friend had threatened suicide unless the baby were offered up to another family.'

'That's all true, Little Sister.'

'So the *feng-shui* is some kind of appeasement ritual?' asked Holly.

Frangi explained, 'Because this mother-child separation began with *feng-shui*, I was informed before I left China by the old priest at the Taoist temple which my adoptive family and I frequent, that I had to enact certain symbolic rituals to bring good fortune and close out this whole terrible episode. Actually, Holly-Jean, I personally don't really believe in any of it, but I thought I should follow tradition.'

Holly shook her head, murmuring, 'Enough of that nonsense for ever.' Then she spoke up. 'I have a new sister then, and Ma has her baby back!'

'That's right. "The dear friend" was she,' said Frangi. 'I was the baby, and the family were surnamed Jan. I chose the Western surname Johns as a sign of respect to your father, Mr Jones.'

'My father?' said Holly. 'What's he got to do with this? He's not your real father, right?'

'No, my real father was killed in the riot in Taipei, along with the other males of the family,' explained Frangi. 'The reason I chose his name is because your father saved Ma. He came along at a time when the only fraternisation was done in the upstairs rooms of bars and brothels. By taking her as his bride he saved our Ma's life. After being shunned in Taiwan she had made it to Hong Kong, but as a young widow in menial service to an ex-pat family in Hong Kong she had few prospects. She was an outcast in the Ho clan of Maioli for many years. The Taiwan clan only accepted her back four years ago when she returned to the island.'

Holly found she was crying copious tears. 'So my dad married her and brought her back to London and I was born in Kentish Town.'

'Ma!' Holly called, opening the door to the fifth-floor penthouse. 'There's someone here I'd like you to meet. Prepare yourself – you've got a very special Christmas present this year. But first I'll make some Oolong *cha*.'

Ma had just finished drying her hair and was wearing a silk dressing-gown when she came into the living room.

'May I present Frangipani Johns,' said Holly, handing round steaming cups of Oolong. 'She is your first daughter, my elder sister.'

Ma opened her mouth, pointing wordlessly at Frangi who stepped forward just in time to catch her as she crumpled into a dead faint while Holly neatly snatched the cup of Oolong on its way to the carpet.

'Families, I ask you,' tsked Holly, pouring fresh Oolong *cha*.